IN GRAY

SARA J. BERNHARDT

For Alicia, Enjoy.

Sara J Bernhardt

Lavish
Publishing LLC

Second Edition

2019 Lavish Publishing, LLC

All Rights Reserved

Published in the United States by Lavish Publishing, LLC, Midland, TX

Cover Design by: OliviaProDesign

Cover Images: depositphotos.com

Paperback edition

ISBN: 978-1-944985-79-0

www.LavishPublishing.com

Contents

For my Adam

Prologue

I AWOKE to the overwhelming stench of gasoline and burning rubber. The blood had rushed to my head, causing an intense ache. I looked around, seeing the car I was in as nothing more than a heap of metal and torn-up leather. I struggled to pull myself through the broken glass of the window. My arms had no strength left in them, and I couldn't even be sure if my legs were still attached.

I couldn't feel anything but the throbbing in my head. Eventually, some of the numbness in my body subsided, and I could feel the heat from the asphalt burning through my shirt.

I was lying in the middle of the road. Nothing was clear. My head was foggy, and I could only remember pieces of how I had even gotten there. A flash of color and a loud screeching wail before my vision went dark—that was the only image I could remember—and I awoke with my head feeling as though it were on fire.

I tried begging my mind to wake up so I could get up from the street, where I wasn't safe. My eyes closed again, and I tried with everything I had to open them. Nothing worked. I could feel myself slipping into a deeper sleep until a voice pulled me out of my head and into reality.

"Miss?"

I knew he was speaking to me because I could feel the pressure of his hand on my shoulder.

"Miss, can you tell me your name?"

I tried again to open my eyes but couldn't. I choked out my name. My throat burned as if I had swallowed hot coals. My ears rang with reverberating thunder through my entire body when he spoke again.

"Daisy," he said, "you are going to be all right."

I was able to pry my eyes open to see hazel ones staring intently into my own...and glass. There was so much glass scattered all over the road. I tried to focus again on the eyes in front of me. It was a boy, no older than my seventeen and a half years. He had clear, fair skin and dark, shaggy hair almost hiding his gaze.

"Listen to me. You're going to be all right."

I tried to reply, but it took all my energy just to tell him my name. I could feel my eyes closing again even as I struggled to keep them open.

"Stay with me," he pleaded. I could hear panic creeping into his voice. "Daisy, stay with me. You're going to be all right!"

His voice echoed in my head. I knew he was saying more to me, but I couldn't understand the words. I just listened to his voice, keeping me awake and alive. As his voice faded, a rhythmical beeping sound took its place—a maddening, almost piercing noise. I sat up, realizing I was in an uncomfortable hospital bed. I opened my eyes, and even before I realized I was screaming, the nurses had rushed into the room and held me down. I struggled in their grasp, trying to get free.

"Daisy, you need to calm down," I heard a woman say. "You need to just relax."

A nurse came in with a syringe and poked me in the arm with it. I growled in anger but began to feel very sleepy and weak. I was no longer able to struggle and had no way of expressing the terror I felt at seeing what was in front of me.

Chapter One

THE SKY WAS GRAY. It was always gray. I looked up into the cloud-covered heavens, searching for the sun. I could see it there behind the clouds, its rays penetrating the atmosphere—but they were gray. I sighed, drinking in the warmth from the summer afternoon. I could feel the heat but was unable to see the light. I diverted my gaze to the planter just beneath the windowsill... daisies—my mother's favorite, which I guessed explained why she named me after them. I stared at them as if willing them to change—all those gray little flowers with their gray petals in gray soil. I glanced at my hands. Just as I thought—still muted and dull. I once had beautiful, honey-colored hair and blue eyes—blue like the sky I could no longer see. Now, I was gray, just like everything around me.

I knew it wasn't easy for my mother seeing me this way. I had tried for a very long time to pretend I was all right with things. When my mom's friend got married, I failed miserably. I ran from the room in tears when trying to pick out matching ribbons for the bridesmaids. My mother had tried to convince me to stay home, but I was persistent and kept telling her I would be fine. I was wrong.

I knew then I could never be normal, no matter how hard I tried to be. I felt everyone who looked at me knew something was wrong with me. They saw me as something less than themselves. I would always be judged for my differences. One simple occurrence in my life had changed me completely.

The night fell quickly; I missed the colors of sunset. Only the shadows around me grew darker.

I knew I must have been asleep because I was seeing things that weren't possible.

The color was almost blinding, yet it was beautiful. Even as I feared it might destroy me, I didn't dare close my eyes. The sun blazed, illuminating the fields, showing the colors all the more vibrantly. I pulled my blond hair over my shoulder and smiled at the shiny, lustrous color I could clearly see. The wildflowers of purple and blue swayed in the wind, and the newly grown strawberries almost glowed scarlet in the overwhelming sunlight. My gaze was fixed on the landscape before me. Even the places where the grass had died and the foliage was brown, it was the most miraculous shade of brown imaginable. I felt enthralled and blessed. I soon found myself in tears. I wanted to keep the vision before me forever, but I felt myself being pulled almost violently away.

I felt waking numbness...and the vision faded, leaving me alone in the gray morning of another warm summer day.

It was the first time since the dreams started that it wasn't frightening. The feelings of dread and anxiety weren't there. I knew that wouldn't last. The fact that the dreams had come back meant that eventually they would turn into nightmares. The dream, I knew, was more than just a dream in itself. Only the visions were in color. The vibrancy told me once again I was meant for a task —a task for which I had no choice. They started less than a month after the accident—after the color drained from my life forever. I knew there was more to it than the things I did and the people I helped. I knew, as I had from the beginning, that *he* was the source of it all. *He* was the one I was meant to seek out.

My mother always knew when something wasn't right with me. The second I sat at the table, before even taking a single bite of the omelet she had made, she mentioned it.

"Daisy?"

I looked up, not wanting to deal with what was coming.

"Are you okay?"

I sighed. "Yeah. I'm fine."

She pulled her eyebrows together and made hard, uncomfortable eye contact. "Have the nightmares come back?"

"No," I lied. "I'm fine." I grabbed my bag and stuffed a couple bucks in my pocket.

"Are you going somewhere?"

"To the café. I'm meeting Jess. I won't be long."

"Dais, remember what the doctor said."

"Mom, I'm fine," I said, trying to hide the annoyance in my voice. "It's a café, not a rock concert."

She nodded, and I rushed out the door. I saw my mom wave to me as she drove by on her way to work.

Since the accident, I wasn't permitted to get behind the wheel. I guess they assumed seeing a stop sign wasn't possible unless it was burning a hole in my retina. According to the doctor, they couldn't risk the head injury causing seizures or blackouts while behind the wheel. If I could go long enough without anything happening, I should be able to get my license back.

Honestly, none of it seemed to matter. It wasn't like I was ever going to feel comfortable driving again.

I walked quickly to the café. One good thing about living in a small town was I didn't need to drive. Cayucos was a cool beach city with little shops lining the streets. With so few residents, everyone knew me and what had happened to me.

The café was mostly empty when I walked in. A couple of older gentlemen smiled at me, and Roslyn, the hostess, said hi. I'd known almost everyone in this town my entire life, but none of them looked at me the same way anymore. It was like they were afraid to say the wrong thing.

"Daisy!" I heard Jess call from the other side of the room.

"Sorry," I said, rushing to the seat across from her. "Am I late?"

She glanced at her watch. "Three and a half minutes." She laughed.

I smiled and reached for the mug in front of me. "Thanks."

"No problem. Extra shot of chocolate."

"You know me too well."

"So what's going on?"

"I'm just feeling a little nervous about the follow-up appointment coming up."

Jess nodded. "Do you want me to come with you?"

I shrugged. "I don't want to make you do that." I was hedging.

"No, it's okay. I don't mind being there for you."

I nodded. "Thanks."

"So are you okay?"

"What do you mean?"

5

She shook her head. "Never mind."

I looked into her black eyes for a moment then averted my gaze. Those black eyes used to be a captivating shade of chestnut that held a kind of sparkle. I supposed they still did, but, of course, I would never again see it. The shine in her jet black hair was now gone, and the dull, flat color was all I could see. I sighed.

"Fine," I finally said. "I'm having the dreams again."

"What?" she almost yelled, causing a few people to turn and look at us. She leaned in closer and lowered her voice. "Since when?"

"Just last night."

"Was…*he* in it?"

I shook my head and took a sip of my coffee. "No. No, not this time. I woke up before anything happened."

"And the colors?"

I nodded.

"Wow." She lowered her head for a moment then looked back into my eyes. "We need to do something about this, Dais."

"Like what?"

"I don't know," she whispered. "But I'm your best friend, and something is going on. I won't let you go through this alone."

"What do you think we can do?"

"I really don't know," she answered. "We need to find him."

"Jess, I already tried. The police tried too. It's like he just…disappeared. They think I'm crazy."

She shook her head. "I know, but I believe you, and I know he's behind all of this."

I nodded. "Where do we start?"

"How about where it happened."

"The crash site?"

She nodded. "Maybe seeing it again will bring back some suppressed memories."

I shook my head. "Jess…if there are suppressed memories, they have been suppressed for a reason."

She took a sip of her coffee before responding. "I know, but if you want to find out what all of this is about, we need to start from the beginning."

"There is one other thing," I said. "Something I haven't mentioned."

She raised her eyebrows, waiting for me to come clean.

"Ever since the accident, I've felt like someone is watching me. I would see a shadow out of the corner of my eye, but when I turned to look, there would be nothing there." I waited for the look in her eyes, for the look that told me she thought I was crazy. It never came.

"Why didn't you tell me this before?"

"Everyone already thinks I'm crazy. Why would I give them any more of a reason?"

"Daisy, I'm not everyone," she said softly. "You know me. I would never think that about you. I know what you have gone through and what you are still going through. You aren't crazy!"

I nodded. "I'm sorry. I just…I like the way you look at me."

She smiled. "What do you mean?"

"That." I chuckled. "That is what I mean. You look at me the way you always have, like nothing has changed."

"You're still you."

I nodded. "Well, everyone else seems to think differently."

She gave me a wry smile. "It's like I said. I'm not everyone."

"So you think we should go back? To the road where I—where it happened?"

She nodded.

"When?"

"What do you mean when?" She laughed. "I was sort of thinking now."

"Now?" I repeated. "Like today?"

"That's what 'now' means, Daisy."

"Thanks for the vocabulary lesson." I smirked at her.

She smiled. "If I give you time to think about it, you'll want to back out, and that can't happen. We need to get to the bottom of this. I am starting to feel like a clock is ticking somewhere."

"Great, like I'm already worried and anxious."

"Exactly," she said. "So why give you time to make it worse? Come on."

I groaned.

She stood up and signaled me with her hand. "Come on. I'll be with you the whole time. I promise."

I reluctantly got to my feet and followed her out to the parking lot. I liked seeing her black Honda, knowing it had always been black and the interior always gray. But I did miss the vibrant yellow color of the dice hanging from her mirror. I ignored them and stared at the floor of the car, where the color was right, where I wasn't again reminded I was broken. I could feel the anxiety creeping its way into my chest as we came closer to the place of my nightmares.

I began squeezing my eyes shut as the fear became a tangible beast ready to pull my racing heart out of my chest. I kept seeing the scene replaying in my mind over and over, making me feel almost sick.

"Daisy?" I heard Jess's voice filled with the softness of compassion.

I tried to clear my head before responding. "I'm okay," I said before she had the chance to ask.

"Are you sure?"

I nodded but still hadn't opened my eyes.

"If it's going to be this bad, we don't have to do this."

I shook my head. "No. No, we came this far. You're right. I need to do this."

"Technically, it's not that far. We're only fifteen minutes from town," she responded dryly.

I felt the tension slowly ease in my chest. "Smart ass," I muttered grate-fully. It had always been that way between us.

Slowly, I opened my eyes, and at first, nothing seemed off. All I saw was an empty black road, the same as any other road I was likely to see. I glanced around, waiting for something to strike a memory.

"We...should get out," Jess said.

I nodded and climbed out of the car. Standing on the road, feeling the sun on my skin, I felt completely normal. I continued looking around, but there was nothing. My eyes moved across all the gray trees and pebbles in the road until something caught my attention. There was a small patch of wilting flowers near the side of the road.

I knew they were yellow. I remembered them. I remembered staring at them once my eyes were open and listening to the voice of my rescuer, trying to stay awake and attentive. I remembered all of it. The visions came back, intense and vivid. I felt as if I had fallen through a wormhole and was back when it happened. I could smell the gasoline and burning rubber. I could feel the stinging in my skin from the broken glass. I could see the colors—all the glorious colors. I tried to pull myself out and back into the empty road with Jess, but the visions were too strong. I was meant to be there.

When I finally saw the boy, I tried asking his name, but it was like I was watching the memory from another's eyes and couldn't change the outcome. I could no longer feel the pain. I was suddenly watching myself in the road, focusing on the details of his face. He was lovely and sweet, but nothing caught my eye. Nothing was off about him except for the urgency in his voice and the fear in his eyes. It was as if he wanted to do more than help me. It was as if he were desperate to save me, as if maybe he knew me. Like maybe he loved me.

I shook off the thoughts, and again I felt the pain. I was ripped away from the eyes of an onlooker and sucked back into the body of the girl on the road, looking into shining hazel eyes. I started choking on my breath as I tried over and over to ask him his name. I felt the jagged glass sticking out of my flesh and the burning in my head. I felt everything. The pain and fear were almost suffocating me. It was happening again. This was no dream. This was the real thing happening to me all over again as though there was something I was meant to discover. My vision became cloudy and dark. I tried to speak, to cry, to do anything to stay awake. My eyes closed, and everything went dark just as it had the first time it happened. I drifted away into a dreamless sleep.

I awoke, hazy and confused, to a familiar voice.

"Daisy?" I heard. "Are you awake?"

I rolled over groggily. "Jess?"

"Yeah. Are you okay? How do you feel?"

I sat up, realizing I was in my bed. "What happened?"

"I was hoping you could tell me," she said. "You were fine one second, and the next thing I know—you just collapsed!"

I sighed. "I thought I was back."

"What do you mean?"

"Being there on that road brought me back to that day. I swore it was happening again."

"That's called a flashback, Dais. It's no more real than a dream."

I scoffed.

"Okay. *Most* dreams anyway."

I sighed and flopped back onto my pillow. "To answer your first question of how I feel...sort of like I just woke up from a car crash."

She smiled flaccidly. "I'm sorry."

"No, it's okay. You were right. I needed to at least try. Just the feelings were so vivid, so...horrible."

"Like I said," Jess began slowly, "no more—"

"More real than a dream," I interrupted. "I know. I'm not so sure though. It felt like I was meant to be there to remember something—only I blacked out before I had the chance. Maybe we need to go back."

"What?" she asked, sounding incredulous.

Forgetting the grogginess in my head, I sat up. "If I felt like I was meant to be there to remember something, then maybe I was. Maybe I need to try again."

"After what just happened? Are you sure that's a good idea?"

"I don't like it either," I said. "But as long as you're with me, I think I could handle it."

"Maybe you can, but what about me? I'm not sure I could stand seeing you like that again."

"Jess, I'm fine. But I can't do this alone."

"You overestimate my strength."

I smiled. "I think you *underestimate* your strength."

"Either way, time to get up."

I groaned. "Not a chance." I rolled over, facing the wall.

"I've got aspirin and lunch for you."

I turned back to face her. "Waffle House?"

She chuckled. "You know it."

I sighed. "Fine. You promise to do this with me, right?"

Jess nodded. "Lunch first."

We headed back down the familiar roads, mostly silent. I could already feel my lunch creeping its way into my throat.

I don't know if I can do this.

Jess stopped the car, and I heard the crunching of gravel as she walked over to my door.

"Daisy? Are you getting out?"

I realized I was still in the car, buckled in and staring at the floor. "Uh, yeah," I said, climbing out of the Honda. I glanced at my surroundings as I had before. I took notice of the emptiness of the road and the stretch of trees dappling the sunlight and leaving little white spots of shadows in the street. I looked at the ground where the glass had torn up my body. I waited for the horrific visions to come into play, but nothing happened. I closed my eyes like I had the last time, envisioning the scene. Still nothing.

"It's not working," I said.

Jess looked over at me and squeezed my shoulder. "Give it some time."

I closed my eyes again and replayed everything I could remember, from the crash to the boy with the hazel eyes. I opened my eyes again and stared at the wilting flowers on the side of the road. The edges of my vision didn't become hazy, and I didn't feel that surreal pull of any oncoming vision.

"Nothing," I said, sighing.

"Are you sure?"

I nodded. "Yeah. I don't think it's going to work this time."

She sighed. "Okay. You feel like coffee?"

"Sure."

Anything to get my mind off of this.

The café was still empty when we walked in, which meant we would be able to talk.

"I don't get it," I whimpered. "I didn't do anything different today."

"I don't know," Jess answered, staring into her cup. "Maybe it wasn't meant to happen this time."

"I don't understand any of it."

She looked back up at me again. "Maybe you should…just…wait for the dreams again. Maybe that's the key."

I nodded. "Maybe."

I took a sip of my coffee and looked around to see if we were still alone. I noticed one of the employees restocking cups and a guy sitting at a table across the way, reading a book. I may have lost the vibrancy in my vision, but I certainly was not blind. I knew the softness of his hair and the childlike round-ness in his face. Even without seeing the hazel of his eyes, I knew—it was *him.*

I almost choked on my coffee. I wasn't sure what to do first, whether I should say something to Jess or just go confront him. I had a thousand questions racing through my head. Would he even remember me? What was he doing here? Why had I never seen him before? I looked to Jess and nudged her in the arm.

"Huh?" She looked up at me.

I tried to speak, but for a moment, I couldn't find my voice. I looked over to where he was sitting, and his table was empty.

"What?" Jess asked. "What is it?"

I wasn't sure what to say. She would definitely think I was crazy now.

"Nothing," I said.

"Nothing? Come on, Dais. What's up?" Her voice was filled with confusion.

"It's nothing," I said, getting up from the table. "I think I just need some time by myself."

"Okay. Are you sure?"

"Yeah," I answered, trying to keep my face unreadable. "Yeah. Thanks."

"Call me if you need anything, okay?"

I faked a smile. "Promise."

I rushed out of the café and headed down the street, searching for the boy. The sidewalks and streets were just as empty as the coffee house—no trace of him anywhere. I felt the sting of tears welling in my eyes. Maybe I *was* crazy after all. People don't just appear at random times and disappear at will. Maybe I was simply seeing things. Maybe my head injury was more serious than we thought.

Chapter Two

I SAT IN THE CAR, fidgeting with a thread dangling from a hole in my jeans.

"Daisy?" my mom asked. "Doing okay?"

I nodded. "I'm fine, Mom."

She made a face but didn't push it. "The doctor said you should be all right you know."

"I am all right."

She stayed silent for the rest of the drive.

We walked into the waiting room, and Mom signed us in. Jess was sitting in one of the chairs, reading a magazine.

"Hey," she said as I walked over. "You feeling okay?"

"Yeah," I said. "Normal."

When the doctor called me in, Jess was allowed to come with me into the office. I knew Mom wanted to be there, but she was trying to give me some space. She knew I hated how she hovered. I sat on the uncomfortable bed covered in paper that crinkled and tore. Jess sat in a chair beside me. I started feeling anxiety creeping in but tried to push it away. I sighed, and Jess grabbed my hand.

"It's okay," she said. "Just relax."

I nodded, taking a few deep breaths to calm my nerves.

My doctor was an older man with thick, white hair and an even thicker English accent. "Are you experiencing any headaches?" he asked.

"No," I said. "Nothing like that."

He shone a light in my eyes. "Have you been avoiding loud sounds?"

I nodded. "I was never one for clubs or concerts."

"Good," he answered. "Now, with this form of monochromacy, more commonly known as color blindness, it is caused by damage to the retinal cones. Unfortunately, it is irreversible."

I nodded. "I already knew that."

"So far, it seems you have healed elsewhere," he said. "Your CAT scans and X-rays came back normal. There were no signs of brain damage or internal bleeding. Unfortunately, you may have some minor memory impairment, but it should only affect memories of a couple of days before and after the accident."

"I think I remember everything," I said.

"That's a good sign. Just continue to avoid bright lights and loud sounds."

"I will."

"Okay. I will need to see you back here in one month."

I nodded and walked back into the waiting room.

"What did he say?" my mom asked immediately.

"Everything is fine," I said. "He said everything came back normal."

She smiled and put her arm around me. "Good."

I needed to clear my head. My thoughts were overwhelming me, and nothing was going to change by sitting at home, stressing over it. I had no destination in mind; I just knew I had to get out. I walked aimlessly, paying no attention to street signs or buildings. I walked until I could feel blisters forming on the soles of my feet.

I sighed when I recognized the field and the little silver strawberries growing on a nearby vine. I knew I would end up here; I just wasn't yet sure why. The dreams always came true, at least the ones that were in color. I tried to imagine the colors of the butterflies and hummingbirds hovering over the flowers—the flowers, which I knew were purple and blue. I felt my knees buckle as the dream flashed through my memory. I let myself fall lightly to the ground, not worrying about the dirt, and succumbed to sinking into my memories.

The memories were crisp. I could still smell the gasoline and feel the tremors of fear racing through my veins. There was no sight, just the over-whelming stench.

Nobody had seen the boy who pulled me from the wreckage. The doctors and my mother said the head trauma had confused me. The injury that had taken the color from my life also caused me to see things and remember things that never existed. At the time, I believed them. That is…until the dreams started. The dreams were always in color. Even though the crash had ruined my eyes, my mind still remembered them. No matter what the dreams entailed, I always found myself living them mere days afterward. The dreams were more than just dreams, and he was always there—the boy who had saved me, the boy who nobody could remember seeing. I knew he was real, and my mind showed him more vividly than my imagination ever could. He was more than a figment of my damaged mind. I had to find him.

This time, as I stared at the landscape before me, I knew what was going to happen. This was about to get more than only uncomfortable; it was about to get violent.

I sat in the dirt for what felt like hours, waiting for something to happen—something I feared was going to be gruesome. The breeze stirred the flowers and ruffled my hair, but apart from that, everything seemed so—dead. I remembered the first time a dream had come to life. It was a month after the accident, and I was led to the lake just outside of town. I rescued a seven year old girl from the water. The second time, I pushed a man out of the path of a speeding truck. I could still hear the screeching tires, the same as that horrible sound that consumed me the day I lost color.

My memories came to a halt when I heard voices, and a strong sensation coursed through my limbs, almost as if I were being electrocuted. It was time. The voices were muffled at first, and I could only make out the tones —one angry, one pleading. As I approached closer, I saw a boy not much older than seventeen. He appeared to be bleeding, judging by the dark streams running down his cheeks. He was on his knees, begging to be released.

"Please," he whimpered. "You don't understand."

"I understand perfectly," I heard another male voice jeer.

"It's not what you think. Just listen."

"There is nothing left to say!"

I felt the shock return through my muscles. The pain took me off guard, almost knocking me to my knees. I knew it was my cue.

"Hey," I called as I approached, silently praying the assailant didn't have a gun. "What's going on?"

"None of your concern!" It was the voice of the attacker, who I now could see was large and very muscular, armed with a good-sized kitchen knife.

"Actually, that's where you're wrong," I said. Fear intermingled with the waves of shock, causing me to feel almost sick.

The attacker turned to look at me, his round eyes full and angry. He held the knife so tightly his knuckles were white. I pulled out my cell phone.

"Three numbers," I said. "Three numbers and you go down for assault. If you aren't careful, you go down for murder as well."

He growled deep in his throat. "This isn't over," he hissed, shaking the knife at his victim. "Wherever you go—I *will* find you."

He took off in the other direction, and I felt my breath explode in a sigh of relief. I turned to leave, but the boy called to me.

"Wait."

I turned back to face him, taking notice of the horrific shades of what must have been bruises on his face, accentuating the light hue of his eyes.

"You're welcome," I murmured.

"No. Please wait," he called. "Are you Daisy?"

I froze for a moment. My mouth hung open. "What?"

"You are, aren't you?" A smile spread across his face. "You're Daisy!"

The sensation of shock was still tingling through my limbs, making me unsteady on my feet and cloudy in the head. I tried to think before responding, but nothing came out.

The boy I saved was doing nothing but staring, still with a huge grin on his face. He had light eyes, which I could tell even without the color must have been blue. His hair, which appeared a dark shade of white, must have been a sandy blond and slopped with hair gel.

"Who are you?" It was the only thing I could say.

He didn't reply right away. He lowered his eyes to the ground and looked up again. His smile had become flaccid, but he still looked happy, perhaps even amused.

"Well?" I pressed.

"The name's William. Samuels, if you want to know."

"And you know my name how?"

"Hmm... That's a hard one to answer."

I saw a silent chuckle shake through him. "It's a simple question. It can't possibly be hard to answer."

"Well, maybe not," he said. "I'm just not sure you would believe me."

I widened my eyes and leaned in inches from his face. "Try me."

He sighed and lowered his head. "Fine," he started, his voice losing its casual tone. "I had this...dream."

"A dream?" I tried to keep my voice even.

He nodded. "Yeah. Like a vivid memory almost. Only it had never happened before."

I knew those words, as they were the same ones in my head since I'd started having the same dreams. I knew then—I was in danger.

"Please," I pressed. "Tell me more about the dream."

"I don't remember it," he said. "Well…not all of it. I just remember seeing you…here. You told me your name was Daisy. Other than that, I don't remember a thing."

"Don't you understand?" I spat. "If you are having dreams about me, that could mean I'm in danger."

His face became a collage of confusion and possibly fear. "What?" His voice sounded throttled.

"That's why I'm here. My dreams are to save people—the way I saved you."

He shook his head and averted eye contact. "That doesn't make sense."

"It may not make sense, but it's a part of my life now."

"Then what are the dreams for?"

"I told you. To save people."

He gave me a strange look but didn't say anything.

"Look, all I know is after I almost died, I started having dreams that basically force me to either save people or watch them die. In other words, dreams that force me into something I never asked for."

"At least you're doing something beneficial," he said. "The only thing that happened to me is an unexplained flash of a future event that holds almost no significance. Why is that?"

"You think I know any more about this than you?"

"You must," he said, exasperated. "You've been experiencing this a lot longer than I have."

"I don't understand it either."

"Well, maybe we can try to figure it out together. I'm scared."

"*You're* scared. I'm the one who could be in danger."

"Then maybe we should get out of here," he said with a smile.

"We?" I almost laughed. "No. There is no '*we.*' I can't help you." I turned to leave.

"But you can try," he called.

I turned back to face him.

He was smiling again. "Can't you?"

I sighed, remembering seeing the boy from my dreams at the café. I knew he was real. I knew I couldn't be crazy. Maybe this William could help me find him.

"Maybe I can," I said. "But I need your help too."

His smile broadened, which didn't seem possible until I saw it happen. "Name it."

"I'm looking for someone. Maybe you have seen him before. Maybe in a dream?"

He nodded. "Do you know his name?"

I shook my head. "No, but I know what he looks like."

"Okay. What does he look like?"

I paused, searching my memory for a moment. "Dark, shaggy hair and hazel eyes."

He lifted his hands. "And?"

"And that's it."

"Gotta give me a little more to go on here, Daisy. You just described half of Cayucos."

I grumbled under my breath. "Never mind."

"Wait," he retorted. "Wait. I can still help."

"How?"

"Just because I don't know this person doesn't mean I won't see him here in town or even in one of my crazy dreams. After all, I saw *you* in a dream."

"Which I still can't figure out the reason for."

"Thanks, by the way," he said, "for saving me."

"Hey, what did you do anyway?"

He waved me off. "Nothing. Just a misunderstanding."

"Seemed like a lot more than that to me."

"Really," he pressed. "It's nothing."

I dropped it, realizing he clearly didn't want to talk about it. I, however, was not about to give up on finding out what I had gotten myself involved in. If he wanted my help, I would need to know what cause I was assisting.

Chapter Three

IT WAS LATE the next morning when I remembered I was supposed to meet Jess at the café. I rushed out the door without even taking notice of what clothes I put on. When I got there, she was reading a novel with a half-naked man on the cover.

"Hey," she said, grinning widely.

"What is *that*?" I teased, gesturing toward the book in her hand.

She chuckled. "Just some trashy romance novel I picked up while waiting for you."

"Yeah. Sorry. I overslept."

"Did you have a dream?"

I shook my head. "No," I whispered, "but I do have something I need to tell you."

She stared at me for a moment as if she were trying to read my mind.

I sighed before beginning. "I…saw him," I whispered.

"*Saw* him?" she echoed. "Who? You mean…do you mean *him*?"

I could barely look her in the eye. A nod was the only reply I could muster.

"Wait. When?" She kept her voice quiet, but I could hear the urgency in it, bordering hysteria.

"Umm…recently."

"Recently?" she hissed. "Come on, Daisy. I know you better than that. Is that why you rushed out of here so fast the other day?"

"Uh, yeah."

She sighed heavily. "I knew it. I knew something was going on with you. Why didn't you tell me?"

"He just…disappeared. I thought I really was going crazy. I didn't want you to think so too."

"We talked about this," she said. "I would never think that about you."

I nodded. "I know. I'm sorry."

"Well, tell me about it."

"There isn't much to tell," I started. "I saw him as clear as day, and then he was just gone."

"Did you see him here?"

I nodded. "At that table." I pointed to the empty table behind her.

"And?"

"And when I tried to tell you, once I turned back, he was gone. I tried following him outside, but it was like he just vanished."

"That doesn't make sense," she said. "Why now? Why are you seeing him now when you hadn't before?"

"I wish I knew. In a town this size, I can't imagine him being able to hide."

"Really," she mused. "We know almost *everyone* in Cayucos."

"There is one more thing I also need to tell you. Remember the dream I had a few days ago?"

She nodded. "It…it happened?"

"They always do."

"Well?" she pressed, raising her eyebrows at me.

"I saved a boy from some jerk with a knife."

"A knife?"

"Shh," I warned. "Yes, but don't worry. I threatened to call the cops, and he took off."

She let out a long exhale. "Wow."

"That's not all. This boy…he decided not only to tell me his name but mentioned he knew mine."

"Wait…what?"

I shook my head, trying to find the right words. "We shouldn't talk about this here."

She nodded. "Come on. We can talk in the car."

I followed her out to the parking lot and climbed into her familiar car, again trying to ignore the dice hanging on the mirror.

"Okay." She exhaled slowly.

"He called after me as I was turning to leave, telling me he knew my name."

Jess furrowed her brow, looking as if she was desperately searching for something to say.

"He saw me in a dream," I murmured.

Her eyes suddenly grew wide. "Whoa…what?" she yelled. "What kind of dream?"

I shook my head. "I don't know. He said he doesn't remember anything about it but me."

"This is so weird. What are the odds of someone else here also having premonitions?"

"I know. Things are starting to get extremely weird. I *know* we have to find the one who pulled me from my car. He *must* be behind this."

"That's not so easy when he keeps disappearing."

"Yeah," I murmured. "Tell me about it."

"Are you sure you're safe?" she asked. "I mean, if he saw you in a dream, that could mean—"

"I know," I interrupted, "but nothing has happened yet, so maybe his dreams are different."

She nodded. "Let's hope so."

I found myself at the medicine cabinet for the third time, downing a dose of cough syrup before finally feeling tired enough to sleep. I clicked off the bathroom light and crawled back into bed beneath the blankets. I sighed, closing my eyes, hoping I wouldn't be disturbed by another dream.

I opened my eyes again, realizing I must have been dreaming when I saw bright yellow strands of hair billowing around my face. The sky was blue with streaks of red and purple clouds reaching across the horizon like ribbons. I recognized the long stretch of road in front of me and the wilting flowers near the edge where I had crashed. A sick feeling grew in the pit of my stomach, and I prayed there wouldn't be another flashback.

"Daisy?"

I whirled around at the sound of my name, almost crying out.

"It's okay," he said. "It's me."

I stared for what felt like hours at the perfection of those familiar hazel eyes—eyes that had haunted my dreams.

"Who are you?"

"You know who I am." His light brown hair shone almost golden in the fading daylight.

"You…saved me. Why?"

"Why?" He laughed and took a step toward me. "Do you think I had a choice?" He huffed and lifted his hands. "Do *you* have a choice?"

I opened my mouth to reply, but no words came out. I felt the air being violently sucked from my lungs, and I woke, gasping for air, alone in my bed with tiny rays of sun casting unfriendly, colorless shadows on the walls of my room.

I sat up, running my hands over my mess of hair, still feeling a lack of oxygen in my lungs. I replayed the dream in my head and flung my hand to the nightstand, grabbing my cell to call Jess.

"Hello?" she answered sleepily.

"Jess, wake up. It's me. I need you to pick me up—now."

"Wha…? Daisy?"

"Yes!" I snapped. "Wake up."

"Okay, okay. What's going on? Are you—?"

"Yes," I interrupted. "I'm fine. Just get here as soon as you can." I raced to my closet and threw on a pair of jeans and a sweater I knew once was blue. I slipped on some sandals and went to wait for Jess at the curb.

She sped down the street, causing a terrible screeching sound, and slammed on her brakes at my driveway. I hopped in the car.

"To the road," I said. "Hurry."

"Daisy, what's going on?" Her voice was flat, but I could hear a manner of fear behind her words.

"I'll explain on the way," I said. "Please…drive."

She nodded. Her dark hair was thrown back in a messy, looped ponytail, and there were dark streaks of makeup smeared under her eyes. She was dressed in gray sweatpants and a tank top. I realized she must have jumped out of bed without as much as a second thought.

"Thank you," I said.

"For what?" She glanced at me, then back at the road.

"Just…for always being there."

She smirked. "Of course. Now, what's going on?"

"I saw him in a dream," I said automatically. "At the road. I have a feeling he's still there."

I glanced at her foot as she pressed harder on the gas pedal. "Okay. If he's there, we'll find him. Did he say anything else?"

I nodded. "Sort of."

She glanced at me again. "Meaning?"

"He said he didn't have a choice in saving me," I started. "He said he doesn't have a choice any more than I do."

I saw her expression go blank for a moment, then saw a look of understanding flicker across her face. "Does that mean he…?"

"Is like me? I'm thinking so."

She sighed. "That's so freaky. I mean…what are the odds?"

I almost laughed. "In this town? I'm beginning to think anything is possible."

Jess braked harshly, and we immediately got out of the car, scanning the road. Off the side behind the wilting flowers was a tree. I knew it had once been bright colors of orange and red in the fall. I spotted a shape emerging from behind it. A dark coat ruffled in the breeze. I knew it had to be him.

"There!" I shouted, pointing to the tree.

"Is...is that him?"

"Yes!" I yelled, taking off in his direction.

I could hear the crunching of gravel as Jess followed behind me. I pushed myself faster until I reached the place I had seen him. Jess appeared at my side, out of breath. We both peered around. Again, he was gone.

"Where did he go?" she murmured.

I grumbled, bowing my head. "Damn! He was *just* here. How does he just vanish like that?"

Jess shook her head. "This guy is starting to get on my last nerve."

"You're telling me?"

Sighing, I turned away and headed back to the car.

"Sorry for waking you up like that." I buckled my seat belt.

Jess chuckled. "I don't blame you. It's not like he's hard to miss."

I nodded. "I don't understand why he keeps avoiding me. Don't you think he would remember me?"

"I don't know. Do you remember the people you save?"

I nodded. "Usually."

She shrugged. "Maybe he just doesn't recognize you."

"Maybe."

Chapter Four

"DAISY?" he called me from across the room.

I looked up, taken off guard for a moment. I recognized the light hair and eyes that appeared almost white. He was dressed casually in a shirt that must have been blue, judging by how the shade matched his jeans.

"William," I said. "That's your name, right?"

He grinned and took the seat across from me. "Yeah. I'm glad I found you here. I was wondering if you've had any more dreams about me."

I shook my head. "It doesn't work that way. I would only dream about you if you were in danger."

He chuckled synthetically. "Yeah, well…"

"Well what?"

"Nothing," he said. "No dreams. That's a good sign."

"What is it you're into?" I demanded. "Seriously. Am I going to have to save your stupid ass again?"

"Whoa." He laughed, raising his hand. "No need for name calling."

"Well, whatever it is you did, you should have learned from it the first time."

"I did, but you heard the guy. He plans on coming after me again. He won't give up just because you stepped in once."

I sighed. "What did you do?"

"Can't you just accept that I don't want to tell you?"

"Not really. Not if we still plan to get to the bottom of this whole dream mystery together."

"We?" He chuckled. "I thought you said there was no 'we.'"

"Shut up," I sneered. "Grab a book and help me."

"Help you with what?"

"With figuring out if there is a name for this…thing I have."

"Is that thing 'being crazy'?" he snapped at me, almost losing the playful tone he had displayed before.

"If you aren't going to be helpful, then leave."

He raised his hands in front of him. "Fine. Dreams, right? Premonitions?"

I nodded.

"Okay. I'll go get some books then."

We sat silently, flipping through encyclopedias on dream studies, which sounded more like superstitions than anything. William gave up on books somewhat quickly and slipped his phone out of his pocket to search online.

Sticking to my preferred books, I found they were full of beliefs of evil creatures who feed off nightmares or suck the life from a human victim while they dream. After a while, I still hadn't found anything on the strange ability I had.

"Hey," William said quietly, pulling me from my frustration.

"What is it?"

"I'm not sure," he mused, moving closer, showing me what he was reading. "After no luck with dream science, I decided to take my chances with psychic abilities and actually found something."

"What does it say?"

He turned the phone horizontally and zoomed in closer. "It says that premonitions are a very common ability among people."

"What about the fact that I started getting them after my accident?"

"Mmm, nothing like that, but…do you see ghosts?"

"Ghosts? No."

"It says here that a near death experience can sometimes enable people to see or communicate with the dead."

I shook my head. "Nothing like that."

"Do you have any other abilities or damages that may be involved? Like something else that happened from the crash?"

I thought for a moment about mentioning the trauma that had ruined my eyes. I glanced at him and liked the way he looked at me, simply waiting for an answer without a single sign of either sympathy or judgment on his face.

"No," I said softly. "Nothing."

"It seems to me like you simply have an ability that your brush with death brought on. You're like…psychic."

I looked to him again, noticing the excitement in his light eyes.

"Is that supposed to be exciting?"

He laughed. "Well, yeah, of course it is. It's the coolest thing."

I scoffed. "Well this 'cool thing' is more of a huge problem. I never asked for it…and I don't want it."

"Well, Daisy, you don't have a choice. If this is like…your calling, or something, don't you think you should listen? I mean, you have the chance to save lives. How many people do you know can have such a positive impact on the world?"

I sighed and lowered my head. "It should be for someone else, not me. I'm not a hero."

He smiled. "You *are* a hero, Daisy. You saved me. And I'm sure you saved many others."

I looked away from him. His words sank in, and I realized he was right. The dreams were not going to stop just because I wanted them to. I could not will this away. As much as I hated that the accident had completely altered my life, I knew it all meant something. If this was my fate, then running from it would only make things harder.

"Fine," I said. "But there is another thing I haven't mentioned."

"What's that?" he mused.

"There was a boy. He saved me from the crash."

"Is he the one you're looking for?"

I nodded. "He's in a lot of my dreams, but every time I see him, he somehow disappears. I'm trying to figure out how he's related to all this."

He shook his head. "I don't know. Maybe he's some sort of dream creature."

"Dream creature?" I sneered. "You mean the kind that's a hybrid of seven different animals and eats nightmares? C'mon, William. You are supposed to be *helping*."

"Was just a thought."

The day was warm as I walked down the streets. I could feel the sun on my skin. The light made the shadows seem fainter and the gray hues appear almost white with silver sparkles. I gazed around at the trees and planters of the nearby houses, no longer thinking about where I was headed.

I eventually ended up at Jess's house about thirty minutes later than I intended. She came to the door before I even knocked.

"Hey," she said.

I smiled and stepped into her house. The smells brought me back to when we were kids. The house was the same as it had always been. The kitchen was straight across from the front door, with a little rectangular table with four wooden chairs. The drapes I knew were burgundy and hung over a window above the kitchen sink. I eyed the sliding glass door that led to a small back yard, exactly like mine.

We headed up the staircase to the left of the entry way. Jess had one older brother who had moved out a few years ago, meaning we should be able to talk without worrying about being overheard.

Her room was once bright with pale pink walls that matched the flowers on her comforter. Her bed had a wrought iron frame that would gleam and shine when the sun from her window would peek in. I took notice of the light-colored shadows in the room that told me it was still as bright as I remembered it.

"Where is your mom?" I asked.

"Don't worry," she said. "She's working late, and Dad is in India."

"India?"

She waved me off. "Yeah, some research thing."

"Okay. Good."

"So what's going on?"

"Well, I talked to William," I said.

"William? As in the stupid ass whose life you saved?"

I laughed. "Yeah, that one."

"Why?"

I shrugged. "He found me at the café."

"What did you talk about?"

"We were looking into what my dreams might mean."

"And?"

"He thinks I'm psychic."

She narrowed her eyes for a moment. "Psychic sounds a little...heavy."

"I was thinking the same thing."

"I didn't say I disagree though."

"You think I'm psychic?"

She shook her head. "I don't know. What else would you call it?"

I shrugged. "No idea."

"What about your rescuer?"

28

"No more ideas on that," I said. "William thinks he may be some sort of dream creature, but the only information I found on those described fantastical shadow monsters."

She laughed. "Yeah, I think we can both agree he's not one of those."

"Then what is he, and why, or better yet, *how* does he keep disappearing?"

"Well, are you sure you actually saw him?" she asked.

"When? At the road?"

"Yeah. Are you sure there was someone there?"

"Why are you asking me that? You saw him, Jess. You followed after him."

She shook her head. "You started running toward a tree, and I followed *you*. I didn't see anyone."

"Wh..what? No. I know you saw him."

"Daisy, I didn't."

"Jess, I remember. I remember you looking right at him."

"It wasn't him I was looking at, Daisy. I was just looking toward the tree where you were pointing. I didn't see a boy."

My head felt like it was spinning. I flopped down onto her bed and grumbled.

"What's wrong?"

"Maybe I am going crazy."

"You aren't going crazy," she answered apathetically.

"Well, nobody but me has ever seen him," I said, sitting up again. "He's always disappearing."

"That doesn't mean he isn't real."

"Yeah, well, it means something."

"Something, sure. I am still willing to help you figure out what."

"I know." I sighed. "I'm hoping William can help too."

"How much do you know about this William character anyway?"

"Almost nothing."

"Then maybe you shouldn't meet up with him by yourself."

I nodded. "That wasn't really the plan. He just showed up."

"Well, call me next time, okay?"

"Sure."

"So, have you had any more dreams?"

I shook my head. "No. None of *those* dreams anyway."

She sighed. "Is there anything you know of that brings them on?"

"No. And as much as it seems like having another dream would help, I would much rather *not* have one."

She nodded. "I know."

"So what do I do?" I asked. "Wait for the boy to magically disappear again?"

"I'm as lost for ideas as you are. But give me some time, and I'm sure I can come up with something."

"Okay, but, Jess…?"

"Yeah?"

"I don't want to be alone tonight. Would it be okay if I stay here?"

She smiled. "You know you are always welcome here. I'll get some snacks, and we'll make a slumber party out of it."

I laughed. "Sounds good."

"So, have you thought about what you are going to do after summer?"

I scoffed. "No. I mean, not really. I plan to take a year off. I think that's what my mom wants anyway."

She nodded. "I had the same idea, although I know that's *not* what my mom would want."

"We can come up with some plans together. With what I'm dealing with, I want to have someone with me."

"You know you are not that different, right?" she asked. "I mean, not to say you aren't special, but you aren't…*special*. You know?"

I laughed. "I know, but my mom still thinks I should give myself some time to get used to things before going back to school. I mean, college will be stressful enough on its own."

"Yeah, tell me about it. I would rather wait and room with you than try to settle in by myself with some random roommate who may end up with pink hair or be obsessed with slasher films."

I laughed. "I'm with you on that."

Jess turned on all the lights in the room as soon as it started to get dark.

"So I read this weird thing online," she started, tossing a few more potato chips in her mouth.

"Yeah? Like what?"

"Well, here." She pointed at her screen. "It says people who have dreams of the future like you are in fact psychic."

"Okay, so I'm psychic. That doesn't explain anything about my rescuer."

"I know," she murmured. "That one is a mystery."

I sighed. "I have to see him again. I have to get him to talk to me."

"Well, obviously he doesn't *want* to."

"I have to do *something*! Next time I see him, I'll just have to do some-thing to make him want to talk to me."

"Like what?" She laughed. "Take your top off?"

I smiled and threw a chip at her. "Maybe."

"I don't know if there would be much to see."

"Hey!" I cracked, still laughing. I smacked her with a pillow.

"No need for violence." She snickered.

"Come on. Be serious for a minute."

"Okay, okay." She inhaled slowly and made eye contact. Before saying anything, she sputtered out another fit of laughs.

"Jess!"

"I'm sorry. It *was* pretty funny."

I just glared at her.

"Okay. I'm serious."

"Okay. I really need your support right now."

"What do you mean?"

"I'm just…I'm afraid to fall asleep."

Her smile instantly faded, and she wrapped me in a hug. I sighed into her chest.

"It'll be okay," she said. "I promise."

Chapter Five

NO DREAMS DISTURBED me that night, but I was obviously distracted during the morning.

"Daisy?" Jess questioned, stepping from the bathroom back into her room.

I looked up.

"Well?"

"Well what?"

She sighed. "Were you listening to me?"

"Um, no," I answered. "Sorry. What were you saying?"

"I just want to know if you want to shower first."

"Oh. No. It's okay. You go first."

"Okay. Are you going to stay?"

I nodded. "If that's okay. I still don't want to be alone."

She nodded. "I won't be long."

I fell backward onto the bed and closed my eyes. I didn't want to risk falling asleep again, but my entire body and mind felt exhausted. I'd kept waking up at odd hours of the night when I was afraid I may be starting to dream, so I didn't get nearly enough sleep.

Jess was back in less than twenty minutes, wrapped in a towel.

"All yours," she said. "You can borrow something, and I'll wash your clothes for you."

"Thanks."

I stepped into her tiny bathroom and examined myself in the mirror. I was never displeased with the way I looked, but I missed the pink shine in my lips and cheeks and the vibrant hue of my yellow hair. More than anything, I wished to once more be able to see my sky blue eyes contrasted with my dark brown lashes and eyebrows. As hard as it sometimes was, I was thankful I could still remember that.

When I walked back into Jess's room, she was sitting on her bed, reading a book.

"Hey," she said, not looking up from the page she was reading. "I left you some clothes on the chair."

"Thanks."

I picked up the jeans and tank top from the armchair and squeezed into them. Jess was always a bit thinner than I was, but we were of similar build, so we shared clothes regularly.

"Feel like coffee?" Jess asked, finally looking up from her book.

"Yeah. We going out?"

She nodded. "Yeah. I'd like to get out. Besides, my dad broke our coffee pot last week."

I chuckled.

Walking into the coffee house was the same as any other day beside the fact William was sitting at our usual table, staring at the screen of his laptop. *Great.*

"Hey," he chirped as we walked in.

"Um, hi," I stammered. "Jess, this is William. William, meet Jess."

He smiled, offering his hand. Jess reluctantly took it and studied him for a moment.

"Find anything else out?" he asked.

I shook my head. "No, not yet."

"Okay. Well, I'll keep looking, but I gotta head out."

"Sure. See you later then."

He quickly packed up his laptop, and Jess and I took our normal seats.

"Yeah, I don't trust him," she said immediately.

"Why not?"

"I don't know. I mean, don't you get a weird vibe from him?"

I shrugged. "I think he might just be a little…different."

"Maybe. But until you know what he did that would make someone want to hurt him, I'd keep him at a distance."

I nodded. "Yeah, I have to agree."

. . .

The café was quiet, and all the shadows seemed a little lighter than usual. As I sat with Jess, chatting and laughing about unimportant things, I started to feel normal again. I glanced at the counter where they served the coffee and tried to remember the colors. I could tell the logo must have been blue. I stared for a long time, just appreciating what I knew was a step forward.

"What?" Jess asked.

"Huh?"

"You're smiling," she said.

"Am I?"

"Yeah. What are you thinking?"

"I was just noticing the blue color of the logo on the coffee cups."

A huge grin brightened her face. "You can see that?"

I nodded. "Not like you can, but yeah, I'm getting better at it."

I saw a silent laugh shake through her. "That's great. Really." It was visible in her face how pleased she was.

"You know I love you, right?"

She smiled. "Of course. I love you too. What made you say that?"

"I don't know anybody like you, Jess. Everything that I've gone through, you've put yourself through too."

"Daisy, I'm your best friend. That's what I'm here for. When you are sad, I'm sad, and when you are happy, I'm happy. You never have to thank me for that."

I smiled. "I just want you to know how much I appreciate it."

"Of course. Always."

"You're the best."

"You know, I'm not the only one," she said.

I could almost hear an accusing tone in her words. "What do you mean?"

"Your mom. She loves you, Daisy. She wants to help you."

I nodded. "I think I should spend some time with her."

"Yeah, I agree."

"I've been pushing her away lately. I don't think that's going to help."

She nodded, taking a sip of her coffee. "It's hard for her, but you're right. Not talking to her and distancing yourself will only make things worse."

"I wish she could believe I was all right," I said, drooping slightly. "Things aren't easy for me, but I am all right."

She nodded. "Maybe you just need to show her that."

"I've tried," I said with a sigh.

"Well…try again maybe?"

I gave her a wry smile. "Yeah."

Talking to my mom was just as easy as it had always been, at least her questions about school and friends and interests. When she moved into the more uncomfortable topics, things became very tense very fast.

"Have you been having any headaches?" Her face showed an obvious look of worry. I knew she didn't want to ask. She was afraid how I would react.

I kept my composure and just shook my head.

"Are you sure?" She sounded a little less worried.

"Yeah. I'm fine."

"Any other changes?"

I looked into her light eyes and smiled. "Well, I recognized the color of the coffee logo."

"Really?"

"Blue. I was right too."

A huge smile spread across her face, and her eyes brightened. "Could you, you know, *see* it?"

I sighed and shook my head. "I'm not getting better, Mom. I'm just…learning."

Her smile fell. "Oh."

The feeling of her disappointment flooded out of her and into me. I hated being the reason she was unhappy.

"I'm all right, Mom. Really I am."

She smiled gently and placed her arm around me. "I know. You're strong."

I let myself lean against her chest a little. She ran her fingers through my hair as she had when I was little.

"Let's get lunch," she said. "Does that sound good?"

I smiled genuinely and nodded. "Sure."

Her smile widened as she stood up from the couch and grabbed her purse from the coffee table.

"Come on," she said, waving me up. Her smile never faded as we drove to the diner.

She seemed to agree talking about less serious matters would be good for both of us. We talked about Jess and about our plans for taking the year off. Her response wasn't exactly what I expected.

"Are you sure you want to do that, Dais?" She glanced at me then back at her menu.

"Yeah. I thought you'd be pleased."

"Oh, it's not that," she said, placing her menu on the table. "I just don't want you to make the decision because of how *I* feel. Decide because of how *you* feel."

I nodded. "I think you're right though. I think I want to get used to things a little more before dealing with the stress of college."

She nodded. "I think that's a good idea."

"And Jess wants to wait too so we can room together."

She smiled at me in amusement. "Yeah? And what does Wendy think about that?"

I laughed. "I don't think she's told her yet. Knowing her mom, she'll flip."

My mom laughed quite loudly. "Yeah, but knowing Jessica, that won't stop her."

That made *me* laugh.

The rest of the day went smoothly. We were able to talk about my mom's job at the insurance office and more about what my plans were for school when I decided to go back. We discussed a possible journalism major, although I had never thought seriously about what I wanted to do. The accident distracted me from the rest of my life. I knew things would work out. I just had to not let this thing I was going through define me. It all sounded so easy in my head. Living it was another story entirely.

Chapter Six

"DAISY, do we have to do this?" Jess complained while pulling her dark hair into a sloppy bun.

"Come on," I said. "It'll be fun. It's been such a long time since we went out—just to go out."

"What are you talking about?" she whined. "We go out all the time."

"Yeah, to the same café," I answered. "I want to just go relax and talk about something other than…well, you know."

She grumbled. "Fine, but if I get sunburned, it's your fault."

"If *you* get sunburned, I'll be barbecue."

She laughed and shook her head. "Okay, which one?"

I looked at her, and she had a different swimsuit in each hand, dangling from a hanger. I couldn't see the color. I wondered if she'd forgotten. I concentrated for a long moment, studying the shades of gray and the contrast of the polka dots on one and the stripes on the other.

"The green one," I said, "with the white polka dots."

She laughed. "The—this one?" She lifted the hanger of the green suit higher.

I nodded. "Well, yeah. It is green, isn't it?"

She laughed again. "Ni-i-ice," she said, extending the word. "Now what color is the other one?"

I stared again. "Hmm. I'm thinking dark blue, maybe purple, but it's not quite black."

She smiled and nodded her head. "Dark blue. Amazing."

I laughed and flopped down onto my back, into the soft cushion of her bed. "It feels good to be feeling almost normal again."

"Oh, please." Jess laughed. "You don't want to be normal."

"Well, I don't want to be a freak."

"You've always been a freak." Her eyes brightened, and she suppressed a snicker.

I sat up and chucked a pillow at her.

She broke into her high-pitched giggle that almost reminded me of shattering glass. I loved it. She only laughed like that when she was truly happy.

"Then you're a freak too," I said.

"I'd have to be to put up with you."

I smiled but didn't have anything clever to toss back at her. "Would you change already?" I asked, still with a smile in my words.

"Yeah, yeah," she said, walking into the bathroom.

"You know, you may want to put on some sunscreen," she called from the bathroom.

The air itself felt hotter than usual, but the sand was cool under the surface. I buried my hands in it, feeling the coolness seeping into my skin. Jess's voice broke the silence and pulled me from my thoughts.

"So you haven't talked to William again, have you?" she asked.

I turned to look at her, smiling at her big round sunglasses covering half her face. "No. Not since the time I introduced you."

"Hm-m. I just think there is something going on with that kid."

I shrugged. "Maybe. Or maybe having a dream about me just…really rattled him."

She sighed and turned away. "Maybe."

"I mean, think about it," I continued. "He had some random dream of someone he has never met, and the very next day, that person saves his life."

"Yeah?"

"It's pretty strange," I said. "I know I'd be scared and looking for answers too."

She nodded. "I know. That's not what I'm concerned with. There was something else. There was something…off, maybe missing."

I sighed. "I hope you're wrong. I am still hoping maybe he can help me."

"Me too."

"Can we do one thing for the remainder of the day?" I asked.

She looked to me again. "Sure."

"Talk about anything *but* him and my dreams?"

She smiled. "Of course."

I looked out into the horizon, wishing I could see the orange hue in the water reflecting the sun. All I saw was a little silver stretch of water, a lighter gray than the rest. Jess pulled me from my thoughts.

"Do you remember that prank we pulled on Josh Hamilton in middle school?"

I burst out laughing. "Oh God," I shrieked. "I forgot about that."

"How could you forget?"

"He screamed like a girl when all those poppers went off."

She shook her head, still laughing. "I thought he'd swear off New Year's Eve parties for the rest of his life."

"You always were the more creative one," I said.

"That's not true." She chuckled. "I've always just been more of a bitch."

I found myself in another fit of laughs. "*That,* I can agree with."

Jess smiled and placed her hand on her chest. "I am the queen."

"I miss that," I said.

"Middle school?"

"Oh God no," I answered with a chuckle. "I mean us—being silly and crazy without a care in the world."

"I guess that changes when you get older."

"Well, it doesn't have to."

She smiled. "Well then, let's use this year off to find creative ways to terrify complete strangers."

I laughed. "Deal."

"You know, college may have many of the same sort of jerks whose lockers we could put weird shit in."

"Probably."

We headed back to Jess's house once we started feeling hot and sticky from sweat. It still wasn't dark, but the impending thought of sleep made a lot of anxiety creep into my chest—the kind one feels when waking up from a nightmare shaking and soaked in cold perspiration. I tried to shake it off, but Jess noticed—like she always did.

"You doing okay?"

"Yeah," I said. "I just have a bad feeling about tonight."

"What do you mean?"

"I'm not sure. It's been a week since my last dream, and I'm feeling that familiar sense that one will come tonight."

She sighed. "Do you want to stay over?"

I shook my head. "It's okay. I think my mom wants me home tonight."

"Well, call me. Let me know what's going on, okay?"

I nodded as she pulled into my driveway. "Sure. No problem."

The dream was in color, but it looked as if I'd been transported into a pastel portrait.

Everything seemed light and chalky. I looked around the little grass field with white wildflowers billowing in the breeze. I felt something brush my leg and jumped, backing away. I looked at a little gray kitten staring up at me.

"Oh, hi," I cooed, kneeling down to pet it.

"Hello," the cat sang back.

I shrieked, jumping back again. "Did...did you just talk?"

"Don't be frightened of me," he said.

I kept my distance, but the cat crept closer, trying to close the space between us.

"What are you?"

He laughed in a deep, husky voice. "I'm a cat."

"I can see that. That's not what I mean."

"It's just me, Daisy. I won't hurt you."

I heard him say my name, and my memory assaulted me with the crash, and I felt almost sick from dizziness. "You... It's you."

He chuckled again. "It's me."

"How...how can this be?"

"It's a dream," he said.

"I'm dreaming?"

The cat didn't answer, just stared into my face. He had hazel eyes that did not appear like the eyes of a cat but looked very human.

"It is you," I said. "Why are you here?"

"I wanted to see you."

"As a cat?"

He chuckled. "Yes."

"Why?"

"Because I wanted to be a cat. Is that so strange?"

"Yes," I replied immediately. "People don't just decide to be cats one day and then become them."

"I do," he cooed.

"Then your dreams are even weirder than mine."

He purred, rubbing against my leg.

"That's weird," I said, shaking him off.

He laughed again and pranced away. He turned back to face me. "Keep your loved ones close."

I meant to ask him what he meant, but I was already awake with that odd feeling of panic racing through my limbs. I couldn't decide why I was so alarmed and frightened by a talking cat. Even though this dream was in color, I knew it wouldn't come true. I tried focusing on that to keep my mind at ease long enough to make it to Jess's. I raced to her house and started pounding on the door. She opened it up, her eyes wide with concern.

"What's wrong?" I could hear panic in her voice.

"I just need a friend. Please."

We headed up to her room, and as soon as she closed the door, I broke into tears. She leaned in and hugged me without shooting off a wave of annoying questions.

"Here, sit," she said and led me to the armchair beside her window. She sat across from me on her bed.

I wiped my eyes with the back of my hand, trying to calm down. "I'm so sorry."

"No, it's okay. Talk to me."

"I had a dream."

She nodded.

I sniffled and took a deep breath, trying to prevent the rest of my tears from falling. "It wasn't even that bad. I'm just so…so—"

"Frustrated?"

"Yes," I answered. "Exactly. Frustrated!"

"And the dream?"

"It scared me, and I don't know why."

"Was it in color?"

I nodded. "Yeah, but it can't come true."

"Why's that?"

"Because there was a talking cat."

"A talking *cat*?"

I nodded. "Weird, right?"

"Creepy," she said.

"That's what I thought."

"Daisy, that would have scared me, too."

"That's not all. The cat was him."

"Dream boy?"

I nodded. "He said he wanted to see me."

"Then why the hell was he a cat?"

I chuckled. "I asked him that, and he said it was because he wanted to be a cat."

"Okay. Now this guy is annoying *and* creepy."

"You're telling me."

"Well, at least we know it won't come true."

I laughed. "Let's hope so."

"Did he say anything else?"

"I almost forgot. He said to keep my loved ones close."

"Whoa!" She raised her hands. "Creepy times two."

I sighed. "Yeah."

"Maybe it was just a nightmare."

"I wish I could believe that, but I'm not that lucky. Not to mention the dream *was* in color. The colors were dull, but they were there."

"What do you mean dull?"

"Like pastels," I said.

"Less vibrant?"

I nodded.

"Hm-m."

"Does that mean anything?"

Jess shrugged. "No idea."

I sighed. "Can I stay here again?"

She smiled. "Of course."

Chapter Seven

I HEARD Jess stir and looked over at her. I was hoping she may have been awake just so I could talk to her a little longer before falling asleep. Putting off the inevitable didn't make a whole lot of sense, so I tried to let myself relax. When sleep finally did come, I was awake before I even realized I had fallen asleep. Jess was lightly shaking me.

"Get up, sleepy head," she sang.

I groaned. "Sorry. It's been a while since I have had any restful sleep."

"Coffee will help."

"You know, someday you are going to die of caffeine withdrawal."

She laughed. "I just need to get a job so I can afford my habit. My dad won't be giving me money forever, especially when he finds out I'm taking the year off."

I laughed. "Yeah, we both need jobs."

"Well, I'm not broke yet. Come on."

I got up to order the coffee. As I reached into my bag to pull out a few dollars, I felt someone brush against my shoulder. Automatically I looked up but didn't see anyone there. I turned around but found I was alone at the counter.

"Miss?"

I looked to the cashier.

"Can I help you?" she asked.

"Uh, yeah, sorry." I ordered our drinks and sat back down.

"What?" Jess asked as I slid her mug over to her. "What's that look for?"

"Uh, nothing really," I said. "Do you ever feel like someone is watching you?"

"Not really. I mean, I guess I can tell when someone across the way is staring at me, but I don't feel like I'm being followed."

I slouched down in my chair. "I do."

"Still?"

I nodded.

"Do you think it could be him?"

"I think it could be my own paranoia."

She smiled thinly. "Let's just enjoy the day, all right? I'm here, and I'll kick the ass of anyone who tries to mess with you."

I giggled. "I know it too. What if it's a talking cat?"

She laughed. "We'll see."

I looked over at the table where I first saw the boy, and as usual, it was empty. I sighed to myself. Jess followed my eyes.

"What?" she asked, glancing behind her at the table.

"Nothing."

"You didn't see him again, did you?"

"No," I answered, almost laughing. "I promise. I just thought there was someone next to me at the counter, but when I turned around, no one was there."

"Hmm. I didn't see anyone but you."

I nodded. "Like I said, I'm probably just being paranoid."

She pulled her eyebrows together. "Did you...did you see someone?"

I shook my head and took a sip of my mocha. "No. I just felt someone bump into me."

"Oh. Well, maybe they just walked past you and you missed them when you turned around."

I chuckled and shook my head. "It's fine. It's nothing."

Jess just nodded.

That night, I knew my thoughts had exhausted me, and I was finally able to fall asleep. As I slipped into a dream, I heard that voice again, the voice of the cat.

. . .

"Keep your loved ones close."

The weak sun shone white in the gray sky, and I found myself in an ordinary field, searching for the cat, the source of the voice. A screaming wind came tearing from the west, stripping away the grays and whites to reveal effervescent color and that same meadow where I spoke to the cat-boy hybrid. I couldn't see his coat bobbing about in the tall green grass, but that didn't mean he wasn't there. The chill up my spine and the heavy feeling in my gut told me I wasn't alone. I could feel the hairs on the back of my neck stand up as I felt a pair of eyes trained on me, and an itch started between my shoulder blades.

My reflexes kicked in, and I broke into a panicking sprint. I could hear my heart beating in my ears and felt heat rush to my cheeks. I was back in the meadow but couldn't see the cat. I glanced around. I was alone, seeing only tall grass and little white flowers dancing in the dull sunlight. My limbs began shaking from anxiety. The ice in my veins had not warmed, and my breathing became quick and labored. I turned to check behind me, but still there was no cat. I spotted a figure across the meadow. I couldn't tell if it was him, and I feared if I were to approach him, he would vanish like he always had. I raced in his direction, feeling the soft grass beneath my feet. I kept running even as my muscles began to ache. As I drew closer, I saw it wasn't him. I stared for a moment at the beautiful, dark, glossy hair and the eyes that held a familiar kind of shimmer.

"Jess?"

She looked up, and I moved closer.

"Jess, what are you doing?"

She opened her mouth to speak, but no sound came out. She gripped her fingers around her throat as if she couldn't breathe and began softly heaving. Her chest rose and fell with each attempt. I took a step forward, wanting to help but unaware of what was wrong. I reached for her, not sure why or what I was trying to do. As my fingers closed around her shoulder, an almost inhuman howl tore from her lips. I jumped back, and a surge of blood erupted from her mouth, splashing the grass and leaves with dark crimson. The blood in my veins turned acidic, and my entire body burned. I could feel the scorching heat in my head, just like the day of the accident.

Jess fell to her knees. Her body ripped horrible gags from her chest, and blood was still dripping from her parted lips. My pulse raced, and confusion coursed through me. *I heard a scream that must have been coming from me, but it did not sound like my voice. It sounded desperate and poisoned with terror. It wasn't a high pitched shriek but more of a low, almost painful-sounding wail. I screamed until my throat burned, and I fell to my knees in convulsing sobs. I couldn't take my eyes off of Jess as the heat from her blood soaked into my shoes.*

Her body slumped into the grass, crushing the foliage. I pulled myself to my feet and took another unsteady step toward her. She was lying on her back with eyes that no longer gleamed, that no longer saw—dead shallow eyes staring up into the sky. I tried with everything I had to pull myself from the dream, to wake myself up.

I flew up in bed, soaked in sweat. I tried to regulate my breathing, but the panic was still almost suffocating me. I realized then what the cat had meant from the very start. *Keep your loved ones close.* I took one last deep breath, and I reached for my phone to call Jess.

"What's up?" she asked.

"Jess, lock your doors now."

"What?"

"Lock your doors and windows. Don't move. I'm coming over." I hung up before she replied.

I ran outside and pulled my old bike from the shed, hoping the tires weren't flat. I didn't worry about the strings of spiderwebs clinging to the handlebars and pedals. I rode as quickly as I could to Jess's house. I threw my bike down on her lawn and pounded on the door.

She opened up to let me in, then locked the dead bolt and the chain lock.

"What's going on?" she asked.

I shook my head. "Is everything locked up?"

"Yes. Even all the windows. Why?"

"Stay here. I'm going to look around."

"Daisy, what's going on? If there is someone in the house, the last person who should be looking around is you."

I glared at her, but I knew she was right. If anyone could take care of themselves, it was Jess. "Fine."

She quietly stalked into the kitchen, and I followed her. She slid a large knife from the block and peered around the corner. She signaled me to follow, and we reached the dining room. She shut all the curtains and checked the living room.

"I just came from upstairs," she said, "and that was clear."

I nodded. "Just…don't leave the house."

"You are staying, aren't you?"

"Are you kidding me?" I choked. "Of course I'm staying. 'Keep my loved ones close,' remember?"

Her mouth fell open. "Oh my God. Did you have a dream?"

I fell onto the beige couch next to her.

"You did, didn't you?" I could hear tears behind her words.

"It's okay," I said. "Yes. I saw you in a dream, but you're fine."

She sighed. "Are you sure?"

"Jess, I'm sure. Remember, I see people so I can save them."

She nodded. "It's just…I saw you too."

"Wait—what?"

"I had a dream too, and I saw you."

"What do you mean?"

She shook her head. "It was weird. I was picking flowers, which is something I would *never* do and—"

"Flowers? In a meadow?"

She jerked her head toward me in surprise. "Yes. How could you have known that?"

I didn't answer.

"Did we have the same dream?" Her voice had lowered almost to a whisper.

"I don't know. What happened next?"

"Nothing," she said. "You asked me what I was doing, and I woke up."

I couldn't frighten Jess more by telling her about the pain, the blood—the death. I just nodded. "Yeah. We had the same dream."

"Wow. Do you know why?"

I shook my head. "I have no idea."

"That's too weird."

"We need to stay close for a few days," I said. "Don't eat anything strange, don't drive, be careful when showering, don't cook with gas or knives… Just don't do…anything."

She nodded but didn't say a word.

The day was dull, but my paranoia remained very intense. We sat in Jess's room while she surfed the internet and I read some books from the library, constantly peeking out the window.

"Find anything?" she asked.

I dropped the curtain back into place. "No, not yet. I keep finding more and more stories about mystical monsters."

"Like what?"

"Ghouls, ghosts, demons, and weird hybrid dream monsters."

She sighed. "Me too."

"Maybe we are looking way too far into this. I mean...I have a gift—that's apparent. Maybe this boy is nothing more than my imagination."

She stared at me, hard. "Is that really what you feel in your heart, Daisy?"

I huffed. "No."

"That's what I thought. Let's just keep looking. It's clear he's stalking you."

"Do you think he plans to hurt me?"

She shook her head, not taking her eyes off her screen. "I'm not sure. You dreamed of me. Maybe he's planning to hurt *me*."

I peeked out the window one more time and almost lost my breath. By the sidewalk, looking up at the window as if he knew I was there, was a little gray cat.

"Jess," I hissed.

She grunted a response.

"Jess, look."

She got up from her bed and looked out the window. "So?"

"It's a cat."

"Yeah, I see that." She chuckled. "It's probably the neighbor's."

"I don't know. It looks like the cat from my dream."

"Daisy, come on," she groaned. "Do you actually expect it to talk?"

"I don't know what to expect. I'm going outside. Lock the door behind me. I'll be right back."

"Are you sure you should do this?"

I sighed. "Just lock the door."

I stepped out into the gray afternoon and looked at the cat still sitting at the curb. He looked at me, but I could not be sure of the color of his eyes.

"Hello." I waited with angst, expecting a human voice to emerge.

The cat meowed up at me and took a few steps closer to nuzzle my leg.

It's just a cat. You are such an idiot, Daisy.

I patted the cat on the head and started back to the house. Jess let me in, and when we got back to her room, the cat was still looking up toward the window.

I knew I couldn't leave Jess alone, so I texted Mom to let her know I wasn't coming home again. I figured sleep was impossible, so I stayed up, sitting in Jess's armchair, staring out the window. The cat had left but recently appeared again at the curb. He was still gazing up at me. It was seeding crazy ideas into my head, so I closed the curtain and focused on listening to Jess's breathing, making sure everything was normal.

I must have fallen asleep in the chair because when I opened my eyes, Jess was shaking me.

"Hey!" She grinned. "You fell asleep in the chair."

I stretched the kinks out of my back. "Yeah. What time is it?"

She glanced at the digital clock on her nightstand. "Ten thirty." She grabbed a towel and turned back to me before disappearing into her bathroom. "Can we *please* go out today?"

"Jess, I don't think that's a good idea."

She sighed. "Daisy, it's been over a whole day, and nothing has happened."

"Sometimes nothing happens for a week."

She sighed. "Just come with me, and you can make sure nothing happens. Please?"

I mentally weighed it for a moment. I was not comfortable leaving the house, but Jess coughing up blood in the middle of a field was unlikely to actually happen.

"Fine," I said, "but we have to stay together."

She nodded. "We always do."

Chapter Eight

THE NIGHT WAS WARM, and I kicked off the constricting blankets and rolled to my other side, trying desperately to get comfortable. I could hear Jess lightly snoring beside me.

I got up and crept into Jess's bathroom, fumbling through the medicine cabinet without turning the light on. I found the cough syrup and took a gulp straight out of the bottle. I slinked back to bed, trying not to wake Jess. The medicine was enough to make my eyes feel heavy. The shadows grew dark, and I slipped into unconsciousness.

It must have been either very late that night or very early the next morning when I awoke, feeling I was being watched. My eyes darted open only in time to see a hand come down over my mouth. I was unsure if I was awake, but slowly my mind cleared, and the primal instinct of survival kicked in. I tried to scream, but the hand over my mouth was solid and strong. My heart was pounding as if it would tear through my chest. My entire body felt hot with anger and fear. I kicked and flailed, hoping the attack would wake Jess. I saw the black shadows in the room turn to gray with light and felt Jess jump from the bed. I could see the assailant had a ski mask on, making it impossible to see his face. The man tried reaching for my arms to pull me from the bed.

Jess didn't say a word. Without warning, his hand was ripped violently away from me, and he lurched back, howling. His back arched, and he stumbled into the wall. I saw thin, dark lines running down the length of his limbs. He slumped to the floor, unmoving.

Jess was standing wide eyed and shaking. Her entire body seemed to be shivering. With fear still coursing through me, I saw the kitchen knife in her hand, dripping dark liquid.

I threw myself over her bed and reached into her nightstand, shuffling through the contents of books and diaries, searching for her pepper spray. Jess was still frozen.

"Jess," I called.

No answer.

"JESS! Snap out of it!"

Her eyes became clearer, and she turned to me, dropping the knife.

"Where's your pepper spray?"

"Attached to my keys."

She dug through her purse and tossed me her keys. I got up from the bed and nudged the man with my foot. He didn't budge. I reached down to remove his mask, and he rolled over, grabbing hold of my wrist. I shrieked and pressed down the trigger on the pepper spray. He screamed again and scrambled for the door. I tried once again to reach him and rip off his mask, but he was already stumbling down the stairs, trailing blood as he headed for the door.

I couldn't breathe at first. I just stared at the blood, gasping. My body was shaking, and Jess had dark stains of tears on her cheeks.

It was a long time before either of us said anything. Jess fell into the chair, and I ended up on the floor. It must have been early morning, and her mom must have been at the hospital since nobody came running to our aid.

"We need to clean this up," Jess whispered, her voice barely audible.

I nodded but couldn't lift myself from the floor.

"What kind of criminal doesn't have a weapon?" she added.

"A stupid one…or…inexperienced."

She huffed. "Why would he do this?"

I knew who she meant and just shook my head, still staring at the dark stain of blood on the carpet. "I don't know. After saving me, he does this?"

"We need to clean this up, now. Before Mom sees it."

I nodded. "What about that carpet cleaner we picked up last year when we spilled that bottle of wine?"

She chuckled halfheartedly. "Yeah, I still have some."

She stepped into her bathroom, and I could hear her shuffling through the cabinets, some things crashing to the floor.

"Got it," she said, standing beside me on the floor.

I still hadn't taken my eyes off the blood.

"Daisy?"

I finally made eye contact. "Sorry. I'm still trying to figure out what to make of this."

"I know," she said softly. "This isn't good at all, but we need to take this one step at a time. Step one is scrubbing all this blood off the carpet before it sets."

I cleared my throat. "Yeah. I'll get a brush and some towels."

The drops of blood on the staircase came out pretty easily, but the puddle in the middle of Jess's bedroom was too deep into the carpet to get out. We scrubbed for over an hour, and there was still a light gray stain.

"My mom will definitely notice this." She walked out of her room, and a thud echoed through the hallway. "Daisy, a little help please?"

I stepped into the hallway and saw her tugging a rug from the linen closet. I knelt down to grab the other end to drag it into her room. I could tell it must have been white, which would match the pink of her walls and bedspread. Her mom wouldn't think twice of Jess redecorating.

"Good idea," I said.

"It works," she answered with a sigh.

It wasn't yet light, and neither of us had spoken a word in a while. Jess was curled up in the chair, and I was under the blankets of the bed, facing away from her.

"We can't stay here," she finally said.

I sat up. "Where else should we go?"

She shook her head. "Not here. I locked everything—the doors, the windows. Everything."

I sighed. "My mom is home. She always knows when something is wrong. I can't risk her finding out about this."

"She wouldn't believe us."

I nodded. "I know. She still thinks everything bad is because of my injury, but still—I feel we need to deal with this without involving our parents and, potentially, the police."

"Then what do we do?"

"I don't know. Sleep in shifts?"

Jess huffed. "If I can sleep at all."

"I'll take first shift. I will stay in the hallway with the knife and pepper spray. Okay?"

She nodded. "Okay."

I moved Jess's armchair outside her door and kept the living room light on in hopes it may ward off any more strangers. I was wide awake and couldn't have slept if I wanted to. I sat with a reading light, skimming through a romance novel I found on Jess's nightstand. I couldn't concentrate much on the words. I kept looking up every few seconds to make sure I was still alone. I soon realized there was no sense waking up Jess. I wasn't going to sleep no matter what. I figured I'd let her get as much rest as possible.

I saw the light silver peeking through the windows—the sun was coming up. I stood up and stretched, feeling the knots in my back loosen. I wrapped my blanket around my shoulders and entered Jess's bedroom. She opened her eyes as soon as I walked in, gasping.

"Just me," I said.

She groaned. "Is it my turn already?"

"No, it's okay. I couldn't sleep, so I stayed up. It's morning."

"What? You let me sleep?"

I nodded.

"Thanks."

"No problem. I may need a nap this afternoon though."

"I'm fine with standing guard during the day. Nothing else weird happened last night, right?"

I shook my head. "Nope."

"Good. That's good."

It was noon when I finally passed out in Jess's bed. I wasn't even aware of how tired I was until my eyes wouldn't stay open. I drifted off and into a dream.

The sun was warm, and I pulled my purple sweater tighter over my chest. I buttoned it, not because I was cold but because it felt so good to be warm. I was out on the street, walking toward my house. Colors were everywhere, and I felt like a kid again. The trees loomed overhead, their bright green and yellow leaves almost sparkling in the sunlight. The flowerbeds adorning the nearby houses were filled with a plethora of bright shades. I walked slowly, just enjoying the scene. When I got to the door of my house, even the handle was warm from the sun. I kept my hand on it for a moment, just letting the feeling consume me. When I opened the door, cool air ruffled my yellow hair, and I followed the entryway into the kitchen.

The house felt empty at first until I heard my mother call me from the living room. "Is that you, honey?"

I found her sitting in front of the TV, watching some sitcom. "Yeah, just me."

She turned to smile at me, and something wasn't the same about her. Her eyes seemed darker and distant, almost empty. Her smile seemed forced, an imitation of what it was, like a stranger trying to be my mom. She didn't feel like my mom at all.

"Are you okay?" I asked her.

Her smile didn't fade, and her voice was overly cheerful. "Why wouldn't I be okay?"

"Um"— I shook my head—"no reason."

"Here, sit next to me."

I took a seat on the couch, and she put her arm around me. Her body felt cold and her skin thin like parchment. She seemed almost—dead.

I jolted awake, gasping for air. Jess immediately rushed to my side.

"Tell me!" she demanded.

"My mom," I cried.

"What?"

"My mom!" I repeated. "We have to go. Now!"

Jess yanked her bag off her desk and followed close on my heels. We could get to my house in fewer than five minutes if she drove like she normally did.

"Step on it," I said.

"Duh," she replied tightly.

She sped off down the street, knocking me into my door. I pulled on my seat belt, struggling to fasten it with how terribly I was shaking. I couldn't stop fidgeting.

"Can't you go any faster?" I hissed.

"Do you want to get there alive?" she replied, but I saw her press her foot a little harder on the gas pedal, her knuckles white on the wheel.

When we got to my street, I could feel panic and adrenaline coursing through me at the sight that greeted me. The place was flooded with cop cars, their cold, gray flashing lights drawing morbid terror toward me; an ambulance was backed up on my driveway. So many people were running around, barking into their radios, diving in and out of my house. I jumped out of Jess's moving car. I pushed past the caution tape, my sneakers slapping the pavement, desperate to get into my house. A man in a dark uniform blocked me.

"This is my house!" I screamed, trying to shove by. "I have to get to my mom. Mom!"

"It's too late. It's a crime scene now," he answered firmly.

The words rang in my ears, and my head felt cloudy. I was dizzy, as though my entire world just spun off its axis. I could feel my legs give out. I dropped to my knees, the brutal, unforgiving concrete quickly sucking the remaining heat from my body, making me cold—so cold I'd never be warm again. I held my head in my hands as if that could keep me together. I could hear the muffled voices echoing through police radios. The drumming sound of feet was almost maddening. *Tap. Tap. Tap. Tap.* Over and over again until I had to cover my ears, hating the strangers invading my home—violating my mother's sanctuary and mine.

A female officer strode toward me. "Are you all right? Do you need medical attention?"

I looked up blankly and unsteadily got to my feet. I felt as if my legs were made of rubber and I'd collapse at any second. I struggled to speak, but nothing came out. I could feel bile sneaking up my throat, choking me. I tried again, and my voice came out throttled and hoarse. "This is my house. I need to get to my mom. I need to make sure she's okay," I said desperately. "Why w-won't they let me g-go inside?"

"Okay," she started calmly, speaking in a soothing voice. "Can you tell me your name?"

"Daisy. Daisy Carmichael. Where is my mom?"

"You're Donna's daughter?"

"Yes," I snapped back. "Where is she?" I asked, forcefully edging toward my home.

I knew the answer before she said a word and could feel my stomach drop out.

I saw her face shutting down and sorrow creeping into her eyes. "I'm so sorry," she said. "There was a break-in. Your mother was at home at the time... I'm sorry, dear. She...she didn't make it."

Grief overflowed inside me, and I couldn't feel anything else. The sobs tore from my chest. I felt arms around my shoulders supporting some of my weight as my legs started to give out and realized Jess was at my side.

"What happened exactly?" I heard her ask.

"There was a break-in," the officer started. "We aren't sure if it was supposed to be a burglary at this time or not, but she was attacked. It looks like she put up a fight. She had defensive wounds on her arms, and a lot of furniture was destroyed in the struggle. I am so sorry. Do you know who could have done this?"

"We don't," Jess said.

"Miss Carmichael?"

I looked up, barely meeting the officer's eyes.

"Do you know of anyone who would want to hurt your mother?"

I shook my head.

"When was the last time you saw her?"

"Um…the night before last…b-before going to bed. I…I came over to Jess's early yesterday morning."

The officer nodded. "I need both of you to come down to the station to answer a few questions. Standard procedure so we can rule you out."

"That's fine," Jess said. "We'll be there."

And we were. What else could we do?

They had me in a tiny, dimly lit room by myself, asking me the same questions over and over. Did I know anyone who would want to hurt my mother? Did I know anyone who would want to break into my house? Where was I when it happened? When was the last time I saw her? It felt like I was in there for hours. Once they were done with me, I waited for them to let Jess go before we headed home.

Jess parked in the street; the driveway was still full of first responders. Movement caught my eye as we approached my home, and I saw two men wheeling a body covered in a sheet out of the house. I felt my body jerking almost involuntarily toward them. Jess pulled me back, and I started screaming uncontrollably.

"Daisy, no," she cried. "No. You don't need to see that."

I continued to scream. "She needs me! My mom needs me! Please! Oh God, please!"

My cries were deep, dreadful sounding moans. I yelled and cursed at Jess to let me go, but she held me firmly.

I needed to go to my mother and tell her I loved her. I needed to run to her to wake her up. I didn't want those horrible people touching her. I didn't want them here at all.

I could feel my vision whitening and the despair thrust into my chest when the realization hit me that I would never again be with my loving mother. I fell weak in Jess's arms. I had stopped screaming, but the sobs were still suffocating me.

"Shh," Jess coaxed. "Daisy, just keep breathing. I'm here. Everything is going to be okay."

For the first time, I knew—nothing would ever be okay again.

Jess helped me wobble to my feet and put me in the car. I was in shock and sat silently, unable to speak a single word.

"Daisy?"

I didn't even flinch at the sound of my name. I sat unmoving. I heard Jess sigh, and she reached over to buckle my seat belt.

"I'm calling my mom," she said. "I'll be right back."

I didn't answer. She stepped out of her car and shut the door. I was glad. I didn't want to hear her say it out loud. I didn't want anybody to say it. I heard her voice, sad and frantic as she told her mom what happened. I couldn't understand the words, but the pain in her voice only made mine worse.

The car door opened with a loud, deafening sound and closed again in a crash so loud I had to cover my ears.

"Daisy?" Jess asked softly, her voice cutting through me. Everything echoed eerily. The sounds were still reverberating through my bones like soft hums ringing in my ears. She didn't try to speak again. I kept my hands over my ears as her engine roared to life. I winced at the pain in my head.

My face was wet and sticky from tears, but they continued to fall, slowly and plentifully down my cheeks. My whole body felt sore and tired. I just wanted to wake up. I wanted it to be a dream. I wanted to wake up in my mother's arms with her telling me it was just a bad dream and everything was going to be okay. I couldn't wake up no matter how hard I tried. Then I just wanted to sleep. I wanted to sleep and never wake up again. I wanted this horrible event to be over.

Chapter Nine

THE WOMAN'S voice was far away and muffled. "With situations like this, we have to think of the best solution for the child."

I sat in the hallway in an uncomfortable plastic chair. Jess sat beside me, holding my hand.

"I understand," her mother answered. "It is what Donna wanted. If those are her wishes, I am more than willing to oblige."

"Fantastic," the woman answered without an ounce of enthusiasm. "We can get the paperwork taken care of and place the minor in your care immediately."

I shuddered knowing Jess's mom had to deal with taking care of me now. I would only be a minor for a few more months. I feared what would happen to me then. I wondered if I would still have a place to stay. Jess stroked my shoulder, but I barely felt it. Everything was quiet and surreal. I couldn't even be sure I was awake. I glanced at Jess for a moment, trying to force myself to feel alive. Her eyes were red and puffy, and her cheeks were wet with tears. I looked away, unable to deal with seeing her grief for what I was feeling. There was just too much—too much darkness, too many vacant voids inside me, trying to pull me apart...too much loss and fear. I couldn't handle any more. I couldn't handle even being awake.

I didn't remember the drive home or climbing the stairs to Jess's room. I sat slowly on her bed, with my mind still replaying the horrible images from the day—my mother's lifeless body covered in a sheet, the cops flooding my home, my own screams. The tears had dried up, but my chest was still tight with sobs tearing at me, trying to escape.

Jess didn't say a word. She just sat in her chair, gazing out the window. She treated me as if I was fragile—made of glass. I felt cold, dead, like stone. Nothing could break or penetrate the cold exterior constricting me.

When Jess finally spoke, it wasn't so painful to hear. Her words were soft. "No matter what happens, Daisy, you will always have a place to stay."

I looked into her eyes for a moment. It was as if she read my mind, knowing I had been asking myself where I would go. I just nodded. She came to sit beside me, and I let myself fall against her chest as she embraced me.

The funeral was only two days later. The sun was shining bright, warm—and sickening, as though God was mocking me with the beauty of that day.

The masses of black fabric blurred together into a sea of shadow. I was alone in my own head, not even listening to the priest reciting the eulogy. It was always just me and my mother. We had no other family. The only people here were work friends, old college buddies, and Jess with her mom. It seemed too empty, too forgettable.

I don't even remember getting back to Jess's house. I curled up in her bed, still in my black dress, and cried myself to sleep.

The next morning, I awoke still feeling heavy and cold as ice. I curled up in the blankets and replayed my memory, wondering if it had been a dream all along. As the grief flooded into me, I knew it was in fact real, but I wanted to go to sleep until things were back to normal.

Jess was already awake, again in her chair, reading a book. I didn't say anything to her. I didn't even let her know I was awake.

Days passed this way. They began to blur together in a haze of depression and pain. I felt empty and alone. For the first time in my life, the accident wasn't the worst thing to have happened to me.

It was late in the afternoon when Jess woke me up.

"What?" I groaned.

"It's past noon," she remarked.

"And?"

She sighed, and I felt the pressure of her weight on the bed. "Daisy, you need to get up."

"I don't need to do anything," I answered curtly.

"Daisy, I know this is hard, but you can't stay in bed like this. You are going to make yourself sick."

I sat up but kept my head down. "I don't know what else to do."

"It's been over a week."

I shook my head. "It's all been one long day to me."

She put her arm around me. "She wouldn't want this."

"What do you mean?"

"Your…mom," she answered, struggling with the words. "She would want you to move on and live your life."

"I feel like I don't even *have* a life anymore." I finally managed to look at her.

"I know, but you do."

I sighed. "So what do you want me to do?" I almost snapped at her.

"Well, you can start by taking a shower and eating something." She smiled and pinched my stomach. "You're withering away."

I let out the huff of an almost-laugh, and my lips curled upward.

"There," she said. "That's what I want to see."

"Okay. I'll take a shower."

"You may want to use some extra conditioner so you can pull a brush through that."

She was smiling, but I didn't laugh. I pulled myself out of bed and sauntered into the bathroom. My feet barely scraped across the floor, and my back hunched over as if I were crippled from age. My eyes were heavy, and I felt almost as though I didn't know where I was—just…simply lost.

There was a very strong sense of something missing. Every moment and every action seemed to be missing a certain meaning and motivation. Things had lost their reason. Why was I doing any of these things? Why does any of this matter anymore?

I tried to heed what Jess had said about what my mother would have wanted. She was right. My mom always wanted me to be happy and take care of myself. I wasn't doing either. I should live in a way that would make her proud of me. I should live for love and happiness. That is what she would have wished for me. Even as it sounded wonderful in my head, I knew it was going to be very difficult to actually do. I wrapped myself in the robe hung on the door and walked back into Jess's room. It didn't feel right shuffling through her closet and dresser drawers for my own clothes. I guessed while I had been in bed, Jess had divided her space.

"Your clothes are on the left," she said, pointing to the other side of her closet.

"Thanks."

I threw on some jeans and a tank top and already felt a little better. I brushed my teeth and drank a glass of water Jess had set on her nightstand. My entire body was frail and dehydrated. I only realized how sick I felt once I started feeling better.

"Come on downstairs," Jess said. "Mom brought some lunch."

I grimaced.

"You can't live on chocolate and Diet Coke."

"Yeah, I know. I'm just not very hungry."

"You haven't felt hungry in days, Dais. You need to eat."

I didn't argue. I followed her down the stairs, feeling weakness in my legs that threatened to give out at any moment. I pulled myself up into a bar stool and rested my head in my hands.

"Well, you look pretty," Jess's mom said, walking into the kitchen from the back door with two paper bags.

I faked a smile but didn't say anything.

"It's good to see you up and about," she continued.

She was trying too hard to be nice. I was certain I looked half dead. She walked behind the counter and placed the bags on the bar in front of me.

"I hope you like Italian," she said.

"Oh, *I* do," Jess chirped, slightly bouncing.

"Italian's great," I managed to answer, trying to force some emotion into my voice.

"Good. I'll get some plates."

I tried to act interested as I ate, smiling or nodding at certain remarks. It was difficult to swallow. After not eating anything substantial in so long, food only hurt. After I got through the first few bites, it became easier, and I realized how hungry I was.

"Well, you definitely have your appetite back." Jess snickered, staring at my empty plate.

I smirked. "Yeah, I guess I do."

I was in her room when Jess walked in and shut the door.

"Okay," she said. "Since you aren't ready to go out, I got all the best."

"Like what?"

She reached into a plastic bag. "I got chips and our favorite dip. I grabbed some chocolate and DVDs—with only the most beautiful men."

I smiled. "Thanks. So, movie night?"

She nodded. "Yup."

"Feels like high school."

She giggled. "Only better, since we aren't in high school."

I scoffed. "You can say that again."

Jess was staring at me solidly as though she wanted to say something but couldn't find the words.

"What is it?" I asked.

"Just…" She trailed off, breaking eye contact.

"Just say it," I demanded.

"Okay, but don't get mad."

"I'm not making any promises."

Her lips tightened for a moment until she spoke again. "After the meeting with social services, they recommended counseling. Do you remember that?"

I shook my head.

"Well, I think it might be a good idea."

I scoffed. "I'm not going to therapy," I snapped. "I'm not crazy."

"It's not like that. It's normal for people who deal with tragedy to talk to someone. I would go with you. My mom has actually gone a few times."

I shook my head mechanically. "Not happening. I want to deal with this on my own."

"But you aren't dealing, Dais. You were in bed for over a week, and you've barely spoken since I got you up four days ago."

"I don't know what else to do. I can't even bring myself to talk to *you*. Why would I want to talk to a stranger about all the intimate details of my life?"

She sighed. "What do you want to do then?"

"I want you to give me some time to get through this my own way. I want you to keep being you and being supportive, but I don't want you to pressure me into talking about it…with anyone."

"Fine. Is there anything else I can do?"

"No, but I was thinking about calling the precinct. I want to know what progress they've made."

She didn't respond, just handed me the phone and the business card of one Officer Boyd.

"Hi, Officer Boyd. This is Daisy Carmichael. I was wondering if there are any updates on my mother's case."

"Hi, Miss Carmichael. I'm afraid we've exhausted all our possibilities at this point. Despite evidence to her fighting back, no DNA evidence was recovered. No unexpected fingerprints were found at the scene, so we're assuming the assailant wore gloves. I'm sorry, but due to the lack of physical and forensic evidence and the fact that there were no witnesses, I'm afraid we have hit a stalemate."

"You can't keep looking?"

"Unless we can find more evidence or get a new lead, there isn't much we can do. If you remember anything you think may help us, Miss Carmichael, no matter how small a detail, please contact us."

I sighed. "So that's it?"

"I'm sorry."

"Thanks."

I ended the call, dropping my cell on the bed. "They've stopped investigating," I murmured, unable to make eye contact. "I guess the case has gone cold."

"I'm so sorry, Daisy."

"I don't understand. How can they just give up?"

She came to sit beside me on the bed, put her arm around me, and just let me fall apart.

It was another four days before Jess was able to convince me to go out.

"It's just the café, Dais. You know this place."

I nodded. "I know, but I'm not sure I can handle it."

"I know you can."

I sighed but didn't reply.

"You gotta live your life. I'll be right there with you."

"And if I want to leave?"

"We'll leave," she said. "No questions asked."

"Promise?"

She nodded. "I promise."

"Okay," I mused.

She smiled brightly, but I could tell she was containing her enthusiasm.

Our usual table at the café was empty, and the place seemed relatively quiet. There weren't too many familiar faces, which was a relief. With the recent tragedy, it only gave people more of a reason to look differently at me.

Jess ordered the coffee and sat back down.

I took a sip and exhaled deeply. "It sort of feels good to be here. I almost feel like myself again."

"Good. How's the mocha?"

I smiled. "It's great. Thanks."

"No dreams, right?"

I shook my head. "I would have told you."

She shrugged. "You weren't saying much of anything."

"I know, but I would have told you that."

"Just checking," she said with a smile.

I looked up at the counter, staring at the logo I knew was blue. It didn't make me feel as happy this time. I was still feeling a bit numb. I looked away and tried glancing at something else. When my gaze moved to the table to my left, my breath was instantly forced from my lungs.

He was there—the boy who saved me. He met my eyes and immediately got up from the table. I stood up without even thinking and followed him out of the coffee house. He quickened his pace toward the parking lot, and I started running, rage coursing through my entire body. My legs were weak, but I kept running, fuming with frustration and hate. The parking lot was empty save for him only a few yards in front of me.

I caught up with him, and with all my strength, I shoved him into a car. He moved away from the car, and I shoved him again.

"Hey," he grunted, moving his hand to his chest. He opened his mouth to say more as he backed away slowly. "Stop," he finally said.

I saw him move in slow motion, and I had no way to control my volume. "Who the hell are you?" I screamed.

"Quiet down," he replied, panicked, as if I was going to cancel out some kind of secrecy.

"Don't you dare tell me what to do! Who are you?"

"You know who I am," he said, still with his hands in front of his chest as if I was going to attack him again.

"You saved me."

"Yes."

"Then why this?" I cried. I could feel the sting in my eyes from unshed tears.

"What are you talking about?"

"You will not play games with me!" I yelled, pointing an angry finger at his chest. "If you saved me, why did you kill my mom?"

SARA J. BERNHARDT

"Whoa!" he exclaimed, raising his hand. His eyes widened. "Daisy, I didn't! I swear. I couldn't have!"

"How am I supposed to believe you?" I took a few steps toward him, and he backed away again.

"What reason would I have?" he asked. "I save people, Daisy...like you. I'm not a killer!"

"Why have you been avoiding me?"

"Avoiding you?" he mused, finally dropping his hands. "What do you mean?"

"At the café and the road," I snapped. "I know I saw you, and you always somehow disappeared before I got to you. Care to explain that?"

"You...you saw me?"

"Yes! And don't try telling me I didn't."

"You're sure? You *remember* seeing *me?*"

"Of course. Now why have you been avoiding me?"

"Daisy, I can't do this here. I shouldn't even be talking to you."

I paused for a moment. "What?"

"I have to go."

"No! No, you can't leave! I have questions only you can answer."

He nodded. "I know, but right now, I have to go. I will find you, Daisy. I promise."

I opened my mouth to answer, but I heard Jess yell my name from the other side of the parking lot. When I turned back to the boy, he was gone.

"Hey," Jess mused, out of breath. "Everything okay? You ran out of there pretty fast. I couldn't find you."

"I...I'm sorry. But I saw him."

"What?"

I cleared my throat. "I saw him. I saw him. I talked to him. He is real, Jess. He was real all along."

Her hand was covering her mouth. She grasped my wrist and led me to her car. We got in, and she instantly started with the questions.

"What did he tell you?"

"Not much. I accused him of...well...my mom."

"Yeah?"

"And he swore he didn't do it."

"You don't believe him, do you?"

I shook my head. "I don't know. I mean...I know I shouldn't, but there was something about him, something in his eyes that made it hard not to."

She narrowed her eyes. "What do you mean?"

68

"I don't know. I can't explain it. I don't think he killed my mom, Jess."

"Then why is he stalking you?"

I shook my head. "I don't know. He said he would find me again. He said he had to go."

"And?"

"And…he disappeared again."

She huffed. "Of course he did."

"It just doesn't make sense," I peeved. "I mean, after all of this and everything I have gone through, why would he just leave me like this?"

Jess shook her head, and a few tears spilled from my eyes.

"Oh, Daisy, don't let him do this to you. You don't need to cry. It'll be okay."

"There is just so much pain right now. I can't handle dealing with any more crap."

She nodded. "We will figure this out. Just remember you are never alone."

I nodded and slouched in my seat. She started the car and looked at me again.

"Do you want to go home?"

I nodded. "I think so."

"We still have chips and dip."

I laughed. "Maybe we can stop by the store to restock on chocolate."

She smiled at me. "Glad to see you are back to your old self."

"Hey." I giggled. "I never stopped eating chocolate."

She cocked her head to the side. "Yeah, that's true. That's about all you were eating."

I smiled, but the thought of being so sick and in bed only made me uncomfortable. If it weren't for Jess, that's where I would still be.

"Thanks," I said, "for getting me to go out."

"Of course."

"I mean it. Staying in bed was not helping me."

She nodded. "I know, Dais. I'm glad you are feeling better."

"Better, but things aren't the same."

"I know that," she said. "I understand that moving on doesn't mean we forget or that we pretend it didn't happen. You know me better than that. I will always be here for you, on the good days and the bad days."

When we pulled into Jess's driveway, I spotted the cat again. The little gray kitten was sitting on the porch, watching me as we strode up to the house.

"Hi there," I said, kneeling down to pet it, still half expecting it to talk back. Without the color, I couldn't tell what his eyes looked like. "Jess, what color are his eyes?"

"What?"

"The cat. What color are his eyes?"

"I have no idea," she said, confused. She knelt down and looked into his little eyes. "Like…green. Greenish with brown, I guess."

"Like hazel."

She nodded. "I guess."

"I didn't know cats could have hazel eyes." I looked to Jess, and she had a very accusing look on her face.

"Daisy, are you serious? It's a freakin' cat. Now can we go eat our snacks and watch Chris Hemsworth?"

I chuckled. "Yeah, yeah. But he doesn't have a collar."

"Daisy, he's the neighbor's cat. You can't kidnap him."

"Are you sure?"

"Well, he's not my cat, and he's here all the time. He has to be the neighbor's. Now stop being weird." She laughed when she said it, but I knew she was serious.

We got back to her room, and she sprawled out on the bed.

"Put a movie in?" she questioned.

I smirked at her and popped in a DVD. I peered out the window by her chair and still saw the cat staring up at the window, actually making eye contact with me. I looked away, feeling invaded and somehow uncomfortable.

I shook off the feeling and got into bed beside Jess to eat ourselves sick on junk food like we were back in middle school.

"Up for another movie?" Jess asked, still munching on chips.

I glanced at her for a moment, but my only thoughts were of my mom. "I don't know."

"You okay?"

I shook my head. "I'm just feeling really depressed right now."

She frowned and handed me a piece of chocolate.

I smiled. "Thanks."

"Do you want to talk about it?" Her voice was soft, as if she were speaking to a child.

"I'm okay. It's just…the movie is over, and we are running low on snacks, and yet…I can't go home to see my mom. I miss her so much." Finally the tears spilled over.

Jess pulled me into a hug but didn't say anything. She just let me cry without the least bit of annoyance or frustration in her touch. I was thankful to have Jess with me, but it just didn't feel like enough. I missed my mom so much already; I feared how horrible it would be five years later…or ten. I sighed, pulling out of the hug.

"I'm sorry," I said, wiping my eyes with the back of my hand.

"No," Jess cooed. "Daisy, don't you ever apologize for this. You have nothing to be sorry for."

I nodded. "I know. I just don't want to be like this."

"There is nothing wrong with feeling sad sometimes. If you didn't have days like this, then I would be worried."

"I guess. You can put in another movie," I said, "and pass the chips."

"You sure?"

"Yeah. Something else to think about."

Chapter Ten

IT WAS the worst time for Jess and me to walk into the café and see William at our table again.

"Do you want to leave?" Jess whispered.

I shook my head. "No. I can't avoid him forever."

He waved us over with his usual ear-splitting grin.

"Hey," he said.

I faked a smile, and Jess pulled an extra chair over to the table.

"Any more dreams?" he asked.

I shuddered, not wanting to think about any of it. "No."

"Any more theories?"

"William—not a good time, okay?"

His face fell. "Oh. Right. Your… I'm sorry. I…wasn't thinking."

I nodded. "It's fine."

"I'll just let you know if I find anything."

I nodded, and he headed out the door.

"Wow," Jess murmured. "You totally just iced him."

"I did not."

"Yeah, Daisy, you did." She snickered.

I shrugged. "I don't want to deal with him right now."

"That was obvious."

I slouched down in my chair. "I wasn't *that* mean, was I?"

She shrugged and waved me off. "You were fine."

I took the moment to appreciate how well Jess knew me.

"So, I told my mom about taking the year off," she said.

"Yeah? What did she say?"

She chuckled. "She said it's a good idea."

"What?"

"I know." She laughed. "She thinks you need me."

"Ah. Well, maybe I do."

"My dad will be back Tuesday. I haven't told him yet."

"Do you think he will be all right with it?"

She shrugged and took a sip of her coffee. "Not sure. I think he may be understanding—considering the circumstances."

I nodded. "Yeah, let's hope."

"We should do dinner," she announced, completely changing the conversation.

"What do you mean?"

"You know, hit up a diner."

My memory flashed with the last day I had spent with my mom. "Um, I don't know."

"We can go anywhere you want," she added.

I made a face but didn't say anything.

"I'd just like to do something a little different tonight."

I could feel how bored she must have felt staying in with me for so long, and then when I am finally willing to leave the house, we just end up back at the café. It was difficult for me to refuse her after everything she had done for me.

I sighed. "Anywhere but Ruddell's."

"Hoppe's?"

I nodded. "Sure."

Her eyes brightened, and I followed her out to the parking lot. I noticed she had removed the yellow dice from her mirror. I almost sighed in relief. "What happened to the dice?"

"Huh?"

I gestured to her rearview mirror.

"Oh, they were getting dingy."

I didn't notice. I wouldn't have noticed.

When we got to Hoppe's diner, I was beginning to feel a sense of happiness in the pit of my stomach. It was the first time I had really felt anything remotely related to joy in a long time.

"I don't know what I would do without you," I said, glancing at Jess.

She smiled. "Hey, what are friends for anyway?"

I mirrored her smile. "Getting each other to eat chips and dip and soda until they barf?"

She laughed. "Damn right."

I giggled and shook my head, opening my menu.

When our waiter came to take our order, I found myself awkwardly staring. I knew him, although I couldn't figure out why. He knew me as well.

"Daisy?" he questioned with a bright smile on his face.

"Sam!" Jess interrupted.

"Jessica, right?" he asked, looking at her, still smiling.

"Just Jess."

"I remember you," he said. "Daisy, your locker was next to mine freshman year."

I giggled. "Right. I remember."

"I sat behind Jess in literature the same year."

Jess nodded. "I'm surprised you remember me. You were never really there."

He shrugged. "You're kinda hard to forget," he said, giving her a crooked smile and a very solid gaze.

Oh, please.

"Were you the ones who put all those poppers in Josh's locker?"

We both burst out laughing.

"I knew it," he murmured. "I tried telling him it was you, but he didn't believe me."

"I never realized it was a secret," I said.

Sam laughed. "It wasn't. I just think Josh didn't want to admit he was pranked by a couple of girls."

"Don't underestimate Jess," I said. "She's evil."

Sam shook his head. "Trust me. I never messed with you in high school for a reason."

"I am the queen," Jess said again, pausing between the words.

Sam laughed again and turned his dark gray eyes to Jess. "What can I get for the evil queen?"

"A number ten for me," she said.

"Wait," I started. "If you're the evil queen, then what am I? Your goofy sidekick?"

"I'd say…her advisor." Sam chuckled.

I smiled. "Accepted. I'll get the same."

He sauntered off toward the kitchen.

"He's kind of cute," Jess said.

"Oh, please," I sneered. "Sam? You're back to that?"

"Hey, he's always been cute."

"He's always been…Sam."

She shrugged. "I liked him."

"I know that, Jess. I remember. It seems like you still do."

She smiled. "Maybe I do."

We got back to Jess's house, and things started flooding back to me. I realized how anxious I was to meet the boy again. He said he would find me.

"Maybe we should go back to the café," I said.

"Why?" Jess asked.

I shrugged. "I think that's where he will expect me to be."

"I don't know if that's a good idea."

"Jess, I have to know who he is and what all of this means."

She sighed. "Okay, but can we go tomorrow instead?"

I nodded but honestly wasn't keen on the possibility of having another dream before I got to talk to him again. I felt the familiar pull of one coming on. I kept it to myself, deciding not to worry Jess.

I saw his chocolate brown coat tail swaying gently in the warm summer breeze. He turned to face me, his hazel eyes full of stories and secrets. His smile meant a lot of different things, but I couldn't define which one I was seeing.

"Is this a dream?" I asked.

His smile widened. "Can you see color?"

I nodded. "I was hoping maybe it was real."

"It is still real," he said softly. "All of this is real, Daisy."

"Who are you?"

He opened his mouth to speak, but I interrupted him.

"Don't tell me I know who you are. If I knew, I wouldn't be asking."

He raised his hand. "My name is Lucas. Lucas Black."

"And you are?"

"I am me. I don't know how else to answer your question."

I sighed. "Fine. Another question then. Why am I dreaming of you, and why are you stalking me?"

"Stalking you? No, Daisy. I'm not stalking you."

"You are. I see you around all the time, and you just disappear."

"I-I don't know how…"

"Don't know how what?"

"I don't know how…you remember."

I was preparing a reply as his face withered away like smoke, and I found myself wide awake. I tried to keep my eyes closed and slip back into the dream, but it was gone. I focused everything I had on bringing back the image of him, but nothing worked. I stayed in bed, unable to sleep with his words echoing in my head. *I don't know how you remember.*

What could that mean? He saw me crash. Did he really think my head injury was that severe? So much that I was only at the café every day because I was reliving the same day? It didn't make sense. I knew I had to find him, and I couldn't wait until morning.

I threw on the clothes still in the corner from yesterday and headed out the door. The shadows were dark, but without the contrasting colors, it made things easier to see.

I rushed down the street, my entire body quaking with anxiety. I kept my feet moving, not knowing where I was going, only knowing I hadn't gotten there yet. I felt the familiar discomfort of blisters forming on the pads of my feet and realized I was at the field—the field where I rescued William.

Lucas was there, exactly like he was in my dream—back turned to me, coat ruffling in the breeze. He turned around with the same smile on his face.

"I told you I would find you," he said.

"*I* found *you*," I argued.

"Fair enough. I merely guided you."

"I need to know what happened to my mom."

"Daisy, your mom was killed by a burglar. It was a tragedy, but I was not involved."

"I feel it in my blood. I feel it in my bones—my soul. There was more to it than that. I know it."

He waved me off. "Perhaps. If that is the case, it's not to my knowledge, and it wasn't my doing."

I just nodded, unable to come up with a response. I had this annoying urge to trust him. I was incapable of believing he was lying. It was digging at me, causing my anxiety to swell until it was pressing down so strongly it was threatening to crush my chest. My breathing became rigid and labored.

"Daisy? Are you okay?"

I looked into his eyes, and even without the color, I could tell they were hazel. I knew them so well, I knew *him* so well, and yet—I didn't know him at all. Everything about his face and voice, everything about the way he moved, it was as if I really knew him.

"I'm sorry if I frightened you," he said, "in the dream."

My eyes locked into his, and I almost lost my breath. "What?"

He looked away. "I didn't mean to scare you."

"Wait—did we have the same dream?"

He looked up again. "You could put it that way."

"What does that mean?"

He sighed but said nothing. My head was spinning. This was more than I could deal with, and I didn't know how much longer I could handle what was coming.

"Please tell me what's going on."

"Daisy, I know what dream you had because…" He broke off, sighing again.

"Because?"

"Because I…I gave it to you."

"You what?" My voice came out swollen with sarcasm.

"I'm telling you the truth," he said, "though I'm sure you won't believe me."

"For some reason, I have a hard time *not* believing you."

The corners of his mouth curled up in a slight smile. "I have no reason to lie to you."

"So, what do you mean you gave me the dream?"

"I mean just that. You didn't dream of me as much as…I came to you in a dream. It's not easy to explain, but I have no other words than that."

I pressed my fingers to my temples. "So…you're a-a dream creature?"

He chuckled. "I don't know if I would say *that*."

"Then what are you?" I pressed.

"It's a lot to tell, Daisy, and there are still answers I need before I can explain everything."

"Then at least tell me one thing?"

"What's that?"

"The cat?"

"Oh." He sounded like he was suppressing laughter.

"Oh?"

"Sorry. Yes, the cat. I was…looking after you."

"What's that supposed to mean?"

"I've…" He looked over his shoulder. "I've said too much."

"No. Wait, please."

He looked to me and back over his shoulder again.

"Please. What do you mean you don't know how I remember seeing you?"

"What?" He was still distracted, glancing behind me and turning around.

"In the dream," I continued. "You said you don't know how I remember."

He shook his head. "I can't, Daisy. I-I have to go."

"No. Please. Please don't leave again."

"I'm sorry. I have to."

Chapter Eleven

JESS JUST STARED for a moment before saying anything.

"This is Lucas," I said.

Jess nodded, still staring coldly. A darkness washed over Lucas's features as he timidly shook her hand.

"Nice to finally meet you," Jess said, her voice cool and flat.

I gave her a look. *Be nice.* I knew she was just as confused and angry as I was, but asking too many questions would only scare him off.

"We're just trying to figure out what this thing is I have," I said.

Jess looked to me. "I still think you are psychic."

I smiled. "Maybe."

Lucas chuckled almost silently, bowing his head.

"What?" I asked, narrowing my eyes at him.

"Nothing."

"You don't think I'm psychic?"

He smiled. "I guess psychic works."

I sighed. "It happened after the accident."

His eyes became distant but solid at the same time as though he wanted to listen but was worried about what I may say.

"You were there," I said. "You saved me."

He nodded. "I know, but I have nothing to do with your ability."

"Then why am I suddenly 'plagued' with this?"

He shook his head. "I'm trying to find out."

"Wait," I snapped. "How? And why?"

He waved me off. "I can't tell you everything yet. I will explain soon. I promise. All I can tell you is I need to take care of some things so I can find out what's going on."

"So, this does involve you?"

He shrugged. "I know it does."

"Because you saved me."

"Because of other things, Daisy."

"Because you have the same gift?" I asked. "And...dreams?"

"I will explain it all to you later," he said. "I promise."

"I think you should do some explaining now," Jess snapped.

"I know you deserve answers," he said. "I understand there are things you need to know. All I can say is there is a time and a place, but it is not now and not here."

I just nodded, unable to argue.

"I have to go," he said. "But I promise to meet you again as soon as I have some answers."

Jess made a sound, but I wasn't sure what it meant. He got up to leave, and I watched him like a hawk as he walked out of the building and around the corner.

"I'm not sure about it," Jess said.

I gazed back to her. "What do you mean?"

She shrugged. "He's talking to you like..."

"Some sort of wizard?" I laughed.

She smiled. "Exactly."

I shrugged. "He's a little different. But I think he can help."

She nodded. "I hope so."

"Can we get out of here?" I asked.

She huffed. "Definitely!"

Jess sighed and plopped onto her bed. "My dad's back."

"Oh?"

She nodded. "My mom's picking him up at the airport. He wants to do a family dinner. That okay?"

I shook my head. "It's okay. Do your family thing."

"Daisy, I'm not asking if you are all right with me going. I'm asking if you are all right coming along."

"Oh," I breathed. "I'm not sure."

"You're family too. He specifically invited you."

My face fell. "Really?"

She nodded. "Of course."

I sighed. "Yeah, I think I can handle dinner."

"He won't...talk too much about...you know."

I nodded. "Good to know."

The door downstairs creaked open, and Jess flew toward her bedroom door and raced down the stairs. Before her dad had even dropped his bags, she was in his arms, lifting her legs off the floor. He laughed cheerfully, and my heart burned with longing. As much as I loved Jess, an anger flushed through me, jealous, resentful of what she had.

"Daisy," he said, peering at me still at the top of the stairs.

I smiled.

"It's good to see you again."

"You too, sir."

"Sir?" He laughed. "Daisy, we're family. You can call me Rick."

I nodded again. It was the only response I could muster.

"Well, we have reservations, honey," he said to Jess. "So go get ready and don't take years."

She was all smiles. "Yeah. Come on, Dais. I'll do your hair."

She raced back up the stairs. I followed her back into her room. She walked to her counter and immediately started smearing makeup on her already perfect skin.

"Do you really need all that?" I asked.

She smiled, looking at me in the mirror. "It's not every day I have an excuse to get pretty."

"Jess, you're always pretty."

She chuckled. "Whatever. I'm doing your makeup after mine."

I rolled my eyes.

"Arguing is pointless." She snickered.

"I know."

After covering my face with what felt like a pound of makeup, Jess turned my hair into a mane of curls and gave hers a nice crimped style. We headed for the door right as Jess's dad was whispering about how long we were taking.

"Ready," Jess squeaked.

"Good. Let's go," he answered.

We headed to the car. It was at least a thirty-minute drive to the restaurant.

Walking in, my eyes rose to the crystal chandeliers hanging from the high ceilings. Suit-coated, white-gloved waiters gently wove through round tables draped with light-colored cloth, serving the customers. I felt completely out of place even in the dress I had borrowed from Jess. Each table had a candle and an elegant vase of fresh flowers. Jess's dad told the hostess the name on the reservation, and she led us to a table. The place settings looked like real silver, and even the salad forks were chilled.

I was relieved when I saw the menu seemed normal. It wasn't French or Mediterranean or anything else I couldn't read. I settled for chicken, as it was the most familiar thing listed.

I was mostly quiet until the conversation moved to me.

"Are you taking care of my beautiful daughter?" Rick asked, looking to me.

"Dad, please!" Jess interrupted.

"I think *she's* doing more of that. She's taking great care of me," I said.

"We take care of each other, Dad."

"I'm just making conversation." He smiled and winked at me.

I returned the smile and lightly laughed when I saw how red Jess's cheeks were.

"Unbelievable," she murmured. She looked at me and shook her head but was still smiling.

The rest of dinner was nice and normal. I was tuning out most of the conversation and talk about Rick's time in India. I couldn't stop thinking about Lucas. I couldn't stop replaying his words, wondering how he was involved in what was happening to me, wondering if maybe he had something to do with who broke into Jess's house—and mine. I tried to focus on being polite but was noticeably distracted. With what I had been through, I was hoping nobody would take offense.

When we got home, Jess immediately washed her makeup off and insisted I used her overpriced makeup remover and face wash.

It was easy to fall asleep even though I could not stop thinking about Lucas. The morning came peacefully without any dreams.

"Last night was nice," I said to Jess as I pulled on a pair of jeans. "Thanks."

"You don't need to thank me, Daisy," she said, flopping into her armchair. She pulled her legs into her chest like she used to do when she was a kid.

I nodded. "You've been a really great friend."

She smiled. "I try to be. It's not like I would want to be a lousy friend."

I chuckled. "Thanks for trusting me about Lucas."

"Hey, if you say he's telling the truth, I believe you."

"Well, what do you think?"

She shrugged. "I don't know, Daisy. Maybe if I heard it from him, I could form an opinion."

"Well, I know he didn't come right out and deny he was involved in what happened to my mom, but what about the other things he said?"

"What are you talking about?"

I narrowed my eyes, slightly confused. "The other things we talked about."

"What things were those?"

"You know. The…" I broke off.

She raised her eyebrows, waiting for me to finish.

"Yesterday at the café."

She nodded. "Yeah, I know we talked."

"Okay, good. What do you feel about what he said?"

She planted her feet on the floor and leaned in as if trying to get a closer look at me. "Daisy, I really don't know what you're talking about."

"What?"

"Did you have a dream last night?"

"What? No. Stop changing the subject."

"I'm not," she said. "But I think you may be confusing a dream and what happened yesterday. Lucas wasn't there."

"What?" I bellowed. "Of course he was. You spoke to him, Jess. You looked at him."

"Daisy, you're scaring me."

"*You're* scaring *me*."

"What's going on?"

I covered my face with my hands. "I don't know," I whispered.

"Are you feeling like usual?"

"Jess, I'm not sick. I know you saw him."

"Daisy, I have never seen him—not at the road and not yesterday."

I remembered her reaction at seeing him at the road and the way she responded when I mentioned it the next day. I grabbed my shoes off the floor.

"Where are you going?" she asked.

"To the café. I need to check something out."

"Are you okay?"

"I'm fine."

"Are you getting headaches again?"

"No, Jess!"

"Fine. At least let me drive you."

I nodded, and we headed to the café. As soon as we walked in, I went to the register.

"Can I help you?" the woman at the counter asked.

"I'm sorry to bother you," I started. "This might sound a little strange, but do you remember the young man I was here with yesterday?"

She made a face, seeming to be searching her memory. "No. I don't think so."

"You don't remember me being here?"

"No, I remember you," she said. "You were sitting with Miss Grayson like you always are. I didn't see a young man with you, but I was working. I may have just not noticed."

"Thanks."

"Is everything all right?"

I nodded. "Yes, everything is fine. Thanks."

I sat at the table, next to Jess. "She doesn't remember him either."

"Daisy, that's because he was never here."

"Jess, I *know* he was."

I heard his words echo through my memory. *I just don't know how you remember.*

"Oh my God," I breathed.

"What? What's wrong?"

"The dream," I said.

"Which one?"

"The one where he said he doesn't know how I remember him."

Her eyes became far away for a moment, and something registered. Her face became rock hard. "Are you...are you positive he was here?"

I nodded. "You two talked, Jess."

She shook her head. "I don't remember."

I lowered my head for a moment. "What *do* you remember?"

"I remember talking about you being psychic and about how we hope Lucas can help."

"That's it?"

She nodded. "What did I miss?"

"You don't remember me introducing him?"

She shook her head.

"Oh God. Okay. I introduced you, and you even shook his hand. You said you were glad to finally meet him."

She shook her head. "What else?"

"You said you thought I was psychic when I mentioned I was trying to figure out what ability I had."

She nodded. "I remember that part."

"Okay. He somewhat agreed but insisted he has nothing to do with it."

"Go on."

"I asked him why I am having these visions, and he said he was going to find out. He told me himself that he is involved."

"Involved how?"

"I don't know," I said. "He said he doesn't know yet and will tell me when he gets some answers."

"Daisy, this doesn't make sense. Why can't I remember any of it?"

"I don't know. But I'm not crazy. I know he was here, and I know he saved me."

"Maybe this is why nobody believed you before," she said.

"What do you mean?"

"Daisy, it's obvious. The only thing that makes sense is—one, you're crazy, which we both know isn't true. Or two…"

"What, Jess?"

"Nobody believed you before because—because nobody *can* remember him."

My blood ran cold, and I almost lost my breath. "Nobody but me."

Chapter Twelve

"MY HEAD IS KILLING ME," I whined.

"You…you have a headache?"

"Not that kind of headache. I've just been staring at the screen too long."

"Oh," she said. "Yeah, me too."

"Find anything?"

"Not a thing."

I sighed. "Maybe we should go back to the field?"

She shook her head. "You can go. You can always call me if you need me, but I don't want to have something happen and not remember it."

"Are you sure?"

She nodded. "The idea of not remembering just scares me too much."

"Okay. I'll let you know how it goes."

"Be careful, Daisy."

"I'll be fine."

Once I got to the field, I found that I was alone. A cool breeze blew my way, causing a chill to run through me. I hugged myself to stay warm and started feeling anxiety creeping into me. The field was empty and gray as if it had never been anything more. The tall grass leaned and danced in the light breeze, and this time, I knew I wasn't alone. The familiar feeling of being watched almost consumed me.

"Lucas?" I called. "Lucas, I know you can hear me." *I have no idea how, but I know you're here.*

"Daisy."

I spun around, gasping, raising my hands defensively.

"I'm here," he said.

I sighed heavily.

"Sorry I scared you."

"You can't sneak up on people like that."

"*You* called *me,* remember?" He smiled, and it lit up his entire face. The look of his shaggy hair brought me back to the day he saved me. I could see the glint of his eyes, even without the color. His perfect smile left me speechless. I just stared at him, feeling a strange sense of familiarity; it was like I knew him.

"What is it?" he asked.

I shook off the feelings. "Nothing."

He gave me an accusing look. "Are you sure? What are you thinking?"

"Nothing."

He stared into my eyes for a moment as if trying to read my mind. I felt exposed and invaded, almost like he could.

"Then why am I here?" he asked.

I sighed before responding. "I need to ask you something, and you have to tell me the truth."

He replied with a nod.

"Why can't anyone remember you?"

He bowed his head for a moment, and I heard a long exhale. "Yes. I thought you might ask me that."

"Well?"

"Well, honestly, Daisy, I was never aware it would come up since I have no idea how *you* remember me."

"Yes, you mentioned that. Why wouldn't I remember you? And why does nobody else?"

He shook his head. "I don't know."

I felt heat rush to my cheeks and an urge to smack him upside the head. My entire body felt hot with frustration, bordering on anger. I was so sick of the confusion, the questions. He was the only one who had answers, and even now, he was withholding them. I tried to calm my nerves, but my hands were shaking. Rage boiled up, and I found myself shouting at him.

"That is not an answer! There is no way that you don't know!"

He raised his hands. "Daisy—"

"Just stop," I cried. "Please. You know I can't help but believe you, but I know that logically everything you have said is a lie."

He shook his head but didn't say a word. He turned his back to me. "I don't know how to make you believe me," he said softly, almost with sorrow behind his words. "Or if there is any reason you should…"

"It was you, wasn't it?" I said, my voice finally soft. "The dream…the one about Jess."

He turned back to face me. "Yes."

"Why?"

"I was only trying to warn you. I didn't mean for it to be so violent. I only introduced the idea. Your imagination and thoughts filled in the details."

"Why would I see Jess that way?"

He shook his head. "Fear perhaps. Clearly dreams are not always your wishes, Daisy. They are sometimes your fears as well."

I shook my head, trying to make sense of everything. There were still so many questions. "You said you were trying to warn me. Of what? Did you have something to do with the man who broke into the house?"

"No! No, of course not. I only had a feeling something would happen. I was only trying to protect you."

"Wait—you had a *feeling*? You expect me to believe that?"

"Yes," he snapped immediately. "Is it any stranger than your dreams, Daisy?"

I opened my mouth to speak but realized instantly he was right. I asked the only other question I could.

"Why?"

"Because I don't want you to be hurt."

"Why do you care? You saved me the day of the crash just as I save people. Why can't you just move on? I do."

"I'm not you, Daisy. I always want to look out for you."

I remembered what he had said before about watching over me. "Tell me about the cat."

He turned away again. "I…I can't."

"What do you mean you can't?"

"Daisy, you shouldn't even remember," he said, facing me again. "The fact that you do has already caused so much…hysteria in my world."

"I don't understand."

"You have to forget me," he said. "It's the only way things can stay sane."

I shook my head. "I can't forget you. You…you saved me. I will always remember you."

"You didn't the first time."

I narrowed my eyes. "What?"

He exhaled heavily. "You didn't remember, Daisy. Not the first time."

I just stared at him, trying to read him, trying to figure out exactly what he was hiding from me.

"You have met me before—many times. By the next day, it was as if I was never there."

"You've saved me before?"

He shook his head. "Not exactly. I...I can't explain it to you right now, but...we've met."

"That's crazy. Why can I remember you now?"

"I really don't know."

"Is there something wrong with me?"

He chuckled. "No, Daisy. There is nothing wrong with you."

My stomach was in knots, and I felt like I was going to be sick. "Who are you, Lucas?"

I saw a half-smile pull at the corners of his perfect lips. "Nobody. Daisy, just forget me."

I shook my head. "I can't. You are the only one who knows what's happening to me."

"There is nothing wrong with you."

"This...thing, the dreams... I don't want it."

"It's not up to you."

"Is it up to *you*?"

He froze for a moment like he was shocked by what I said. "What? No. Of course not. I have the same gift, Daisy. I wouldn't force it on anyone. It chose you."

"It?"

He nodded. "The gift. It came to you just as it came to me."

"Why?"

"I don't have all the answers."

"You have to help me."

He sighed. His voice was filled with a sort of compassion when he spoke again. "I know. You remember me. That means something. I will find out what is happening, but I cannot promise you'll like it."

"I still need to know. And there is one more thing."

He just stared, waiting.

"I have this...friend. He...remembers dreaming of me before I saved him."

"Yes. Why are you surprised by that?"

"That doesn't seem odd to you?"

"Oh," he breathed, placing his hand on his forehead. "Daisy, your head trauma from the crash…"

"What about it?"

"It's normal for them to dream of us before we save them. It's just something that happens."

"Wait. So…so I dreamed of you *before* I crashed, but…but I don't remember?"

He nodded. "The head injury must have taken some minor memories."

I pressed my fingers to my temples. "That's so strange."

"Let me find some more answers. I will come find you again."

I nodded. "How are you going to find these…answers?"

"Remember, Daisy, there are some things that I just cannot tell you yet. There are some things that only by *not* knowing will you be safe. You have to understand that."

He turned away, and before I had time to protest, he was gone.

Be safe. Was I not safe?

I always knew somewhere deep within me that I had met him before. At the crash, he spoke to me with such kindness and concern. It was clear he knew me. I walked slowly up to Jess's room, trying to fight back tears. I was so lost and confused, and nothing was getting better. I flopped down on her bed.

"Hey. Are you okay?"

I looked at her and nodded.

"What happened?"

I sighed. "Apparently, I know him," I said, without realizing she would have no idea what I meant.

"What?"

"I mean…he told me I have met him before. That I just don't remember."

"When? When did you meet him?"

"I don't know. He doesn't tell me much."

"That's nothing new."

"Jess—we aren't safe."

"Wait. What?"

I shook my head, exhaling slowly. "I don't think we're safe."

She sighed. "That man… Was that—?"

I shook my head. "No, I don't think that was him, but I know he is involved. In fact, he admitted he's involved."

She got up from the chair and sat beside me on her bed. "What do we do?"

I shook my head. "I don't know. I wish I did."

Chapter Thirteen

IT WAS JUST after noon when I walked into the café. I slung my book bag onto the chair to my left and stared at my folded hands resting on the table.

William took the seat across from me before I even saw him come in. He was smiling like usual, his eyes big and cheerful.

"Hey," he said, setting a book on the table. "What did you find?"

"Not a lot. But I think I know why you dreamed of me."

"Really?"

I nodded. I knew I had to keep Lucas out of things for obvious reasons. I couldn't have the rest of the town thinking I was crazy again.

"I saved someone else, and he dreamed of me too," I said, trying to keep the lie out of my features.

"Well…what does that mean?"

"I think it's just something that happens. I think when a dream comes to me, the people I save are often linked to me in some way, and they see me like I see them."

He sat back in his chair and huffed. "Ah. Weird."

I nodded. "Yeah."

"Well, what about your friend?"

"Jess?"

He chuckled, brightening his eyes. "No. The person you were looking for. Did you find him?"

I shook my head. "No."

"Hmm. Sorry I couldn't be more helpful."

I waved him off. "It's no big deal, really. It seems both of us are safe, at least for now."

He nodded. "Well, if I happen to see who you are looking for, I guess I'll give you a call."

"Sure. Thanks. Look, I gotta go. I have plans with Jess."

He nodded. "We'll talk later."

I faked a smile but had no intention of talking to him again. I grabbed my bag and headed for the door. I wasn't even focusing on where I was going as I walked, and I realized I had stopped at my house—my mom's house. Caution tape still clung to the trees and bushes, and the door was padlocked. Tears filled my eyes, but I couldn't bring myself to get any closer. I turned away, feeling the emptiness returning, feeling the need for my old room and my old familiar home. There was a longing that seized me, pulling me into the memories of my mother and how much I loved her.

I turned around and started back to Jess's house, which I guessed now was my house too. I fought the tears as I walked, hoping not to concern Jess with anything more than what we were already dealing with. It felt as though my actual heart was aching. I tried as best I could to push away the feelings before I got home.

Jess was sitting at the bar in the kitchen, with a bowl of cereal and a magazine.

"Hey," she said with a mouth full of corn flakes. "So, I was thinking we could either do a beach day or a shopping day."

"Umm...Jess?"

Her face fell. "Are you okay? What happened?"

I shook my head. "It's nothing. I'm just feeling a bit..."

She nodded. "I understand if you are just not having a good day. That's normal."

I nodded. "Yeah."

"Not pressuring you but have you not noticed the date?"

"The...date?" I had been so distracted I hadn't noticed anything.

"It's the seventh."

"Of July?"

She laughed. "Uh, yeah."

I shook my head. "Wow."

"Well?" she chirped. "You are officially eighteen. Shouldn't we do *something?*"

I remembered talking to my mom one night about birthday plans. My chest started burning at the memory. It almost felt like a betrayal to be celebrating without her.

"I'm not sure," I said. "I just keep thinking about Mom. She and I were supposed to celebrate…together."

Jess sighed and put her arm around me. "I think she would want you to enjoy your day. She'll be there, you know."

I smiled. "I guess."

"If you don't want to do this, we don't have to."

I shook my head. "No, it's not that. This is supposed to be a big day. I want to spend it with you."

"Are you going to be okay?"

I shrugged. "I'll try. It's not easy not being with my mom today, but I think I can handle it."

A huge smile lit up her face. "Okay. So, what do you want to do?"

"Hmm. Keep it simple. It's still pretty early, so we can spend the day at the beach and have a nice dinner after. That okay?"

"It's your day. That's fine."

As night came, I felt the recurring panic of not wanting to fall asleep. I lay in bed with the lamp on the nightstand switched on, trying to stay alert. If I didn't sleep, I didn't dream.

Of course, trying to stay awake never worked as planned, and I eventually passed out, still with the light on. The sleep was deep and dreamless, but a hazy, surreal tug pulled me out of it. I opened my eyes, seeing Jess literally yanking me from the bed. Her eyes were big and alert.

"Jess…"

She clapped her hand over my mouth and placed her finger on her lips. I nodded, and she removed her hand. My heart started pounding, and panic was shaking me. Jess pointed to the floor, telling me someone was downstairs. I moved closer to her so I could whisper.

"Maybe it's your parents?"

She just shook her head and pointed to her clock.

5:45 a.m.

Her parents had already left for work. Jess checked the lock on her bedroom door and backed into the far wall of her room with her pepper spray in hand. I reached under her pillow and grabbed the knife before standing beside her, against the wall. The panic was still surging through me like a scorching blaze. Beads of sweat broke out on my forehead, and even through the heat, I could feel my teeth starting to chatter with fear.

The air was still for a moment, and everything went quiet. Not even the sound of footsteps echoed through the house. I could hear our breathing in rhythm and almost feel the fear emanating from Jess at my side.

I gripped the knife tighter in my hand, struggling to keep my grip with how badly my hands were shaking and slicked with sweat. The door creaked open, and I heard a sharp inhale from Jess, and we both raised our weapons in front of us. Small beams of light slithered into the room, and a shape emerged from the doorway.

I started forward, lunging with the knife. My arm was caught instantly, and I felt my entire body hurl backward. The softness of the bed broke my fall, and I scrambled back up. As I got to my feet, the knife flew out of my hand and skidded across the floor. Jess yelped, and I looked her way. The figure had grabbed her by her shoulders and pushed her back against her door. Instinct took over, and I rushed toward him even without the knife. He caught me by my shoulders. I shook and flailed, trying to get free—until I heard his voice.

"Daisy," he said softly. "Daisy, it's okay. It's me."

My entire body instantly relaxed. It was as if I had woken from a nightmare in the comfort of my own bed. Suddenly, I felt like everything was okay. The mere sound of his voice comforted me completely.

"Lucas?"

Jess stood up from the floor, placing her hand on the back of her head. She flipped on the light, and Lucas's face came into full view. He pulled me into his arms before I had time to protest. His firm yet gentle arms pressed me against his hard chest, and I could feel the lines of muscle in his stomach. He held me there for a long moment before I was able to pull myself away.

"It's okay," he said. "You're all right."

"Did you just…save me again?"

He smiled his perfect smile and shook his head, laughing at me.

"What's so funny?" I heard Jess sneer. She crossed her arms in front of her chest.

"I guess I did," he said. "Save you, I mean."

"What the hell is going on?" I asked with a sigh. I moved away from Lucas and sat softly on the side of Jess's bed.

"You're okay," he said. "That's all that matters."

"I won't remember any of this, will I?" Jess asked, sitting beside me.

I stared at her with a lost expression on my face. "I'll fill you in."

She sighed and dropped her head into her hands.

"Who was in the house?" I asked.

Lucas shook his head. "I'm not sure, but there are things you need to know."

I nodded, waiting.

"There are things about me and our connection that I have noted as unusual."

"Please—"

"If you are ready to hear them, meet me at the field."

"Why can't you tell me now?" I peeved.

"Daisy, please," he said. "I can only tell you there—where it's private, where it's safe."

I was unable to find words to argue, but I glared at him.

"You are safe today," he said in response to the look on my face. "I promise you nobody will come after you again."

"Are you sure?" Jess whispered.

He nodded. "I'm sure."

Jess fell backward onto her bed with a huff.

"Meet me at two," he said. "Try to go back to sleep."

As his suggestion reached me, I felt myself already drifting off into a deep sleep.

When I did wake, I was startled at Jess shaking me.

"What's wrong?" I chattered, groggily.

"Dais—what happened?"

"What?"

"Last night. I don't know how—I don't know…"

I suddenly remembered Jess couldn't remember Lucas. "Oh. It's okay."

"How did we get away?"

I hesitated before responding, wondering how I should say it. I figured it was best to just be direct. "Lucas."

"Wait, what?"

"He saved us."

"From…?" She gently shook her head, trying to coax me further.

I shrugged. "I don't know. I'm supposed to meet him at the field today. I hope he will explain everything then."

"Are we…are we safe?"

I shook my head. "I don't know. Lucas promised me nothing would happen today. You will be fine, at least while I'm gone."

She nodded. "Will you…try to hurry?"

"Of course."

The field was as normal as ever, but with Lucas standing in the tall grass, he somehow made it more than that. He was so beautiful and mysterious that my curiosity almost ate away at me every time I looked at him. It was impossible to not feel something when I was close to him…a feeling of longing and desire. It was as if something within me was trying desperately to remind me of some connection I couldn't remember.

He turned to me, and a flawless smile lit his face. He took a few steps forward until he was only inches away from me.

"Thank you for coming," he said softly.

"I had to," I answered. "What—what are you, Lucas?"

"You need to understand I am not supposed to tell you anything," he started. "You need to understand that by telling you, I could be putting you in danger."

"I still need to know."

"You are the only one who can remember me. I am still unsure why that is, but either way—you do. You're special, Daisy."

"You can come into my dreams. You can watch me from the eyes of a cat. You say *I'm* special?"

He smiled. "Yes, well—in my world, those things are quite normal."

"Your world? You've used that term before. What does it mean?"

He pursed his lips. "I don't live in the same way with the same rules as you."

"What are you?"

"People have called us many things throughout the ages: gods, spirits, angels, demons, sorcerers. Over the broad spectrum of ideas, we are as lost for answers as you are. It is truly terrible to not know what you are or where you came from. I am in a very lonely place and don't know how to be anywhere else."

"Because nobody can remember you?"

He nodded and lowered his head. "Nobody but you and…"

"And?"

"And my kind. This curse is not effective on my own kind."

"You still haven't told me what you are, Lucas."

"That's because there is no answer," he said, lifting his hands. "I am lost, Daisy. We all are. I don't know what to call myself. Some call us lugaru. Some call us shifters."

"Wait—you're telling me you're some mythical monster?"

"No, Daisy. That is what others might say—others who don't understand what we are."

"So, the cat…" I started, searching for the words I wanted to say. "The cat was…was you?"

He moved his eyes away from my face. The nod came later, and it was weak, almost unnoticeable.

"You're a…"

"Shape shifter," he said. "I think that is the term they use these days."

"This is crazy. Is that how you kept disappearing?"

He nodded. "I didn't realize you would remember seeing me, but I still couldn't find the courage to talk to you."

"Why?"

"Because it's hard for me. Because when I talk to you, I want to see you again. When you don't remember me, it hurts."

I nodded. "I understand."

He shook his head. "I wish you could."

"I can try."

He gave me a forced half-smile.

"So, you are a shape shifter. Does this mean you aren't human?"

He shook his head. "I'm not sure. I was born in my human form—naked, bald, and crying, just like you."

"How did you know what you were?"

"I don't remember. It was something that was always inside me. It wasn't until later in my childhood that I realized other people weren't shifters. For a long time, I didn't know I was different. I would have preferred it stay that way."

"How did you find out?"

He hesitated before responding. "I wanted to leave. I wanted to live among others as human. I realized when nobody could remember me that I could never have that."

My heart rate quickened, and heat rose in my cheeks as his pain slithered into me as if I were feeling it for myself. "I'm sorry for what you go through."

"Don't be. I have accepted what I am as best I know how."

"But you can never be fully human."

He smiled. "Sometimes I feel safer in another form. Sometimes I feel more normal and more natural than I ever have as a human."

I couldn't wrap my head around the concept of being something entirely different. "Does it hurt?"

"It can," he said. "But the searing pain of breaking bones and tearing through one's skin is nothing more than Hollywood drama."

I nodded. "That's good."

"There are other things you need to know. Like the reason I saved you."

"What do you mean? I thought you have the same gift I have."

He nodded. "I do. But for my kind, that's normal. It's you I don't understand."

"What are you saying?"

"I'm saying that my saving people is more than something that is told to me through dreams. In my world, it is decided by an order."

I shook my head as if that could clear my confusion. "What do you mean? What order?"

"There are two sects in The Order of my world. One deals with saving those who may die before their time. The other…"

"The other does what, Lucas?" I knew the answer before he said it.

"The other…brings death to those whose time has come."

"How can that be their decision?"

"Daisy, it has been this way for eons. Since the beginning of time, there has been a balance."

"It *was* you, wasn't it?" I cried. "My mom."

"No. It wasn't me, Daisy. I am one who saves people. I am not involved. I am not even a member of The Order. I already told you I wanted to leave. I live with my kind, but I am nothing more than the son of an elder. It would take a lot more for me to be part of The Order."

"So what is this 'Order'?" I asked.

"Sort of like a secret police."

"Did they kill my mother?"

He sighed. "I don't know. But I do know they might have something to do with who is after you."

"What can you do?"

"I'm not sure yet. I need to find out what's going on, and I need you to stay strong. There may come a time when I ask things of you, and you have to promise me to do as I say. The only thing I want to do is protect you."

"Why am I so trusting of you?"

He stared at me for a moment, studying my face. "I…I encourage you to believe me."

"What does that mean?"

"It's another thing I have. I use suggestion to encourage you to do things."

"Wait, you can control me?"

"No. No, that's not what I mean. I cannot *control* your thoughts. But I can guide them. I cannot make you do something you don't already want to do."

"But you can make me do things?"

He nodded. "Some things. Only things you already want to do. If you ask it of me, I will never work you like that again."

I nodded. "Please. It doesn't feel right."

"Understood."

I immediately felt a strange sense of anxiety that I had not felt before. I realized the trust I had in what he was telling me was depleting rapidly.

"Do you feel differently now?" he asked.

"A little. This is all too much for me."

"I swear to you it's the truth."

I nodded. "I know."

He looked away as if afraid to look me in the eyes.

"What about things like silver?" I asked.

"What about silver?"

"Can you touch it? Does it hurt you?"

He smirked and pulled a pendant out from under his shirt. "This is silver."

"Why a star?"

"It's a pentagram—a symbol of protection, bringing the elements and spirit within the world into harmony."

"Seems appropriate."

"You reading up on werewolf lore?"

I smiled. "Maybe a little."

"Anything else?"

"Why a cat?"

He shrugged. "Cats and dogs are the most common. They're easier as they are familiar to us. I did know someone once who could shift into a bear."

"A bear?"

"People were always amazed when they saw it. Not all of us are able to pull something like that off. For me, I just always felt a connection with felines, so the cat just sort of happened."

Although my anxiety and uncertainty were practically suffocating me, I felt a sense of awe. I didn't know what to say, so I just smiled.

He mirrored my smile, but it quickly faded. "I need to talk to someone," he said, changing the subject. "Someone who may be able to help. If you are patient, I will make sure everything works out. Go home, Daisy. I will make sure you're safe."

Although I could not know for sure I would be safe, and I knew he was no longer "working" me, I trusted he was being honest.

Chapter Fourteen

A WALK WAS the only way I could clear my head. Sitting at home going over Lucas's story over and over and the lost look of disbelief on Jess's face were only going to make me crazy. It was getting dark, and the air was getting cold. I knew Jess was safe at home. If something were to happen, I expected Lucas to jump in and take care of things again. He promised we were safe for the time being.

I shivered and pulled my sweater over my chest. I felt a freezing drop hit my nose. I gasped and looked up, noticing it was softly raining. I was thinking about heading back when I spotted a boy sitting on a bench under a streetlamp. The rain picked up and began pounding the pavement. I was already soaked, and the boy on the bench had not moved.

I walked slowly toward the bench. The boy, I could see, was not a boy at all but a man. He had a masculine build to his jawline and chin, and the downpour dripped from his shoulder-length hair. I stared at him for a prolonged moment, just studying his face, etching it into my mind. There was something about him that aroused my curiosity. He had lovely light hair that must have been blond and matching eyebrows that were thick and perfectly shaped.

"Excuse me?" I started. "Are you all right?"

He looked up into my eyes and smiled. "Of course."

"If you don't mind, why are you sitting in the rain?"

"The rain relaxes me."

I smiled, unaware of how to respond.

"The name's Kristoff," he said, lending a soft-looking hand.

"Daisy," I answered, shaking it.

He bowed his head. "Nice meeting you, Daisy."

I nodded and was about to continue walking when he spoke again.

"Don't go that way!"

I turned around and noticed he was on his feet with his hands reaching out toward me.

His voice was swelled with tension. "Please. Don't go that way."

Before I had time to respond and ask him any questions, another voice distracted me.

"Hello."

I spun around, startled, and saw an old man in a black hooded cloak, drenched in rain. Wet strands of hair hung messily in front of his eyes. Kristoff put himself between us, as if he were guarding me.

"She doesn't know me," I heard him say. "She doesn't know anything. Please, Moe, leave her out of this."

"You're a fool!" the man said. "Do you have *any* idea what they will do to her? I'm giving you the chance now to leave. Both of you. *Now.*"

"What?" I was outraged but curious.

Kristoff turned around and took my hand. "I'm sorry, Daisy, but you have to come with me. Now."

"What? Where?"

He gripped my hand tighter and started pulling me with him. "Please don't ask any questions right now. Just come with me."

He didn't loosen his grasp at all until we got to his car.

"Get in," he demanded.

I turned away, but he grabbed me and basically threw me into the car. I began shaking uncontrollably.

Who is this man? Why am I getting into a car with a complete stranger?

But I did. I didn't run off or turn away again. It was like somehow I knew I had to listen to him; somehow I knew I had to go with him...wherever it was he was going. I sank into my seat and closed my eyes. He started the engine, and I opened my eyes to look at him. His face was tense, and his light eyes appeared almost turbulent. He didn't say a word, and the silence was over-whelming.

"What's going on?" I asked quietly.

"What did I say?" he spat.

"Sorry."

He sighed. "No. I didn't mean to snap. I'm the one who is sorry. You have every right to know. I'll explain to you what I can. Just wait until we get some-where safe."

I just nodded. *Somewhere safe. So we aren't safe.*

He drove for a long time, and I was really beginning to fear the worst. I wanted to ask where we were going but didn't want to make him angry. His tension was already unbearable. I couldn't help thinking he was taking me to some secluded place to kill me.

Finally, he pulled into the driveway of a very modern, normal-looking house in a quiet suburban neighborhood. He opened my door for me and offered his hand. He was smiling, which was completely unexpected, but I forced a slight smile back. I took his hand and climbed out of his car. It had stopped raining, but the air was still crisp and cold.

"Let's get you some dryer clothes," he said, still with a smile in his voice.

I nodded and followed him inside.

The room was very normal, but there was no TV that I could see. Strange. There was a couch and a loveseat, and across the way was a kitchen with a bar and a round table with four cushioned chairs. There was a window over the sink with pale curtains and house plants on the sill. I couldn't figure out the reason I wasn't frightened. It was clearly not the wisest idea for me to be trusting a complete stranger.

"It's okay," he said. "You can sit. I'm not worried about the furniture."

I half-smiled and nodded, taking a seat on the couch.

"I'll be right back," he said. "I'm going to get you something else to put on."

"Thank you."

He disappeared up the stairs, and I leaned my head back against the couch, trying to relax. So now I was in a stranger's house and had no idea where that was. Great. Jess would just love this!

A light rapping echoed into the living room, and Kristoff came running to the door. I perked up, peeking behind him, trying to see what I may have been up against.

"Yes," I heard Kristoff say softly. "No. He let us go."

I leaned in from the couch as if it would improve my hearing.

"Not long," he said. "I'm not sure, but I know it's not good."

Kristoff turned to me and gave me a strange look. He opened the door the rest of the way, and Lucas stepped into the room.

I was instantly on my feet and rushed to the door to meet him. "Lucas!"

Kristoff's mouth fell open, and he kept switching his gaze from me back to Lucas.

"You…you know him?"

I smiled. "Yes."

Lucas grinned. "I told you," he said softly, looking at Kristoff. "It's only her."

"Remarkable," he answered, studying my face as if I were some exotic animal in an exhibit.

"I'm sorry," Lucas said to me. "This is my brother, Kristoff."

"Brother?"

He chuckled. "Yes. Things did not work out like we thought. He didn't believe me when I said you could remember me. He decided to keep quiet about me, fearing he would only be talking about someone you never remembered meeting."

"Did you plan this?"

"No," Kristoff said. "We weren't planning on you being there. We had to get you away from that place. If you kept walking that direction…" He broke off and lowered his head.

"What?" I asked. "What would have happened? Who was that man? He said something would be 'done to me.'"

Lucas was at my side and put his arm around my shoulders. "Daisy, that man is a member of The Order I told you about."

"Was he the one who broke into my house?"

Kristoff looked to Lucas with an angry expression littering his features.

"I don't know," Lucas said, putting his arm around me. "But I know he wants to hurt you."

"Why?" I snapped, shrugging his arm away. "Why me? What did I do?"

"Daisy—"

"No more!" I yelled. "You need to tell me everything. Now."

"She doesn't know?" Kristoff spat. "How could you not tell her?"

"Tell me what?"

Lucas signaled me to follow him to the living room. He sat beside me on the couch and took my hand. "I wasn't supposed to save you, Daisy."

"What the hell do you mean by that?"

"We have a duty," Kristoff chimed in. "We choose who lives and who dies."

"So do I!" I yelled. "I've saved several people."

"You don't understand," Lucas replied. "That's not your decision to make!"

"Then what makes it yours?" I yelled. "I'm having these dreams for a *reason*."

"The dreams are a mistake—a flaw in the pattern," Kristoff said. "You were not supposed to live."

"What?"

Lucas sighed and dropped his head. "I saved you."

I could feel heat rushing to my cheeks and my pulse racing.

He looked up again, and tears were moistening his eyes. "I saved you, Daisy, but I wasn't supposed to."

"So I...I'm supposed to be dead?"

He nodded, drying his eyes with the back of his hand.

"Is that why these people are after me?"

"We can lobby," Kristoff said before Lucas could answer. "We can lobby for your life."

"What? How?" I retorted.

"We can go to The Order and ask them for your release."

"I don't understand."

"Kristoff is being trained as a member of The Order," Lucas said. "He may have a way to convince them to let you live."

"They need a reason," Kristoff said. "Do you have one?"

Lucas lifted his arms. "Are you serious? Look at her, Kris! She's different. Special."

Kristoff nodded. "I'm just not sure it's enough."

Lucas sighed. "It means something. It has to."

I sat on the couch in an oversized shirt.

Lucas sauntered in, looking like he hadn't slept in days. "Your clothes are in the dryer."

I just nodded, still unable to think of anything to say.

"Will you please say something?"

"What do you want me to say?"

He sighed and plopped down beside me on the couch. "I guess I can't expect you to not be confused."

I shook my head. "I'm scared," I whispered. My voice cracked, and finally I felt the tears spill over.

Lucas wrapped me in a hug. "I promise you we will figure this out. Kristoff is smart. He knows what he's doing. You will be safe here."

"What about Jess and her mom and dad?" I asked.

"They're safe."

"No, I mean...I mean they will wonder where I am."

He nodded. "I know. I will make sure you have a way to contact Jess. You need to make sure you tell her not to call the police. They will only overcomplicate things. We can't be running from them too."

I sighed, and my entire body felt chilled. I was meant to die; it didn't seem like anything else could be in play. Even after what happened to me, I always thought things happened as they were meant to. Seems I was wrong.

"It's getting late," he said. "You should call Jess, but use my phone."

"Where's mine?"

"It's still in your bag, but I turned it off. We can't risk it being traced. Use mine. They can't trace it."

I took his silver cell and rapidly dialed Jess's number. She answered after half a ring.

"Daisy?"

"Yeah, it's me."

"Thank God. Where have you been, and where are you calling from?"

"It's a lot to explain. I just need you to know I'm fine, but I won't be coming home for a while."

"Where are you?"

"I...I can't tell you. Just whatever you do, don't call the police. I'm safe, and I will come home as soon as I can."

"Daisy, what's going on?"

I prepared myself to respond, but Lucas yanked the phone from my hand and turned it off.

"Lucas, what the hell?"

"The less she knows, the better."

I grumbled. "This sucks, you know."

He didn't answer, just stood up from the couch and offered me his hand.

"What?"

He waved me up. "Come on. You should get some rest."

"I doubt I can sleep." I took his hand and rose to my feet.

"You can try."

He led me up the stairs to a small bedroom with a large bed. The bedspread was floral and either blue or purple judging by the darker shades of gray. I sat at the edge, and Lucas came to sit beside me.

"You know, everything will be okay," he said.

I shook my head. "Don't say that," I whispered.

"Why?"

"Because you can't know for sure that it will be."

"Daisy, I won't let anything happen to you."

"You can't control The Order, Lucas. You and I both know that."

He sighed. "I'm here now, and I will protect you."

He put his arm around me again, and I let myself lean against him for a moment before moving away. We were both silent, but my thoughts were almost deafening.

I noticed Lucas staring at me in a very solid way, almost like he was reading my mind.

"You're very beautiful," he said.

I scoffed.

He smiled at my reaction. "Really, you are, with your shiny, yellow hair and eyes like the sky. You look like a summer day."

"I don't see that," I said. "I never will again."

"I have always seen your beauty. With or without color, you are still as stunning as the first time I saw you."

"You…you know…about my vision?"

"I know *you*, Daisy." His eyes softened and held me in his strong gaze, sending a warm flush through my body.

"When was that? The first time you saw me."

He smiled. "The beach…about four years ago."

"The beach? Are you sure?"

He nodded. "We talked, and you taught me how to ride the waves to the shore."

"I wish I could remember."

"It was that first time when I realized how much you meant to me."

"What do you mean?"

"Nothing." He turned away. "You didn't remember me."

"I do now. So what do you mean?"

"Why do you think I saved you, Daisy?"

"Because you had to."

He shook his head. "No. I was supposed to let you die, remember? I saved you because I knew you. Because I loved you."

My heart felt as if it had skipped a beat. I remembered the way his words sounded the day he saved me. I remembered the feeling of familiarity in his voice. I felt a sense of panic back then, but at the same time, I felt like I had always remembered him.

"I know you, Lucas. I have felt since the day I saw you in a dream that I had met you before."

"You remember?"

I shook my head. "No. But my body and my soul? Somehow I remember knowing you."

"Do you remember kissing me?"

My eyes widened.

He smiled and bowed his head. "I didn't think so."

He looked up again, and before I had time to ask him about it, he was pressing his lips to mine. It was strange how natural it felt, how every contour of his lips fit mine like I had kissed him a thousand times before. I did know him, and I cared for him, more than I thought I could remember. He pulled away from me, and I moved back to kiss him again, not wanting him to stop. He pulled away once more.

"Please," I said. "Don't stop. I remember. When you kiss me, I remember."

He brought his lips back to mine, and a flash of color filled my vision.

I was at the beach, feeling the heat from the sun and seeing the blue horizon in front of me. My yellow hair ruffled around my face, and a boy with hazel eyes stood before me with a perfect smile on his face. I felt the heat of his skin when I reached to touch his cheek.

The vision faded and was replaced with a park bench in a dark evening, the sun barely peeking over the mountains. We were laughing, but there was no sound. Flashes of smiles and exchanges of looks rapidly played in my memory. There were so many empty hours filled with the one thing I should have never been able to forget.

Another memory—a laugh, a smile, and finally a kiss, a kiss in the afternoon, standing in the tall grass of our field.

When he finally pulled away, I had soft tears rolling down my face, but I was unable to keep from smiling.

"Did you see?" he asked.

I nodded. "More than that. I remember. The visions…I know I have lived those moments before. They felt perfectly familiar and fitting. I know those memories are mine. I remember."

He pulled me into his chest. "We have fallen in love countless times. But you never remembered."

"And now I do."

"Having you is a miracle. I want nothing more in the entire world."

Chapter Fifteen

"LUCAS, HELP ME SLEEP," I said.

"What?"

"You can, can't you? Since I want to?"

He narrowed his eyes and pursed his lips. "I thought you didn't want me to work you."

I shrugged. "I changed my mind."

He smiled and signaled me to lie down. He kissed me softly on my forehead. I was asleep before I even felt the absence of his lips against my skin. A dull dream played in my head, but as soon as I awoke, it had slipped through my memory like water in cupped hands. My eyes were still closed when I felt a cold hand on my cheek. I sat up, rubbing my eyes.

As I looked at my surroundings, panic instantly shot through me. I was in a bed but not the one I remembered falling asleep in. It was small with a wooden headboard and sheets that were probably gray, even in color. I sprang from the bed and rushed to the door across the way. Strong arms pulled me forcefully, throwing me back onto the bed, smashing my head against the headboard. I groaned, looking for the one responsible. I had never seen him before, but I knew it had to be the man who broke into my house. He was young, and his hair shone a medium shade of gray. His eyes were dark, tense, and focused.

"Who are you?"

"Who I am does not matter," he said, his voice hoarse. "What matters is who *you* are."

I pressed my fingers to my eyelids, as the blow had caused a pressure headache behind my eyes.

"How?" he asked.

"How what?"

"How do you know when someone is about to die?"

I felt some vile tingling in my limbs, as if his intentions were emanating from him. I knew I could not tell him anything. "I don't. I don't know what you're talking about."

He stepped closer and struck me hard across my face. I cried out, reaching my hand to my throbbing cheek.

"The Order wants you," he said, "and whoever turns you in will receive a very hefty reward."

I started silently crying, unable to stop myself. The stranger opened the door.

"Zane," he called, "she's awake."

My head was cloudy as if I were still asleep. I tried to shake off the confusion to be ready for what may be coming.

He entered the room, and my sanity was almost stripped away. I shook my head and blinked my eyes over and over to make sure I knew what I was seeing was real.

"You?" I choked.

He smiled that ever familiar grin. "Me."

"William?"

"No. Weren't you listening?" he spat. "It's Zane."

I shook my head again. "It can't be. How did you bring me here?"

"That's not important," he said, his voice entirely different from the boy at the café. It was swelled with hate and anger.

"You have to let me go," I said through my sobs.

"I don't have to do a thing," he seethed. "All I have to do is turn you over, and everything is forgiven."

"That's what you were involved in?" I asked. "That's why you never told me what you got yourself into?"

"Of course," he said. "I couldn't possibly tell you I had screwed up and a band of shape shifters had tossed me from their council. You would have called me crazy."

"Clearly you're crazy anyway." I had said it before I could stop myself and braced to be hit.

He was visibly fuming, but he didn't strike me. "I let them see me."

"What?"

"I am with the death workers," he said. "My initiation was to take the life of a woman. It was her time. I screwed up, and her son saw me."

"Saw you kill her?"

"He came after me for it."

"I should never have saved you," I grumbled.

"I am not a bad guy!" he shouted. "I was doing my damn job!"

"Why didn't you shift?" I asked. "To get away?"

"Because I am not like your precious Lucas. I am a night shifter. As I was attacked and dragged from my house before dusk, I couldn't."

I understood everything now. "So you want me in exchange for your position back."

"Hey, you're quick," he mocked.

"That can't possibly be enough."

"Well, maybe not in itself, but between you, your mother, and maybe a few others…it will be."

I felt the rage inside me come to life. I forgot about fear and confusion and hurled myself at him, knocking him to the floor.

"You murdered my mother!"

He pulled me off and threw me against the wall. "It was *your* damn boyfriend who saved your life and threw off the balance. I was only evening things out. The Order seemed pleased with my decision."

"You're a bastard," I fumed.

"And you're a dead girl walking."

He left me tied to a chair. How painfully cliché. My wrists were bound behind my back, and my ankles were tied together. When I tried struggling, the ropes cut into my skin. I knew screaming was pointless, and I clearly had no way of untying myself.

I was alone, which at the time comforted me. At least it meant there was no one there to hurt me. I knew I had to think of a way out. I couldn't just sit there, waiting for Lucas to show up. This Zane had been smart enough to get me away from him once before.

Ideas were swarming through my head, but nothing connected. I spotted a lamp on the table beside the bed. I tried with all of my strength to pull the chair closer to it. I was completely unsure what I was going to do, but something told me to keep trying. Some instinct came over me, and I was no longer planning. I was acting on some deep knowledge I was not conscious of before. I dragged the chair a few more inches and pulled the cord on the lamp with my fingers. It fell onto the bed, and I reached behind myself, fumbling with the shade. I felt for the bulb and slowly unscrewed it, still unsure what my intentions were.

I felt around for the metal edge of the bed below the mattress. I found it and struck the bulb hard against it. Nothing happened. I tried again and felt the jagged edges of glass pierce through the skin on my hands. I winced but didn't stop. I used the now broken glass to begin sawing at the ropes binding my wrists.

My fingers kept slipping, and I ended up with shallow slices all over my hands and wrists. The ropes broke free. I untangled my hands and untied my feet. I crept slowly to the door, terrified someone would come in and catch me. I turned the handle, and sure enough, it was locked. I had no way of knowing how to pick locks, and I didn't have any hair pins to try with. I anxiously surveyed the room, searching for anything of use. I was interrupted by the sound of a creaking door and the shuffle of footsteps outside. I scrambled toward the bed and picked up the broken light bulb, holding it out like a knife.

The door creaked open. It wasn't Zane. It was his flunky with the black eyes. I immediately came at him with the glass. He grabbed hold of my wrist, and I dropped the light bulb. He wrestled me to the floor, but I got away, scrambling for my weapon. He grabbed my ankle and pulled me back. I kicked as hard as I could with my other foot, hearing the awful cracking sound of breaking teeth. I grabbed for the glass again and jabbed him in the abdomen. The bulb shattered, distracting him just enough for me to run past him as fast as I could. I felt his fingers brush my ankle as he reached for me one last time.

I took almost no notice of the house as I left. I raced down the streets, with no idea where I was or where I was headed. I ran until my muscles ached and my chest felt like it was on fire. I slowed to a walk, glancing over my shoulder every few seconds to make sure I was still alone.

I noticed the different variations of gray streaks in the sky, telling me the sun was coming up. I was lost and alone, and it was still dark out. Fear set in, but I kept moving, trying to get as far away from that place as possible.

I heard the sound of an engine coming toward me and could see the dim, colorless headlights. The car stopped a few feet from where I stood. I knew it was Zane. It had to be. I prepared myself to turn the other way when a familiar voice called my name.

"Daisy!"

I perked up, and without thinking, I ran in his direction and fell into his arms, instantly in tears.

"You're okay," he said, his strong hand threading into my hair.

"Lucas, they found me."

"It's all right. You're safe now."

"Right on time," I heard Kristoff say from the car. "She was exactly where she should be."

"What are you talking about?" I asked.

"Get in," Lucas said.

I climbed into the back seat, still shaking, consumed with the fear that Zane would come back.

"Daisy, how did you escape?" Lucas asked.

I shook my head. "I cut through the rope with a broken light bulb."

"A light bulb, huh?" Kristoff said in a higher pitch than usual. "What a clever idea."

"I actually don't even know where I got that from. Probably movies."

Kristoff chuckled. "I'll have to take the credit for that one."

Lucas laughed, turning around to glance at me.

"What are you two talking about?"

He laughed again. "Kristoff has this…thing."

"Thing?"

"Sort of like the way I can come into your dreams, Kristoff can do it when you are awake. The only difference is you wouldn't usually realize he's there."

"There?" I echoed. "What do you mean 'there'?"

"In your head," Kristoff said. "The broken light bulb—my idea."

"Wait. That…that doesn't make sense."

"It's like I told you," Lucas said. "Those things are pretty normal in our world. Kristoff was only trying to help."

I sighed, attempting to think.

"The man who kidnapped you is not as smart as he thinks. He's a screwup and an idiot."

"Well, he was smart enough to kidnap me in the first place."

Lucas sighed. "Yeah, that was my fault. I'm sorry. I should have been standing guard."

"How did you know I would be here?"

"It was a lucky guess," Kristoff said. "Judging by the way the roads looked, I guided you in this direction so I could find you. The world looks… very different from your eyes."

I bowed my head. "I hope you will never do that to me unless you have to. I don't like that you can watch my life like that."

"Don't worry," he answered. "I don't like it either. I only did it because

Lucas begged me to. We had to do *something* to find out where you were and to get you out. It wouldn't even work unless you were open to it anyway."

"And now what?" I asked. "What do we do about Zane? I knew him, Lucas. We were friends."

"Whoa, what?"

"He's the one I saved. Remember? The one who dreamed of me. He killed my mother, Lucas. I want him dead!"

Lucas huffed. "That explains a lot. He knew everything all along. He was only befriending you to get as close to you as possible. When he found out you remembered me, he must have known you were the one The Order wanted."

"So what do we do about him?"

"We?" Kristoff murmured.

"*You* will do nothing," Lucas said. "We'll take care of it."

"I have to do something! He killed my mom. I am a part of this now!"

"Listening to me is the best thing you can do right now, Daisy."

"Lucas…my mom!"

He reached back and grasped my hand. "I know, but revenge is not where your head needs to be right now."

I sighed. "It's my family. I want justice whether or not *you* think I should."

"What matters right now is that you're safe, that you're okay."

"I don't feel okay. I want to go back to that place and tear Zane to shreds."

"Like I said, we'll—"

"Take care of it. Yeah, I heard you."

"Just try to trust me, Daisy. I will make sure nothing like this happens to you again."

Chapter Sixteen

IT WAS DARK. The dim light in the room was barely enough for me to see his face.

"How did it happen?" I asked. "The first time."

He smiled. "I was very young. My mother had come in to read me a story. In that trance between sleep and wakefulness, it happened. She was so proud. She called my father into the room. It was a coming of age for me."

"What did it feel like?"

"No words can describe it. It felt very natural and comfortable to me. I wasn't confused or alarmed."

"And it didn't…hurt?"

"There's a sort of ache…at first. It's only until the shift is complete. I don't even feel it anymore. It's something one gets used to after a while."

I nodded, unable to think of what to say. None of it was like anything I could ever hope to experience. None of it made sense to me.

"It wasn't always like that for me," he said. "Things changed when I decided I wanted to go my own way. I know what it's like…to feel you are broken, to think something is wrong with you."

I stared at him for a moment, and even in the dark without the color, I could see the hazel of his eyes. I brushed my fingers across his cheek, feeling the softness of his skin. He closed his eyes and leaned closer to me. His breath was hot and sweet. His lips closed around mine, and I inhaled slowly, savoring the feeling. His body against my own was familiar to me, as if I had found comfort in his arms through my entire life. I admired the feel of his broad shoulders and the hardness of his chest. The thin contours of muscles in his stomach moved against mine as he breathed. I knew his body, his lips, and his mind. I knew *him*...even if I couldn't remember why.

He hummed my name between breaths. It felt as if the sound of his voice was made of something solid that slithered into me, heightening my senses. The sudden urgency in his movements frightened me. I pulled away softly, trying not to ruin the tenderness I was feeling but needing to lessen the overwhelming passion.

"Are you okay?"

I looked away, nodding. "Sorry."

He smiled. "Don't be. I shouldn't have. It's too…"

"Fast?"

He nodded. "Yes."

"But don't leave."

"Wouldn't dream of it." He lightly brushed stray strands of hair off my face, moving it behind my shoulder.

"Can we talk?"

"Of course. What about?"

I shrugged and searched my thoughts for something. "I want to know a little about Kristoff. He seems like an interesting person."

Lucas smiled. "Kris is a character. He was always very competitive growing up. Even as the older brother, he always seemed more like he wanted what I had rather than the other way around."

"I never had any siblings," I said. "I mean, I have my friend Jess, and now more than ever, she is like my sister. But I never knew what it was like to want what a sibling had."

"Sibling rivalry is normal. But with us, it was more of a constant battle of wits, strength, and success, instigated by him alone. Being the person I am, I was never going to back down from a challenge."

I smiled. "I can see that. After how many times I fell in love with you."

A soft shade of gray appeared on his cheeks. I loved that I could make him blush.

"Yes, well, that ended up being a fault of mine. When we fought, it was very hostile. I put him in the hospital once."

I felt the expression of shock creep into my features before I thought better of it. "I'm sorry. I don't mean to look so rattled. I'm just surprised."

"It's okay. Kris was fine. I didn't hurt him that badly, but the fact that I 'won' the fight caused even more resentment toward me. My brother loves me, and obviously I love him, but there is some tension between us."

"He still helped you save me after everything."

He nodded. "He's a good person. It's like I said, he's just competitive by nature. That's one reason he wanted to join The Order and I didn't. It's his way of beating me—of winning."

"His competitive nature and place in The Order may be for the best," I said. "Maybe he really can, as he put it, 'lobby for my life.'"

"I know he can. We just have to try and be patient."

"Lucas, who was that man?"

He hesitated. "What man?"

I sighed in slight frustration. "The man who let us go the night Kristoff found me."

"Oh," he breathed. "*That* man. His name is Moe. Oliver Morris Black, actually, but everyone calls him Moe. He's..." He lowered his head as if searching for the words.

"He's who?"

"He's...my father."

"Your..." I hesitated, unsure of how I was supposed to feel.

"That's why he let you go. He can't betray The Order, but he can't betray his sons either. He's very conflicted, Daisy, and doesn't know what to do. It's best to steer clear of him. As long as he knows nothing, then his not telling The Order about things means he stays in their graces."

I nodded but had no words left to say. There was an entire world out there with rules and order and structure that nobody was aware of. It was puzzling to me that so much could exist without anyone finding out about it.

"You don't need to worry," he said, pulling me from my thoughts. "He's my father."

"He's The Order."

Lucas shook his head. "No, he's a member of The Order. I understand that scares you, but he would not do anything that would hurt me. He knows losing you would destroy me."

When I heard him use those words, I could feel the love he had for me. For the first time, I felt it inside me more than I ever had before. He *did* love me, and even though I didn't know why or how, it was like I had always known I loved him too.

The dream unfolded like the curtains lifting from a stage.

I watched Lucas standing in our field, the blue and purple wildflowers swaying in the wind. The breeze ruffled his chocolate brown coat and tousled his dark locks. He wasn't facing me but appeared to be speaking to someone.

"Lucas?" I mused, taking a step toward him.

He didn't turn around.

"Lucas?"

He still didn't even flinch at the sound of my voice.

I took a few steps closer so I was beside him and saw he was speaking to Kristoff. They both fell silent as I approached.

"Kristoff, what's going on?" I asked, coming closer. I gasped and took a quick step back. Kristoff's face, which was once soft and human, was now twisted into something I did not recognize. His eyes were cold and dead.

His head tilted unnaturally as his empty eyes flicked around, surveying the field. He looked toward me...through me...for a split second before staring back at Lucas. It was as if they couldn't see me or hear me—as if I were invisible.

"Lucas!"

He still didn't move. I called to him, but he didn't heed.

"Kristoff?"

Still nothing. I felt the blood in my veins turn ice cold. I knew something terrible was about to happen. I also knew there was no way I could stop it.

Kristoff lunged at Lucas with a blade. I screamed for him, feeling a sense of urgency, as though there was something I should be doing but didn't know what. I knew this was the cause of the dread I was feeling only seconds before, but I was frozen in place. All I could do was stand there as Kristoff plunged the knife into his brother's chest.

He pulled the blade free from Lucas's body, blood clinging to the gold engravings of the knife. The metal dripped dark crimson onto the grass, staining the meadow.

Lucas's body was slumped in the foliage, blood still pooling under him.

I awoke, screaming. Lucas came tearing into the room like I was being kidnapped again.

"Daisy!" He clicked on the light.

I already had tears running down my cheeks. "Lucas..."

"What happened?"

"I... A dream. You were...dead."

My crying turned to harsh sobbing, and he came to sit beside me and wrapped me in a hug.

"It was just a dream."

"No. It was in color."

He moved away. "In color?"

I nodded. "Only the visions are in color...except the one you gave me about Jess and then the one with the dull colors."

"Dull colors? Which one was that?"

I pursed my lips. "The one where you were a cat."

"Oh." He sighed. "The colors were dull because it took a lot of my energy to come to you as something other than human. You accept me as a human easier."

"Lucas, this was a vision. I can feel it."

He nodded and sighed as if he wasn't sure what to say. "Tell me what happened."

"It was so terrible," I began, trying to control my breathing. "I was in the field, and I saw you there, but it was like I was a ghost, like you couldn't see me. Kristoff was there too, and..." I broke off, trying to catch my breath.

"Go on."

"He...he killed you, Lucas. He stabbed you."

"Daisy, Kristoff would never—"

"I know. But it was in color, Lucas. That means something. Maybe it won't be Kristoff. Maybe it will be The Order."

"Daisy, nothing is going to happen to me."

"You don't know that."

"It was just a dream."

"Then why the colors?"

He shook his head. "I don't know. When was the last time you dreamed in black and white?"

I thought for a moment, looking back. "I think...just right after the accident."

"Daisy, it's possible all your dreams are in color now. I will be fine."

I wanted to believe him more than anything. After all, it did make sense. But I was still shaking from fear and grief. I didn't want to think about the possibility of losing him. It was agonizing. I tried to believe him. I had to, at least until there was another reason why I shouldn't.

I leaned against him. "I love you, Lucas."

I twisted to see the look on his face. I could feel his heart beating against me, and his face turned that familiar shade of gray.

"I love you, Daisy. As I always have."

Lucas helped me go back to sleep, but he didn't leave the room. He was asleep on the floor beside the bed. I would have preferred he sleep beside me, but he insisted on being a gentleman by keeping his distance. I slept well with no other nightmares.

The next morning while I was only half awake, I remembered the dream of Kristoff with the knife. I remembered beautiful Lucas dead in the grass. I winced momentarily and felt the pressure of a hand on my shoulder. I opened my eyes, and Lucas was sitting in bed beside me.

"Are you okay?" he asked.

I nodded. "Yeah. Fine."

"Another dream?"

"No. I promise."

"You can tell me."

I shook my head. "Really. I was thinking about the nightmare I had. It's just stuck in my head for some reason."

He squeezed my shoulder. "I understand. I promise you that everything is okay."

When he said those words, my memory flashed with Zane and waking up in that strange place. Anxiety started filling me up.

"What about Zane?" I asked, pushing myself up, leaning my back against the headboard. "I can't help but be afraid. What if he comes after me again?"

Lucas sighed. "He won't."

"How do you know?"

He turned away as if he didn't want to answer.

"What is it?"

"Daisy…" He paused and looked at me again. "Zane—he's not a threat."

"Not a threat?" I yelled. "He killed my mom and kidnapped me!"

"Look, I'm sorry he got to you like that. I promise that I will never let something like that happen again."

"Lucas, it isn't your fault," I said, finding my composure. "That's my point. I can't help it, but I'm afraid to sleep. I'm afraid not only because I may dream but because I may wake up somewhere I don't recognize. I'm not sure you understand the level of fear and confusion I'm being tangled in right now. Zane was my friend. I had no idea he was anything more than a local boy."

"Daisy, I know what it's like to be confused and frightened, but Kristoff and I are both here and will make sure you are safe."

"Can you promise you won't leave my side at night?"

"Of course. I don't plan on being any farther away than I have to be. I will make sure you are protected until we can sort this whole thing out."

"I want to kill him," I said. "I want to kill him…like he killed my mom."

Lucas didn't reply, just put his arm around me and pulled me close. I inhaled the scent of him, trying to think of nothing else. I wanted to feel nothing but him. This beautiful, mysterious man was such a stranger to me, yet I knew him on such a deep, intimate level. I wanted to be with him. I knew in that moment I wanted to be with him, and only him, for the rest of the time I may have, even if it were only a moment.

"I love you," I whispered.

I didn't know what else to say. It was the truest, most logical thing in my head. All my other feelings were so complex and intense that no words could describe them. There was this burning need to be close to him, this ache to be enclosed in his arms. I nuzzled closer, but it wasn't enough. He kissed my neck, and I felt him murmur my name against my skin, his breath upon me hot and rapid. He ran his fingers through my hair, and I leaned forward to kiss him. His lips were soft and perfect as I knew they would be. I parted my lips softly, and the kiss deepened. I had never been kissed like this; I had never been this close to anyone. I felt the pressure of his body against mine, and before I even realized I was moving, I felt the soft bed beneath me.

"Lucas," I breathed, wanting to say something to him but having no idea what.

He brought his lips to my ear. "Are you sure?" he whispered.

I didn't say a word; I didn't need to. I twisted my head and kissed him passionately, almost violently. I grabbed for his shoulders, pulling him closer to me. I knew he was the only one who deserved to love me this way. He was the only one who I ever wanted to be this close to. All I wanted was the chance to show him that, even if it was only one time.

Chapter Seventeen

THE DAY DRAGGED on in a surreal haze. Lucas stayed with me, talking of unimportant things and trying to make me laugh. It was the only thing that was keeping me sane and not thinking about Zane or The Order.

"Are you sure Jess won't call the police?" he asked.

I almost laughed. "Jess has this thing about cops."

"What sort of thing?"

I shrugged. "I'm not even sure where she gets it from. She's never been in trouble, but she doesn't like them at all."

He smiled. "Okay, so no worries?"

"Definitely not."

"Good. I just hope she doesn't come looking for you. That would be another thing I don't want to deal with."

"Would they hurt her? I mean…if they found out she knew me?"

He shook his head. "If I am honest, I can't be sure, but I won't let anything happen to her. I know how much she means to you. I could never let anything happen that would cause you pain."

I nodded. "I just want this to be over."

"Kristoff will figure this out."

I leaned against him, breathing in his scent.

"It's getting late. Try to sleep."

"Will you stay with me?"

He smiled. "Of course."

I awoke slowly, feeling the warmth of Lucas's arm draped around my waist. I twisted, and he stirred slightly.

"Lucas?" I whispered.

He opened his eyes and instantly smiled. "Good morning."

"You stayed."

"Of course I stayed. Did you expect me to leave?"

I shook my head. "I guess not. It's just nice waking up beside you."

He smiled and reached forward to twist a lock of my hair around his fingers. "I would like to wake up beside you every morning."

I felt the heat rush to my cheeks and couldn't hide the smile on my face. It was such a new feeling being close to him. Even through that sensation, it felt like something that was meant for me, something I had been waiting for. Everything else in my life seemed as if I had just been passing time until I could find him.

I studied him for a moment, noticing the beauty of his human form. I couldn't imagine how strange it would feel to be in another one. I wished I could feel it for myself, to truly understand.

"What is it like?" I asked. "Shifting. I mean, not the process but…"

"Being something different?"

"Yeah. What does that feel like?"

He shrugged. "It's not easy to explain. It doesn't feel strange. It would be like you changing from blue jeans into a dress or a new brand of makeup."

I smiled. "That natural?"

He nodded. "Sometimes it gets frustrating since as another animal, I can't speak. Of course, unless it's through a dream."

"Could I…see?"

He narrowed his eyes for a moment. "See? As in…watch? Watch me shift?"

The tone in his voice had me instantly regretting the request.

"No," I retorted. "No, never mind. I shouldn't have asked."

"No, it's okay. You just surprised me. I have never been asked that before."

"You have only ever been around other shifters."

He nodded. "The shift is a very personal thing. I don't feel like we are anything less than personal with one another."

I felt myself blush, remembering our love the other night.

"So, you'll show me?"

He smiled. "I will."

"Now?"

He nodded. He crawled from the bed, and I took a moment to stare at his perfect body. His skin was clear and soft with the shadows of muscle showing only slightly. When he moved, I could see those muscles flex and tighten. He was truly beautiful.

"Don't be scared," he told me. "It may be hard for you to watch."

I didn't reply, just waited. I almost turned away when he removed his boxers, revealing his entire body. It still felt intrusive.

It happened quickly—so fast I may have missed it if I turned away for even a moment. His face contorted but not in harsh, angry snapping or pulling. The change flowed like mist or liquid, gentle and welcoming. His soft skin grew dark with fur, and his eyes transformed. Parts of his body appeared to wither away as the other form took hold. Before I had time to react, he was sitting on the floor as the familiar gray cat that guarded me at home.

I started laughing. I didn't know what else to do. I was truly in awe. "Wow. Beautiful."

He purred quietly, and I reached forward to touch the ruff on his neck that looked like a mane.

"You're really a cat. Completely."

He hopped up on the bed and nuzzled my cheek.

I laughed and pet him. "Please… This is…weird."

He hopped back onto the floor, and the change came again. The fur withered, revealing his perfect skin, and his human form grew rapidly. I didn't know what to say.

"What do you think?" he asked.

"It's…beautiful. Amazing."

He smiled. "Were you…put off?"

"God no! It was so incredible, Lucas. You are a remarkable creature."

"You said it was weird?"

"I didn't mean you. I meant you nuzzling me as a cat. There was something not right about that."

He chuckled. "Don't worry. I'm not offended. I was teasing."

"Funny," I said sarcastically with a slight grin.

He smiled and rested his head on my shoulder for a brief moment.

"Come on," he said, getting up again. "I'm making us some breakfast."

"Sounds good."

"Looks like Kristoff is home. Make sure you put on more than just a T-shirt." He winked at me.

He pulled on his boxers and left the room. I got dressed quickly and met

Lucas in the kitchen. He was wearing dark-wash blue jeans but was shirtless, almost teasing me with his perfect body.

Kristoff was reading the paper, dressed in a dark blue suit. My mind flashed with the image of him with a bloody knife in his fist. I shook my head lightly and pressed my fingers to my temples, trying to erase the image. When I brought my gaze back, he looked normal again.

He looked up from the paper. "You okay?"

I nodded. "Yeah. You look nice."

"Thank you. I have a meeting with some people from The Order today."

"Meaning what?"

"If you are wondering if I will bring up your case, the answer is yes."

I nodded and sighed, fidgeting with the cuff of my shirt. "Will they listen?"

"They'll listen," he said. "I can't promise that anything I tell them will be enough to grant the request."

"Tell them about the dreams," Lucas said. "Tell them she remembers me."

"I probably shouldn't. You know that, don't you? Besides, it still might not be enough."

"She's different, Kristoff."

He nodded. "Yes, I know, brother. We need to find out why that would matter to The Order."

Lucas turned away, back to the stove.

"I can't be late," Kristoff said. He squeezed my shoulder as he walked past me. "It'll be okay. Give me a chance."

I had been so distracted worrying about myself that I didn't even notice how late it had become.

"I'm sorry," I said to Lucas. "I was not very good company today."

"You were just quiet," he said, grasping my hand. "It's okay. The way you feel is understandable. I love you, Daisy. I will do whatever it takes to make you safe."

I nodded. "I'm scared—terrified it won't work."

"Kristoff knows what he's doing. Try to get some rest, Daisy. Things will make more sense in the morning."

I knew he was only saying what he thought I needed to hear, but either way, it helped. I wanted to believe him. I wanted to believe there was a reason for The Order to keep me alive, that a claim for my life was enough. I fell asleep easily with Lucas beside me.

. . .

I knew it was a dream, but I couldn't wake myself up. I was pulled deep into the tunnels of my mind and could not find my way back. I knew I had no other choice than to let the dream play out.

It started with a kiss. There would have been nothing wrong about some-thing so simple except that when I opened my eyes, it was not my beautiful Lucas looking back at me. I was staring into the gold eyes of Kristoff. I was pulled away from that point of view and was now looking down at myself. I watched myself not only accepting but encouraging affection from the brother of my love.

I knew something was wrong. Not only was the dream in color but some-thing was forcing a dark sense of panic through my limbs. The kiss continued, and I tried to scream at myself to stop—to wake up. I struggled and fought myself in my head—screaming, yelling, and mentally flailing.

I jolted awake. Lucas was beside me with a clear look of terror on his perfect face.

"Daisy, what happened?"

"I… A dream."

"You were screaming. I thought you were having a nightmare."

"I'm fine." I sighed. "I promise."

I couldn't tell Lucas the truth. Even though it was merely a dream, there was this horrible guilt eating away at me. *It was just a dream. Just a dream.*

"What was it?" he pressed.

"It… Nothing. It was nothing. I don't remember. I'm fine."

He raised his eyebrows and stared into my face. "Are you sure?"

I nodded. "I'm fine."

Chapter Eighteen

THE NIGHT WAS DARK. Lucas switched on the light in the living room, but it was still a shadowy, dismal gray. He sat beside me on the couch.

"Kristoff still out?" I asked.

He nodded. "He may have stayed with my father last night. It's a long drive."

I sighed and nodded. "I'm going crazy. I have to know what they said."

"I know. I won't pretend I'm not ready to pull my hair out myself. I do know Kristoff will work this out. He's smarter than he looks." He smirked at me.

I smiled back, hoping it would make me feel better. I wasn't sure if it had. I snuggled closer to Lucas, wanting to just disappear into him. I could feel myself struggling not to cry. I didn't want to make this worse for him.

I concentrated on the beating of his heart and breathed in his scent. He smelled like the woods. I identified the sweet aroma of pine and flowers hidden behind a musty smell of old wood. It was comforting and memorable. I wanted to be there in the woods. I wanted to inhale the scent of the trees and the air where life was in balance.

My drowsy state was instantly shattered by a deafening crash. Before I even had time to consciously react, I was already on my feet. Lucas was in front of me, guarding me from whatever was coming.

I screamed and covered my mouth with my hand, cowering in the corner when a giant animal like a wolf sprang into the room, collided into a bookshelf, and sent books flying. I sank to my knees, with tears streaming down my face. The wolf turned and stared at Lucas, who was still on his feet in front of the couch. I waited for the animal to come toward me, but it didn't. The wolf was knocked back by another force. I rubbed my eyes and stared, frozen. The wolf's throat was clamped between the powerful jaws of a wild cat. It howled and threw the cat forward. They stood face to face, growling and batting at one another.

Lucas raced to me and grabbed my arm. "Upstairs. Now!"

He pushed me forward, and I scrambled up the stairs. I stayed on the landing, staring through the rails. I was trembling in fear and confusion, but I couldn't look away. I felt if I shut my eyes or turned away, something terrible would happen. The animals were reeling over the floor, kicking and biting. Lucas moved very slowly, stealthily, and removed his shoes. I wanted to scream at him, ask him what he was thinking, but I froze. I moved my eyes back to the fight. The cat's coat shone in the dim light, and I could see it had spots—a leopard. The wolf must have been gray with a black stripe down its back.

The cat leaped into the air and collided with the wolf, chomping on its haunch. The wolf howled horribly and went for the throat of his attacker. The leopard twisted, and the wolf's teeth found its neck. The cat hissed and moaned and flailed until he threw the wolf into the wall. He yelped but unsteadily got back to his feet. There were dark smudges on the walls and carpet that must have been blood.

I brought my eyes back to Lucas just in time to see him shift. I found myself on my feet, screaming. The image from the dream of him dead in the grass assaulted my memory. He threw himself into the air, and before landing hard onto the floor, he was no longer human. I was staring at Lucas as a pure and stunning tiger. He pounced on the leopard and tore at its throat. The cat shrieked and headed for the door. Lucas chased it for a few yards, then turned back to the wolf. The cat ran off, trailing blood as he fled. I sank back down as I kept my eyes on Lucas. The wolf slumped to the floor, whimpering. Lucas bent down and nudged its cheek with his muzzle. He made a quiet sort of cry.

I almost wanted to cover my eyes when I saw that unnatural contorting of features and the larger parts wither away like smoke, leaving only Kristoff lying broken and bleeding on the floor. I didn't care anymore about hiding upstairs like Lucas wanted. I came racing to the living room and to Kristoff's side. By the time I turned around to see Lucas, he was already himself again. Lucas handed me a blanket he pulled off the couch, and I draped it over his brother.

Kristoff sat up, covering himself with the blanket.

"You're bleeding," I choked out.

"I'm all right."

Lucas put his hand on Kristoff's shoulder, but Kristoff shrugged it away.

"I had him!" he spat.

"Kris, you were hurt."

"I had him!" he yelled again, standing to his feet. "You should have let me kill him. Thanks to you, he ran off."

"Please sit down," Lucas said. "Let me bandage you up."

"I don't need you for that," he hissed.

He pushed past Lucas and sauntered upstairs. I could hear the clinking of bottles in the bathroom.

Lucas dropped his head and sighed.

Kristoff was grumbling and groaning from upstairs.

"I'm going up there," I said.

Lucas shook his head. "I wouldn't. He's in a mood."

"It's okay."

I lightly knocked on the bathroom door.

"Go away," he snarled.

I pushed open the door and saw him slouching on the tile floor with a bandage in his mouth, trying to use the mirror to clean his wounds.

"Here," I said, approaching him. "Let me."

He sighed and handed me the cotton ball. There was an awful spot of raw, torn-up flesh on his shoulder blade. He winced and groaned as I patted it with the alcohol. He handed me the bandage, and I tried as gently as I could to tape it down.

"How's your side?" I asked.

He pulled up the blanket enough for me to see deep teeth marks on his hip. I put a bandage on that and helped him clean up the scratches.

"Thanks," he murmured. "I'm sorry I scared you."

"It's okay. You were very beautiful."

He looked up and smiled at me. "You think so?"

"Yes. I watched from the stairs. It was amazing."

"You should have been hiding." He sniggered.

I shrugged. "Who was that?"

"You mean the cat?"

I nodded.

"Someone who wants to hurt us."

"Someone like…Zane?"

A strange look flickered across his features but was gone as soon as it came, leaving me wondering if I had imagined it.

"Yes."

It was all he said, but it was enough for my stomach to drop and my throat to tighten.

Kristoff got to his feet. "All better. Check on Lucas, will you?"

I nodded and left the bathroom, trying to ignore the fear still haunting me. I found Lucas downstairs in a pair of jeans, picking up the books and broken glass.

"Let me help you," I said.

"It's okay. Go upstairs."

"Lucas, I'm fine. I want to help."

He glanced at me and continued picking up books. "How is he?" he asked, his voice flat and quiet.

"He's fine."

"Good."

"Lucas…"

"Don't."

"He's just—"

"Don't!" he spat.

I grabbed him by the shoulder. "Stop."

He dropped a book with a thud. "I'm sorry."

"He's just upset. He'll be fine in the morning."

"I wish for once he would thank me…for putting my safety on the line. He's my brother, Daisy."

I moved close and pressed myself into his chest. He automatically wrapped his arms around me. I savored the feeling of his bare skin against mine and kissed his chest.

"Come on," I said. "This'll take all night."

Chapter Nineteen

I LAY IN BED, wide awake, unable to relax. I didn't want to sleep. I kept thinking Zane would come after me as a leopard and tear me to shreds.

"Daisy, close your eyes," Lucas said.

"Can't," I answered.

He sighed. "You weren't supposed to see any of that. That's why I told you to hide."

I shook my head. "I know."

"You did see the way we handled it though. There's no reason to be afraid."

"You don't understand," I began, turning to face him. "I just saw a wolf, a leopard, and a tiger try to kill each other in the living room." I gave him a wry smile.

He tilted his head slightly. "Yes, in your world, that's not something you would see often."

"Ever. That's not something I would see *ever!*"

He smiled. "I understand. But you need to sleep."

"Fine. I'll try."

He kissed my cheek. "Sleep."

"Not going to work, Lucas."

He sighed.

"I'm sorry. I don't mean to be like this."

"It's okay," he whispered. "I just want you to be happy."

I sat up beside him. "Can we talk?"

He smiled. "Sure. What do you want to talk about?"

"You. I mean…I don't know as much about you as I should. I want to know about your family. Your mom maybe."

"Oh, my mom." He laughed. "She was something else. You should have seen her, Daisy. Her favorite shift was into a grizzly bear. She was so beautiful, and nobody messed with her."

"A bear?" I couldn't hide the shock in my voice. "She was the person you mentioned who could shift into a bear?"

He laughed. "Yes. Like I told you before, not many of us can pull off a shift like that, so even most people of *my* kind were surprised when she would shift."

"What…happened to her?"

"Ah, well…" He paused and dropped his head.

I noticed his face had the same look I had when I thought about my mom. "I'm sorry. You don't have to tell me."

"No, it's okay. She's alive, just…missing."

"Missing?"

"Well…gone. I mean…I don't know if she's missing, gone, or dead. She just…left."

"Oh," I whispered. "Oh, I'm sorry, Lucas. I didn't know."

He waved me off. "It's not a big deal. Anyway, I want to know about you —about Jess and your parents."

"It was just me and my mom. My dad died when I was a baby. I never knew him. I have felt like something was missing, which I guess is normal, but I never felt loss like I do now, after my mom."

He nodded. "Did she find someone else?"

"Nothing serious. She said my dad was her one true love. She didn't believe she could love like that again."

"Maybe she was right."

I shrugged.

"How about Jess?" he asked. "How did you meet her?"

"Oh, I've known Jess most of my life. We met in school when we were about five."

He smiled. "You're very lucky to have a friend like that. You both are."

"I don't know what I would do without her. When I lost the color and thought my life was over, she was at my side the whole time. When I lost my mom, she never pushed me or told me how I should feel. It's because of her I'm not still moping in bed, living on diet cola."

He gave me a wry, forced smile but didn't say anything.

"I wish she could remember you. I want her to know you someday."

He frowned. "If you choose this, Daisy, things wouldn't be normal for you."

I shook my head. "I want *you,* Lucas. I can handle abnormal. I can't handle not being with you."

He leaned into me and kissed my forehead. "We will figure things out one at a time. Right now you need to sleep, and tomorrow we can talk to Kristoff about the meeting."

"The meeting! I can't believe I forgot. I was so distracted I—"

"Daisy, relax," he coaxed. "Tomorrow, okay? Please."

I sighed. "I can't believe I forgot."

"Kristoff is sleeping anyway, like we should be. He needs to cool off. Tomorrow."

"Fine. Tomorrow."

It was early when I awoke—still dark. I didn't want to wake Lucas, but sleep was impossible with things rushing through my head. I had to know what happened at the meeting.

As I was tip-toeing across the hallway, I was assaulted by a wave of hot throbbing in my chest. I fell to the floor, and the image of Lucas with the knife shoved into his body entered my mind. I struggled for air, my lungs burning. I squeezed my eyes shut, hoping it would erase the image.

When I opened them, I was sitting up in bed, gasping for air.

Lucas put his arms around me. "It's okay. Just a dream."

I scrambled from the sheets of the bed and rushed to the living room to peer out the window. Nothing but the trees leaning from the wind.

"Daisy, what are you doing?" Lucas's voice came from behind me.

"I was just…" I sighed.

"Just what?"

I groaned and covered my face with my hands. "I don't know. I'm so sorry, Lucas."

"It was just a dream, love. You have been under a lot of stress lately. The dreams won't stop until you relax. Come back to bed."

I followed Lucas back to my room and could hear Kristoff lightly snoring from down the hall. I silently laughed at myself for being so unreasonable. There was nothing more than fear in my mind, giving me crazy dreams. I realized it had to be nothing more than a dream as there was no color in it like there was in my visions. Lucas was right. I needed to at least *try* to relax.

I dug my fingers into Lucas's thick hair and kissed him, trying to think of only the way he made me feel. He accepted and kissed me back, warming me completely and erasing my worries. I thought of nothing but him the rest of the night.

In the morning, however, I was tapping my fingernails anxiously on the table and practically bouncing in my seat, waiting for Kristoff to tell me about the meeting.

"Daisy, relax." Lucas laughed, placing a plate of food in front of me. He pulled his cooking apron over his head and hung it on a hook beside the back door. "You okay?"

"I'm fine. Just impatient."

Kristoff stepped into the kitchen, and I instantly shot to my feet.

"Well?" I asked.

He laughed and looked at Lucas. "Has she been like this all night?"

"Pretty much." He snickered back.

"Come on," I pressed. "Tell me."

Kristoff raised his hand and sat at the table across from me.

"I told them your situation, and—"

"And?"

"Daisy, let me finish."

"Sorry."

"*And* they have agreed to hear you."

"Wait, what?"

"They agreed to see you."

"Wait. I thought that's what the meeting was for."

"No," Lucas said. "He lobbied to get you a hearing. The hearing is where you will go before them and tell them what reason you have for them to renounce their claim. Tell them why you should live."

"But I don't know—"

"We do," Kristoff said, interrupting her. "We know what to say to give you a chance."

"And if they refuse?"

"They won't," Lucas said.

"But if they do?"

"We'll handle it."

"We'll go over everything," Kristoff said. "Don't worry. We also need to get you something to wear."

"I'll take care of that," Lucas said. "I'll find her something nice."

"I'm not a fan of dresses."

"The Order is," he answered. "Sorry, Dais."

I put my hand up. "I won't complain. I want this."

He nodded. "Let's get started then."

"First thing we need to tell you is that The Order doesn't care that you're what Lucas calls 'special.' If I brought it up, it would only make things worse. The dreams and premonitions are a flaw in the pattern. That will frighten The Order more than you want."

"So, I just lie?"

"No," he answered. "You just don't discuss it. Under any circumstance. Understand?"

I nodded. "But…if they ask?"

"Well, lie."

I rolled my eyes.

"Second, *only* speak when spoken to. The Order is full of very important people. I know you like to speak your mind, Daisy—but it's not a good time to be yourself."

I glared at him. If he thought I was bad, he'd never want to meet Jess.

"Just answer their questions briefly and to the point."

"What questions will they ask?"

"Patience," he said. "We will get to everything. Third, always look confident and presentable. I know you will be nervous. That's normal. You need to stand up straight, shoulders back and eyes forward. None of the old head down with fidgety fingers I have seen you do when you're nervous."

I nodded. "I'll do my best."

"The Order is very traditional and old fashioned. Be aware of that. The fourth thing is what they will ask you."

I felt my stomach begin swimming in anxiety and anticipation.

"They will ask you one simple question. Why? That is the only thing they care about. *Why* should they let you live?"

I waited, knowing I was not supposed to interrupt. I was literally biting my tongue to keep from shouting out.

"The answer is simple," he continued. "You tell them that things balanced themselves out when a member of The Order took the life of your mother. Tell them she gave her life for yours and that killing you now would not only be pointless but may throw the balance off all over again."

"That's it? Is that true?"

He shrugged. "More or less?"

"What the hell do you mean 'more or less,' Kristoff? Is it true or not?"

"It is true. Not entirely…but I convinced the members of the council that it is. They need to see you and judge for themselves."

"I don't know. I'm scared."

"Don't be."

"But if they refuse…"

"Really, they won't," he said. "This hearing is just a formality. I already convinced them what to do."

"Are you sure?"

"Yes."

"And will you be with me?"

He nodded. "Lucas and I will both be there as your witnesses. You must never look at us. Remember, eyes forward."

"Eyes forward. I got it."

"We will go over it again later, but right now, I need to get going."

"Where?"

"The Order wants words with me. Don't worry. Everything is fine. I am being trained as a member of The Order. There are many times I will be there."

"Okay," I said. "I'll try to relax."

He gave me a kind smile and left.

Lucas wrapped me in a hug and kissed the top of my head. "How are you feeling?"

"I'm okay, I think. I'm still just a little scared."

"That's normal. Maybe I can make you feel better."

I laughed. "I feel better just being with you."

He kissed me softly, and I reached back and let my fingers tangle in his hair. I felt warm and safe in his arms. He gently deepened the kiss, and the darkness in my vision when my eyes were closed began to change.

At first, I just saw color, all kinds of colors entwining with each other and mixing together to form other shades. I kept my lips moving with his as the colors swirled through my memory.

Shapes came into focus, and I saw Lucas. He was sitting on a park bench, smiling. I heard his voice.

"You won't remember me, Daisy," he said.

I felt my heart drop into my stomach. "I don't want to forget you. I don't want to forget this."

"But you will. And there is no way to stop it."

"But I love you. I know you."

I felt a terrible pain in my entire body as if I were actually there, reliving the moment.

I pulled away from him, gasping for air and falling to my knees. Lucas held me up and led me to the couch.

"Are you okay?"

"I don't know," I said. "I saw something—a memory."

"What kind of memory?"

"We were at the park. You told me I wouldn't remember you."

"You remember that?"

I nodded.

"You really are remarkable, Daisy."

I shook my head. "It was awful. I felt so lost and helpless. Knowing that I can't even keep my own memories—it's a terrifying thought."

"It's okay. You remember me now."

"I'm so afraid of forgetting. I'm afraid of losing you."

"I'm not going anywhere. You won't forget me. I promise."

"How can you be so sure?"

"I don't know." His voice was soft, but I felt a sense of confidence in it. "I just…know. It's like a feeling. I know things are crazy right now, but you and I are one thing I know will be okay in the end."

I sighed, feeling a sense of relief at his certainty. I fell into his chest and savored the time we were together, knowing it was real. He pulled my chin up to eye level and kissed me. There were no painful memories this time, and I let myself give in completely, just loving the feel of him. He moved so he was right against me. I could feel the movement of his chest as he breathed. I could smell that wonderful scent of the forest and the softness of his touch. My heartbeat sped up, and my entire body ached with a feeling so strong I couldn't hold it in. I had to say it.

"I love you, Lucas. I love you more than anything."

"I love you too. More than you will ever know."

I excused myself to the bathroom to splash water on my face. I hoped it would help me clear the confusion from my head.

I walked out of the bathroom to see Lucas scratching at his arm. He sighed and stared awkwardly at it.

"What happened?" I asked, stepping closer.

He pulled his sleeve down. "Nothing."

I narrowed my eyes. "Let me see."

He pulled away. "Really, it's nothing."

"Then why are you hiding it?"

"Because I know how you get."

"Lucas, just let me see it."

He sighed and held his arm out, turning away from me. I pulled up the sleeve of his shirt to see deep scratches on his forearm.

"What the hell?"

"It's not that bad."

"When did this happen?"

"The other night. He swiped at me."

"I didn't even notice. You need to clean this up, or it's going to get infected. I'll do it."

"It's not a big deal," he said. "It just needs to be cleaned. Grab me the alcohol from Kristoff's room, please. It should be on the nightstand."

I nodded and found Kristoff's room down the hall. When I opened the door, I was expecting a beautiful room with Kristoff's personality gleaming from every corner. What I saw was a bland, almost empty space. There was a bed against the wall and a wooden nightstand on each side with cheap, standard lamps. I didn't see the alcohol, so I opened the drawer of the nightstand closest to the door of the room.

I felt my stomach drop. There was what appeared to be a letter opener in the drawer in a fancy sheath. An odd feeling began almost suffocating me. I couldn't figure out why, but I knew I had to see what it was.

I gripped the handle, feeling a sickness come over my body. The coolness seeped through me, chilling my entire body. I pulled the blade from the sheath. My hands began shaking so violently I almost dropped it. I had seen it before. Even without the color, I knew the markings on the blade were gold. It was a knife—the same knife I saw Kristoff kill Lucas within my dream. It *was* a premonition. It had to be.

I was actually dizzy with fear and anger. I felt myself preparing to race to Lucas and tell him what I found, but something stopped me. Something told me to keep it to myself. Lucas wouldn't believe me anyway. He wanted to think Kristoff would do anything for him. If I kept this to myself, I would have a better chance of keeping it from happening.

Chapter Twenty

THE APPREHENSION I was feeling had transformed into something more like an illness. I was dizzy, fatigued, and mentally exhausted.

"You need to calm down," Kristoff said. "I can't take you in front of The Order like this."

"Kristoff, I feel sick, and I look like Miss Muppet," I spat.

"You look lovely," he answered.

Lucas laughed. "I thought you would like it."

I narrowed my eyes. I was in a white, lacy dress with a ribbon, which I guessed was pink, around the waist and tied in a big bow in the back. Apparently, Lucas didn't realize I wasn't six years old.

"Jess would try to throw me in jail if I wore something like this in front of her."

"Okay, stop," Kristoff said. "It's not that bad."

"You should eat something," Lucas added. "It will make you feel better."

I shook my head. "I feel too sick. I can't keep it down."

He looked to Kristoff.

Kristoff shrugged. "Fine," he huffed. "Can we get going then?"

I got up from the table and followed them out to the car. I kept my eyes on Kristoff, making sure he didn't have plans to use that knife any time soon. I wanted to say something to him, but I knew I had to keep the secret at least a while longer. If he had plans to kill Lucas, it would be today. It would be at the hearing.

The drive was long, and I was beginning to feel more than anxious—actually, terrified. We pulled up into the parking lot of what at first glance looked like a park. I scanned the area and saw little sticks in the ground. I looked closer and noticed the sticks were flowers placed in the ground every few yards apart. It wasn't a park at all. He had pulled up to a cemetery.

"What the hell is this?" I snapped.

"You know we have to stay hidden," Lucas answered. "This is where nobody would be watching."

"A graveyard?"

"Well, not exactly," Kristoff said. He put the car in park. "It's more what you would call a mausoleum."

"Oh my God. You can't be serious."

"Relax. It's a family plot."

"Great! So I am going to be begging for my life beside all your dead family members. Way to have a Black family reunion."

"Stop," Kristoff grumbled. "Get out and remember what we told you."

"Head up, shoulders back, and shut up until spoken to."

"Right. Good."

We walked through the graveyard to a freestanding building. It was small but ornately decorated with flowers and flowing design. It was made of dark stone. Lucas knocked on the door as if waiting for the dead to respond. I shuddered.

The door creaked open, and Lucas nudged his bent arm toward me. I took his arm and stepped into the tomb with Kristoff behind us. I didn't want him to stab Lucas in the back when he wasn't looking. I moved my hand to his back. I was sure Kristoff wouldn't have a problem driving the knife through my hand if he had to, but maybe it would make things more difficult than he wanted. Lucas grabbed my hand from his back and hooked his arm with mine again.

"Don't look at me," Lucas whispered.

I kept my head forward. I almost jumped when I heard the door close behind me. It was dark, but there were small lights on a table where people were seated. It was exactly how I would have pictured a council. The walls of the building had plaques with names and dates carved into them. I tried to ignore them. I tried not to remember I was in a mansion of the dead.

Seated at the table, I saw the man from the park—his father. He was staring at Lucas.

"Mr. Black," one of the men started. "What brings you here?"

"The Carmichael case," Kristoff said.

I almost turned to look at him but caught myself and kept my eyes forward.

There were four men and three women, all of whom made me uncomfortable to make eye contact with; they all wanted to kill me.

"Yes," the same man replied.

I tried to make out his face. It was dark, but I could tell he was older, with rimless glasses and white hair. He appeared hard as stone and emotionless.

"Miss Carmichael," he boomed.

I made eye contact. "Yes."

"Why should we let you live after Mr. Black here so blatantly disregarded our orders?"

"Sir, it has come to my attention that a member of The Order took the life of my mother. Because of her death, the world has balanced itself out. She gave her life for mine. If you were to cause my death now, the balance may be thrown off all over again."

The man made a face and looked to the other members of the council. There were whispers and sighs, but I couldn't hear what any of them were saying.

"Mr. Black," he said, "is this true?"

"Yes, sir," Lucas answered. "Zane Edelstein took Miss Carmichael's mother to offset my mistake."

"Understood," he said. "Is your witness in agreement?"

"I am," I heard Kristoff say.

"Very well," he replied. "We can renounce our claim on the life of Miss Carmichael."

I felt my breath explode as if I hadn't breathed in years.

"However," he continued, "you will not be without punishment, Mr. Black."

I felt that same sickness creep back into my stomach.

"Yes," Lucas said. "I understand that."

I couldn't help myself. I looked to Lucas, and his beautiful eyes were rimmed in tears.

"Lucas?"

"Don't fight this, Daisy."

Kristoff stepped forward.

"Take him away," the man said.

Two men closed in and took Lucas by his shoulders and pulled him into what looked like another vault.

"Moe!" Kristoff yelled. "Moe, don't do this! Please!"

I was already screaming Lucas's name. Kristoff grabbed my arm and pulled me away. I stared into the darkness, trying to see what was happening to

Lucas. There were only shadows. I struggled in Kristoff's grasp, trying to get to him. I could hear grunts and pleas. The sound of Lucas screaming flooded into me, making me sick. I wanted to cover my ears, but I couldn't stop fighting to get to him, to try and save him. The screams stopped—and it was then I wanted to hear them again. I needed to know he was still breathing. I knew how The Order punished. I should have known this was going to happen. I lost the will to fight, and Kristoff pulled me out of the vault.

I fell weak in the grass outside the grave walls.

"Daisy…"

"You knew," I whispered. "You knew he was in danger, didn't you?"

"We couldn't tell you."

"This isn't right. It's me who should be dead. Then my mom and Lucas—"

"Daisy, this was his choice. I tried talking him out of it. Moe tried too. He's too damned stubborn."

"You should have let them kill me. I can't live like this."

I felt myself sinking back into that same emptiness I felt the day my mother was killed—that overwhelming loss and helplessness. I began sobbing uncontrollably. Kristoff knelt down on the grass beside me and held me. I let him. Nobody would think twice about someone crying at a cemetery. I had forgotten about the mistrust and the knife he may have been concealing. I could think only of Lucas and what I knew they must be doing to him. He knew that such a mistake could be a death sentence, and yet he didn't do a damn thing to try and stop it.

I would never hold my love again. I would never inhale his scent of wood-lands and flowers. I would never kiss him and remember our past. I would never be with him again. He was gone. The sobs turned violent, and my entire body was shaking. I started screaming. I didn't know what else to do.

Kristoff was pulling me back as I started fighting my way back to the mausoleum. I had to open the doors. I had to do whatever it took to save Lucas.

"Daisy, you need to calm down!" Kristoff yelled.

I fought him still, trying desperately to break free. He held me firmly and pinned my arms to my sides.

"Breathe," he shouted. "Daisy, breathe."

I lost my breath, unable to scream anymore, and fell weak once again with my chest burning and my body shaking. I was completely helpless. I couldn't save him. Nobody could.

Kristoff grabbed me around the waist and picked me up. I was gasping for air, trying to regulate my breathing.

"Breathe," he said again. "Slow, deep breaths."

I couldn't listen. He held me up and walked me to the car. He helped me into the passenger's seat and buckled my seat belt.

Déjà vu, like losing my mother all over again. I just sat, unmoving, staring at the floor. Every sound was amplified and deafening.

Soon the sounds were no longer thunderous; they were nonexistent. I couldn't hear at all. I was lost in my head, unaware of everything. I didn't even know I was back at Kristoff's until I woke up in bed, still wearing the ridiculous dress. I wanted to go back to the day I had met Lucas. I wanted to go back to not remembering him. He would be alive that way, and I would never have to feel the loss I was facing. I wanted to crawl into a dark hole and never come out.

My bedroom door opened, and I pulled the blanket over my head, still fighting back the sobs that were creeping up.

"Daisy?"

I didn't respond. I pretended I was asleep. If I were asleep, maybe he would leave.

"Daisy, do you want something to eat?" I could hear the sorrow in his voice, his words soft and slow.

I shook my head under the blanket. "I want to be alone."

"You need to eat," he pressed.

I clamped my hands to my ears until I was sure he was gone. I just wanted to be left alone.

I must have fallen asleep because the room was darker when Kristoff woke me up.

"Here," he said, handing me a glass of water. "You're going to get sick."

I took a sip and handed it back.

"A little more. Come on."

I shook my head, and he set the glass on the nightstand.

"Daisy, I know you're hurting."

"I really want to be alone, Kristoff."

He sighed. "He was my brother. Did you forget that?"

I finally looked at his face. His light-colored eyes were puffy with dark rings around them. He must have been crying.

"I'm sorry," I said. "I realize you lost somebody too. I just don't know how to comfort you, and the only way I can comfort myself is to not be aware of it."

"You have to wake up at some point, and when you do, it all comes flooding back. You have to deal with this head on. Please, let me help you."

I shook my head. "I don't know."

He put his arm around me, and for some reason, it did feel good. He was warm and human.

"Being alone may not be the best thing for you."

I leaned against him just a little, and the tears spilled over. "I don't know what to do with myself," I said through my sobs.

"I know," he said softly. "You can start with eating something."

"My stomach hurts."

"It will hurt more if you don't eat. I'll make us some dinner, and then you can take a bubble bath. You'll feel better. I promise."

"Why would he do this? I thought he loved me."

"Daisy! He did love you!"

"Then why would he leave us like this?"

"Lucas has always been someone to do what he *thinks* is best for those he loves. Someone had to take the punishment for what he did. He disobeyed a direct order not to save you."

"I wish he hadn't."

He put his hand on my shoulder. "Well, I'm glad he did."

"You are?"

He smiled. "If he hadn't, I would have never had the chance to know you."

I gave him a half-smile. "Thanks."

"Now get up. Fresh towels are in the bathroom with your other clean clothes. You can get out of the Miss Muppet costume."

I let out a breathy laugh. It felt amazing to smile without it being forced.

He left to start cooking, and I dragged myself out of bed and into the bathroom. I felt cold, as though I were made of concrete. I felt solid and impenetrable. I felt the same way I did when I lost my mother—lost, frightened, alone, and angry. Oh, I was so angry. How could he do this to us? How could he leave me alone like this?

I let the bathtub fill up and took the bubble bath sitting on the counter. I didn't read the instructions, just poured the entire bottle into the water. It bubbled over, but I barely noticed.

I leaned back and closed my eyes, trying to relax. My entire body felt sore and tired. The heat helped to loosen the knots in my back and shoulders, and already I began to feel a little better. The grief was still overwhelming, but at least the stress in my body was diminishing.

I was beginning to feel myself slipping into sleep when my mind replayed the memory of Kristoff driving his knife into Lucas's chest. I knew the dream was a vision the first time. How could I have forgotten? How could I have not seen it? Kristoff was always the one competing for dominance over Lucas, and when I remembered the knife in his nightstand—the same one in the dream—I knew. In that moment, it became clear that this was my fault. I should have protected him. I should have tried harder to convince him that Kristoff was dangerous.

I jumped out of the tub and threw on the robe hanging on the door without even bothering to dry off. I stormed into the kitchen.

"Tell me you didn't do it!" I shouted.

Kristoff turned from the stove. "What?"

"Lucas… What happened to him. Tell me you didn't do it."

"Daisy, you saw what happened."

I shook my head. "You had something to do with it. You had to have!"

"Daisy, you're grieving. You aren't thinking clearly."

I pulled my hands into fists. "Don't dare try telling me I don't know what I'm thinking."

"Daisy, stop for a minute. Where is this coming from?"

"Where is it coming from?" I shouted. "You forget who I am, Kristoff. I see people die. I saw Lucas."

His mouth fell open, and he turned off the fire on the stove. "What are you talking about? What do you mean you saw him?"

"In a dream," I said, my voice calmer now that I saw how genuinely surprised and confused Kristoff seemed. I sat at the table, sighing. "Only in the dream, he wasn't just…dead."

"Daisy, what happened?"

"You killed him," I blurted out. "That's it. You killed him with the knife I found in your nightstand."

"My… You went through my things?"

I raised my hands instinctively. "No. No, I went in there to get the alcohol. Lucas had a scratch—"

"Okay, that's not important," he said, joining me at the table. "Why would I kill Lucas?"

"I don't know. You tell me. It was the same knife I saw in my dream."

"Did you see the knife before or after the dream?"

"After."

"Are you sure?"

"Of course I'm sure!"

"Daisy, that knife belonged to my father. I always carry it. You probably saw it before and didn't realize it."

I sighed again and shook my head.

"Daisy, it's normal for your mind to replay things you have seen, even if you don't consciously remember seeing them."

It made sense, but I wasn't ready to believe him yet.

"I loved him. Why would I do this?"

"I don't know."

"I can't fight The Order. You know that."

I sighed again. "You swear you had nothing to do with this?"

He nodded. "I do."

"The dream meant something."

He sighed. "Maybe it didn't. I know that you have premonitions and visions, but you have dreams too, don't you? Regular dreams?"

I shook my head. "Maybe. I'm not sure anymore."

I tried shaking off the fear and mistrust I was feeling. I knew what Kristoff was saying made sense. I knew by the way he looked at me when I accused him he was feeling nothing short of shock and pain.

"You need to relax," he said. "I didn't kill my brother."

"I'm sorry."

"You want someone to blame, Daisy, someone who can pay. I understand that."

I nodded. "I guess I do."

"It's understandable. He saved you. That is what all of this was about."

"Then since I'm not going to die or anything, shouldn't I go home? I miss Jess a lot."

"I don't know. There is still the issue with Zane. I need to put a stop to him before you will be safe."

"But…The Order, they let me go."

He nodded. "That doesn't mean anything to Zane. The only difference is now he wants to kill you simply out of vengeance."

"I didn't do anything."

"Well, you made a fool of him. He tried to kill you. He tried long before The Order released you."

"But if he does, he messes up the balance, right?"

Kristoff nodded. "Don't worry. I'll get hold of him and take him before The Order. They'll make sure he never comes after us again."

"Good."

"Are we okay?"

I nodded. "Yeah."

"Good," he said, laughing. "Because you're covered in soap."

"I'll go rinse off."

"Thanks for getting me to eat," I said, placing my dishes in the sink.

"How do you feel?"

"My stomach still hurts. I miss him."

"I know." He stood beside me against the counter and put his arm around me. "I do too."

I found myself heaving and hyperventilating before I even realized I was crying. I was practically wailing, and it was the only release that felt natural. I fell into Kristoff's chest. He stroked my hair and just let me fall apart.

"It's okay," he said. "Come sit."

He led me to the couch and sat beside me.

"I'm sorry," I said, forcing myself to calm down. "I don't think I can deal with this. I feel so alone right now."

"You aren't," he said softly. He brushed my hair behind my ear, and I felt the timid press of his lips against my cheek.

I turned to look at him, and he was staring at me solidly, leaving me wondering what he was thinking.

"What?"

"I'm sorry," he said. "I don't mean to stare. You are just very beautiful."

"Kristoff…"

"I know. You love Lucas. Everyone does."

"What is that supposed to mean?"

"Lucas always had everything," he said. "I loved my brother, but he always had everything I wanted…including you."

I didn't know what to say. I felt as if my stomach had dropped out and I was going to be sick. This whole time Kristoff was not only protecting me for Lucas.

"I don't—"

"It's okay. You don't have to say anything."

I shook my head and headed to my room. I just wanted to sleep. I wanted to be alone. I tried forcing my mind to drift into unconsciousness. Even if I dreamed…I just didn't want to be awake. I missed the feel of Lucas beside me. I yearned to touch his face and find comfort in his arms. I felt cold and weak. I felt as if a ring of ice was wrapped around my body. I hugged myself to try to feel warm again.

A knock came at the door, and I perked up.

"Daisy?" Kristoff called, opening the door.

"I need to be alone."

"Just two minutes?"

"I'm not dressed."

He entered the room anyway and sat on the edge of the bed. His light eyes were puffy, and streaks of dried tears stained his cheeks.

"I'm sorry," he started softly, "for earlier."

I sat up, and he turned to look at me.

"I felt like I had to tell you."

I didn't know how to respond. I just sat there, staring at his face, trying to see Lucas. Kristoff moved closer, and I felt a sense of panic come over me.

"You told me," I said. "So can I be alone now?"

"What if I need to talk?" he exclaimed. "What if talking is what will make *me* feel better?"

"I'm not very good at…talking. It hurts too much."

He sighed. "Okay. I'll give you some space."

He left the room, and I instantly felt a pang of guilt. Kristoff just lost his brother, and all I could do was feel sorry for myself. I just didn't know what to do.

I tried to stay asleep. Every time I awoke, I would do what I could to fall back to sleep. I didn't know how long I had slept. I had no conception of time. It had all blurred together, like when my mom died. Hours or possibly days passed. And I didn't care.

Kristoff knocked on the door again.

"It's open," I said, trying to be compassionate.

He sat on the edge of the bed. I sat up, trying to think of something to say.

"I know you still love him," he started. "Lucas. I know you will always love him, but…he's gone. If you can just find a way to move on…"

"It's too soon."

"Daisy, do you know how long you have been here? In bed?"

I shook my head. "I don't care."

"It's been days, you know."

I didn't respond.

"You've barely eaten. You're going to get sick."

I remember Jess telling me the same thing when I fell into depression after Mom was killed. I couldn't do this to myself again. I knew I needed to find a way to feel normal again.

"I need…something," I said. "I don't know what, but I need something to make me feel…alive—something to make me feel anything."

"There is one thing I have that might help."

I opened my mouth to speak, but he crushed my lips with his. His lips were hot and sweet, and a sensation of peace fell over me. In a way, it felt right—but I pulled away quickly.

"What are you doing?"

"I'm sorry," he said, bowing his head. "I had to do that at least once."

I looked away, almost frightened of how guilty I felt. I didn't want to be alone, but I knew that it was either Lucas or no one. "It doesn't feel right."

"Lucas is gone."

"And I'm still grieving. Aren't you?"

He turned away, sighing. "Of course I am."

"Then what are you doing? I feel like somehow he's watching us."

"If he could see us, I think he would want this."

"Want what?"

He placed his hand on mine. "I feel that if Lucas can't be with you, he would want you to be happy."

"I know he would want me to be happy," I said, "but I can't be happy with you like this. It just doesn't feel right."

As the memory of his kiss sank into me, I wasn't sure I believed my own words. Something about being close to him felt comforting, felt good. I told myself I was grieving and I was lonely. There couldn't possibly be more to it than that.

"I need to be alone."

He nodded and left the room, closing the door on the way out.

I closed my eyes and imagined Lucas beside me. When I realized I couldn't roll over and bury my face in his chest, I cried so hard I was sure Kristoff would come back. He didn't. I cried myself to sleep again.

I opened my eyes and found myself in the field. The grass was a vibrant shade of jade, and the sky held soft hues of blue and red. I watched my golden locks blowing around my face.

I closed my eyes, inhaling the fresh, crisp air. His voice pulled me out of my thoughts.

"Oh, Daisy. Please don't be sad for me."

"Lucas?" I called out, turning around, searching for him.

"I'm here," he said.

I looked to my feet to see the familiar gray cat with hazel eyes and the fur around his neck that looked like a mane.

"It is you." I knelt on the ground and pushed my hair behind my ear. "I miss you."

"I know," he said.

I almost jumped at how unnatural it felt to see his mouth move and such human words being spoken.

"Please, don't be sad."

"Why did you leave me?"

"I had to."

I felt the tears forming in my eyes. "But why?"

"Daisy, I always have a reason for the things I do even if you don't understand them. I love you. I always have. But I had to save you. Don't you see? Someone had to pay for my mistakes. The only person who should have paid is me."

I shook my head. "I'm sorry. I should have protected you."

"No. You did exactly what you should have. You gave me the only thing I ever wanted. I got to love you, Daisy. I got to love you and leave you memories you can keep forever."

"I love you, Lucas."

"I know," he said. "Remember it."

I awoke in a panic. I brushed my now wet hair from my face and went to the bathroom. I turned on the faucet and filled my hands with cool water. I splashed it on my cheeks, hoping to force some sanity into my head. A knock came at my bedroom door, distracting me.

"Are you okay?" Kristoff called from behind the door.

I opened up. "I'm fine."

"Are you sure? I heard you talking to someone."

"What? I was asleep…"

"Oh. Did you have a dream?"

I nodded. "Yeah, it was just a dream though. It was nothing."

"You talk in your sleep." A smile eased its way onto his face.

"Yeah," I said apathetically, only wanting him to leave.

"So you're okay?"

I nodded. "Thanks."

"Wait, please," he said as I started to close the door. "Are you by any chance ready to talk?"

I looked at his face and could see the pain littering his features. I realized by his tone how desperate he was for someone to talk to. I just sighed and went to sit on the bed. He followed and shut the door.

"Tell me about the dream," he started.

I shrugged. "It was nothing. It was just…"

"About Lucas?"

I sighed. "Yeah. He was the cat."

Kristoff let out a soft laugh. "Yes, he liked that form a lot."

"Do you think that maybe…?"

"Do I think he gave you the dream?" he questioned. "No. I mean, not the way you might think. I think that maybe his memory is staying with you until you are ready to let go."

I shook my head. "No…" I thought aloud. "I feel something more. He said to remember I loved him. He asked me not to be sad for him."

"Daisy—"

"Isn't it possible?" I asked, moving closer to him. "Isn't there a *chance* that he's still alive?"

He opened his mouth to speak but hesitated a moment. "I guess it's…*possible.*"

"So shouldn't we do something?"

"Daisy, I honestly don't think there is a point in any of this."

"We have to try. This is Lucas, remember? Have you already forgotten he's your brother?"

Kristoff sighed, bowing his head a moment before looking back up into my eyes. "Fine. Are you sure it was more than just a dream?"

I nodded. "Yeah. There was *something* different. You have to at least let me find out what. It's worth looking into."

"Okay. Let me call Moe. He can help us."

I sighed. "Are you sure?"

"Daisy, you don't need to be afraid of him. He may be a member of The Order, but he is also my father. He's not going to hurt you. I'm calling him for *help*. There may be something we can do *if* Lucas is still alive."

He left the room without another word. I threw on some clothes and followed him into the kitchen. He had picked up the phone on the wall.

"Moe. Yeah, it's me. We need to talk."

I waited, fearing what he might have been saying.

"Look, Moe, Daisy had a dream. Yes, the girl."

Kristoff glanced at me and nodded, telling me everything was okay. "Yes, I can do that. Twenty minutes. Fine."

He hung up and let out a long exhale.

"What?" I questioned.

He raised his hands. "He's coming over so we can talk. We're going to see what we can do about getting them to release Lucas."

Hope fluttered into the pit of my stomach. "So he's alive?"

"Not so fast. We're still not sure, but Moe seems to think he is. It worked once before. We were able to save you. Lucas is of pretty high status. Maybe his punishment doesn't need to be as severe as with others. I may be able to use my position to our benefit."

I sighed. "Good. Let's hope it's not too late."

Chapter Twenty-One

MOE SAT at the table without as much as a word to me.

Kristoff spoke first. "Daisy, you remember my father, Moe."

I nodded. "Nice to see you again," I stuttered out.

He nodded almost formally. "Let's get started. Miss Carmichael, I need you to tell me exactly what happened in the dream."

"Okay." I exhaled, getting hold of my nerves. "I was standing in a field, and Lucas appeared as a cat."

"Is this field a real place?"

I nodded. "We have met there before, more than once."

"Go on."

"He told me not to be sad for him. He told me he did what he had to do, that it was right even if I don't understand why. That was basically it. He just told me to remember that…that I…I love him."

"Okay, it definitely sounds like something. I can't be sure if I have enough of a reason. What Lucas did was a major offense to The Order. They aren't likely to forgive."

"We can try," Kristoff said. "What are the chances he is still alive?"

Moe sighed. "Look, I… I…know he is."

"Wait!" Kristoff was peeved, his voice turning deep and serious. "What the hell are you talking about?"

I felt excitement grow in the pit of my stomach. Lucas was alive. Nothing else mattered. I almost wanted to scream with joy, but I stayed calm.

"I know he's alive. I've been trying to think of something to do. I just don't know if I have enough of a reason to get him out."

"Do you think the dream…?"

"I think it may have been his way of asking for help," he said. "We have to do something now. He's fading."

I just listened, hanging on every word, knowing my love was alive. The feelings in my body were almost impossible to contain. I was embarrassed by my lack of composure, but slow, soft tears trailed down my cheeks, and I chose not to brush them away.

"Let me get some things together and set up a meeting," Moe said. "I will do everything I can."

Kristoff stood up and opened the door for Moe. When he'd left, he came and sat back down beside me.

"I'm scared," I said immediately.

Kristoff leaned over and pulled me into a hug. I let him. It was easy to find comfort in a warm, human embrace.

"I'm here for you," he whispered.

For the first time since I lost Lucas, I started feeling a bit more like myself. I still had knots in my stomach and shaking in my insides. I was not going to be able to have any semblance of patience while Moe worked on whatever it was he was working on. I had to be doing something. I pulled out of the hug.

"How long until Moe gets back?" I asked.

Kristoff shook his head. "I'm not sure, but it shouldn't be long. He's a high member of The Order. All he has to do is set up a council meeting. He's going to call me in a couple of hours and let me know how things go."

"And if they refuse the hearing?"

"I don't know. They probably won't. It's Moe, remember. He makes many of the decisions himself. I doubt they would refuse him anything."

I nodded, unable to find any words to say.

Kristoff's phone buzzed in his pocket. He answered it, and I moved closer, trying to hear the conversation. All I heard was…

"Yes," Kristoff said. "Understood."

He put his phone back in his pocket and turned to me without a word.

"Well?" I pressed.

"They have agreed to a hearing."

I let out a long sigh of relief. "What reason did Moe find?"

"Well, aside from Lucas being of high status, his dreams help them find many of the people that Sect One is meant to save. Without his premonitions, things will probably fall apart in more ways than they realize. They have been relying on them for a long time."

I nodded. "That's good. That's good. Do I need to say anything?"

"Absolutely not," he cried. "Do not mention anything about your dreams. Remember, they don't like that you're even having them."

I nodded.

"Just do what you did before. Shoulders back…"

"Eyes forward, speak when spoken to."

"Yes. Getting pretty good at this."

I smirked. "I'm ready."

"Good. Because the hearing is tomorrow."

I sighed. "I don't need to memorize anything then, right?"

Kristoff raised his hand. "No. You'll be fine."

It was early when Kristoff woke me up. He barged into my room without as much as a knock.

"Daisy, come on. I need you to get up."

I perked up immediately. "Okay. Do I have to wear the Miss Muppet outfit?"

He smiled. "You know you do."

"You know, maybe I shouldn't go with you."

"Daisy, we need you."

"Why?"

"It always helps to have a witness. You don't have to say anything. Just be there."

"I don't know. I want to kill every single one of them for what they did to Lucas. I might lose it completely."

"You'll be fine." The relaxed tone in his voice was a direct contrast to the excitement in my own.

I shook my head. "No, I won't."

"I'll be right beside you."

I just continued to shake my head.

He moved closer, grasped my hand, and leaned forward, touching his forehead to mine. "Daisy, I won't let anything happen to you."

"I'm not worried about that. I'm just not sure I can keep myself from launching into them."

"We don't have a choice."

I huffed. "Fine. I'll get ready."

I got up and glared at the absurd dress hanging on the bathroom door. I showered quickly and had to resist the urge to pull my hair into a sloppy pony-tail. I turned to the mirror and cringed at how ridiculous I looked and adjusted the petticoat, which was scratchy against my legs. Sighing, I reached back trying to zip the dress. I heard light rapping on the door.

"Doing okay?" Kristoff called.

"You can come in."

He opened the door slowly. He looked at me in the mirror and smiled. "Need some help?"

"Please."

He approached me slowly, moving my hair gently over my shoulder, his touch warm and soft. I shivered, loving the heat on my still damp skin. He pulled the zipper up slowly. I could feel the brush of his fingers against my back.

He moved away immediately, breaking the tension his touch had insti-gated. "Let's go then."

The drive was silent. I was fidgeting with the ruffles on my dress, glancing at Kristoff every few seconds, hoping he would say something reassuring. I couldn't stop my mind from drifting off into the memories of his skin, his scent, and the warmth of his body when he held me. I knew I should be losing my mind, wishing he were Lucas. It was strange how I felt happy rather than guilty to be close with Kristoff. He kept me together when I felt like falling apart. I needed him to remind me that I was still alive, that I could still feel. I sighed, still waiting for his voice.

"Daisy?"

I immediately glanced at him.

He looked to me then back at the road. "It's okay."

"I don't know if I can do this."

"I know you can."

"Kristoff, what they did to Lucas... I can still hear him..." I broke off, remembering the horrible screams I heard echoing through the mausoleum. I could feel my chest tighten with the urge to start sobbing uncontrollably. I tried not to think about it, but I was sure that as soon as I got back to that place, it would be impossible.

"Daisy, you have to stay composed. If you lose your cool, that will only make things worse. After we are done with this, you can go home."

Home. That thought brought visions of my mother into my head. I just nodded, trying to keep my mind focused on Lucas. He was the only thing that truly mattered in that moment.

I kept having short daydreams of hurling myself over the table and tearing the council members to shreds, hearing them scream the way Lucas did. I was so angry, and I wanted revenge. Kristoff pulled me out of my thoughts, opening the car door for me.

"Focus," he said. "Okay?"

I nodded. "I got it. Eyes forward."

We walked through the grass to the building, and Kristoff linked his arm in mine. I immediately started shaking. My entire body was shivering.

"Stay calm," he said. "It's okay."

"I'm not nervous," I murmured. "I'm trying to keep myself from killing them."

"I can't take you in there like this. Take a deep breath."

I inhaled slowly, trying to push the rage down inside me.

Moe appeared at my side before I even saw him walking toward us.

"She going to be okay?" he asked.

"Yes," Kristoff said. "She'll be fine. Right, Daisy."

I nodded reluctantly, and Kristoff knocked on the door. I was practically clenching my teeth to keep my emotions at bay.

The door creaked open, and the council members sat in the dim lighting, exactly as I remembered.

"Mr. Black," the older man said.

I stared forward at the wall behind them, too nervous to make eye contact. I tried to push away the memories of the last time I was here.

"I am here to ask for leniency on the punishment of Lucas."

"Yes, we are aware of your request. Is this your witness?"

"It is."

"Moe, are you in agreement with this appeal?"

"Yes," Moe answered sternly.

"Very well," he said. "What reason can you provide that would convince us to spare your son? He committed a very serious offense."

"Yes, sir," Moe said. "I apologize on behalf of my son and promise to keep him in line from now on. Lucas's dreams are our way of organizing and scheduling Sect One's duties. Without them, things may be more than difficult, perhaps even impossible. Since the disappearance of my wife, Lucas's premonitions are all we have."

I almost shot a look in his direction, realizing he had spoken of Lucas's mother, who had gone unmentioned until that moment. It made sense that she had premonitions like Lucas. I wondered then why he never told me about it.

"Very well," he said again. "You may retrieve your son this evening. You must come alone. Understand?"

"Of course. Thank you."

I almost wanted to jump into Moe's arms, screaming out my excitement at getting Lucas back.

We walked slowly out of the mausoleum, and Kristoff and I instantly began laughing. He embraced me, lifting my feet off the ground. The sense of joy was the strongest emotion I had ever felt.

Chapter Twenty-Two

"I DON'T UNDERSTAND," I said. "Why can't I see him?"

"We have to just give him some time," Kristoff said. "Just try to be patient."

"So what now?"

"I figure it's best for you to go home. You can see Lucas as soon as he's well. I promise."

I sighed. "Can you just tell him I love him, please?"

He smiled. "Of course."

"Oh, man, this is going to be so much to tell Jess," I complained, sitting at the table in a robe.

Kristoff sat across from me, his light eyes holding mine. "You need her," he answered.

I broke my gaze away and stared at my plate in front of me. "I know."

"She'll be there for you, Daisy."

"I just don't know how I am supposed to get everything out. She's going to think I've lost my mind."

He chuckled. "I keep forgetting how different your world is."

"Boring in comparison. I'm just glad to have someone like Jess to share the stories with. I do need her, but…I think I need you too."

His face dropped, and he just stared into my eyes for a moment. "Do…do you mean that?"

I nodded. "I do."

He got up from the table and moved to the chair beside me. "I need you too, Daisy. I always have."

"Kristoff, I still love Lucas," I whispered. "I just want you to remember that."

"I understand. I haven't forgotten."

"What about Zane?" I asked. "Am I safe?"

He grasped my hand. "You're safe. Zane has been ordered to stay away from us. He's forbidden to be anywhere near you."

I sighed heavily. "You did that?"

He nodded. "While you were in bed, I took it upon myself to take him before The Order. I couldn't put you through it."

"Thank you," I whispered, not sure how to express the true gratitude I felt for his compassion for me. He knew how much pain seeing Zane would cause me. "I still want him dead."

"That won't bring you closure, Daisy."

I sighed. "Maybe you're right." I looked away. "I should get dressed. Jess is probably worried sick."

"Will I see you again?"

I smiled, looking up at him. "Of course. I need you, remember?"

"Good. I'll drive you."

"Is this really…over? I mean, Zane and The Order?"

"Yes. It all worked out, Daisy. You're going to be all right."

You're going to be all right. Those words brought me back to the day Lucas saved me from the wreck of my car—the day that changed everything I knew to be true. I tried to shake off the feelings and worry only about getting home.

"Is it okay if I turn my phone back on now?" I asked, reaching into my bag.

Kristoff smiled and nodded.

I turned the phone on. It beeped about eight times.

"Seems like you missed a few calls." Kristoff laughed.

I had three text messages and five missed calls, all from Jess. I opened the first text.

Jess Grayson: Daisy, where are you?? I'm worried sick. I told my mom you were staying with cousins for the whole grieving process.

. . .

Jess Grayson: Daisy, please call me back. I'm running out of things to tell my mom.

Jess Grayson: Don't make me come looking for you.

That last one had been sent yesterday. I decided there was no reason to put off calling her. The phone didn't even get through one ring when she picked up.

"Daisy! Where are you?"

"I'm fine. I'm on my way home now."

"That wasn't my question."

"I will explain it all later. Not over the phone."

I heard her sigh. "Fine, but you are going to have to come up with something creative to tell my mom."

"The cousins was a good one," I said.

"Yeah, only you don't have any. I am pretty sure my mom knows that, Dais. She and your mom were pretty close, remember?"

I sighed. "Yeah. I'll figure it out."

"Hurry, okay?"

I ran back upstairs to make sure I wasn't forgetting anything. I stepped into the bedroom, and strong arms grabbed my shoulders. I shrieked, pulling away.

"It's okay. It's me," Kristoff said, his voice frantic and swelling with urgency.

"What's wrong?"

"Hide."

"What?"

He nudged me with his arm. "Hide!"

I moved back slowly, looking for a place I could conceal myself. The room was just a lot of empty space. I hid in the closet like a child, moving as far back as I could behind the clothes. I pressed my back against the wall and jumped when I heard a crash. Objects hit the door of the closet, and growls sounded through the room. I covered my ears but realized that only scared me more. I moved closer to the door and peeked through the slats.

I saw that familiar leopard I had seen in the living room. I knew it was Zane. He had ignored The Order's law of staying away from us. He was growling at the gray wolf who I knew was Kristoff.

The cat turned toward the closet. I could swear he was looking directly into my eyes. I moved back again, and sweat broke out on my forehead. I knew he could smell me. His nose wiggled as he stalked toward the closet. Kristoff the wolf snarled and sprang onto the cat, knocking him on his side. Zane shot back to his feet immediately and growled in irritation. He did not like Kristoff coming between him and his prey.

Zane swiped at Kristoff and turned back toward the closet. Kristoff closed his jaws around the leopard's leg, pulling him away. The cat screamed and hissed, pulling out of Kristoff's hold. He wasn't going to get to me without first disabling Kristoff.

My limbs started trembling as I watched the animals battle, rolling over the floor and tearing at each other in any way they could. The sounds were worse. The cries, screams, and growls were more terrifying than the dark smudges of blood on the walls and carpet.

I heard an awful cry that must have been Kristoff. I crept back to the door to try and get a look at him. He was on the floor, unmoving. His mouth was open, but he was still in wolf form. A sigh escaped me, seeing his side rising and falling with each breath. But he was not stopping Zane, who was heading back toward me. I didn't even have time to back up to the wall before he had torn the wooden door to pieces, flinging shards of wood behind him.

I shook uncontrollably as hot tears streamed down my face. I couldn't stop thinking about the cat's teeth tearing into my flesh and the force of his body crushing my bones. I had no reason to believe this wouldn't be the most agonizing thing I would ever experience. At this point, death would be a blessing.

He took his time, stalking me like I was a field mouse planning to burrow under the ground. I had nowhere to run. I pressed my back harder into the wall instinctively even knowing that at this point, there was nothing to do but wait.

I heard a soft snarl from behind Zane and began praying that Kristoff had gotten back up. The leopard turned away, and I took the opportunity to try and sneak past him. If I could just get out of this room, I could escape.

He turned around as soon as I made my move. He leaped into the air, and I screamed, covering my head with my arms. Kristoff's wolf form collided with the cat, sending him into the wall—but not without knocking me back as well. I fell, bashing my head on the door of the room. My vision was darkening. I tried to stay alert. *If I can just get out of the room.* I could still hear the snarls and growls but was slipping out of consciousness.

A soft muzzle nudged me in the shoulder. I looked up and through my haze saw the soft, velvet-like face of a tiger. My vision faded, and I saw nothing but darkness.

Chapter Twenty-Three

THAT FAMILIAR BEEPING SOUND, like on the day that ruined my eyes, came seeping into my head. I tried to push away the assault of memories, but it was impossible, and I was far too tired to try any harder. I remembered the glass on the road, shimmering in the sunlight like diamonds. I remembered the burning in my head, and I remembered Lucas—the beautiful boy who saved my life. The memories were vivid, as though it had happened only days ago.

Then I remembered the battle in Kristoff's room. I remembered the leopard and wolf brawling and that same wolf saving my life. As the memories played out, I remembered more.

I remembered the tiger—the same animal Lucas had become the first time Zane came after us. Maybe it could have been him. Maybe I could see him soon. I already missed him so terribly.

I tried to open my eyes, knowing the maddening beeping meant I was in a hospital. Great. I knew Jess was waiting at home for me. *She's going to flip when she finds out I'm here.*

I'm here. Where's Kristoff?

My body was too tired and my eyes too heavy. I tried rolling over, hoping it would force me awake. I felt the familiar tugging of an IV in my arm. The discomfort was enough to pull me from my drowsiness. I opened my eyes and suddenly felt the events of the past few weeks slipping away like a dream. I tried to stay there, in the arms of my love and the company of Kristoff, but it all seemed so far away, and I was starting to forget.

Maybe being away from Lucas was enough for me to forget him again. Maybe I was never meant to remember him in the first place. I covered my face with my hands, begging myself to fall back asleep. Nothing felt real anymore.

I heard the door creak open, and Jess raced into the room when she saw I was awake.

"Daisy!"

"Jess…I'm so sorry."

"What are you talking about?" she hissed, grasping my hand. "Don't be sorry. I'm just so glad you're okay."

"Where's Kristoff?"

She cocked her head, pulling her eyebrows together. "Who?"

"Kristoff. He's… You've never met him, but he should be here somewhere. He was hurt."

"Daisy, calm down. You aren't making sense."

"How am I not making sense?" I cried. "He was hurt, Jess."

"Okay. Was he the one who hit you?"

"Hit me?"

"Daisy…" She broke off and sighed, turning away for a minute. "Daisy, don't you remember? You were in a car crash."

"I… What? A car crash?"

She nodded. "It was pretty bad, but everything's okay."

"I don't understand."

"You need to rest. I'm going to go call my mom, okay? I'll be right back."

She got up to leave before I even had time to reply. I fell back onto my pillow, trying to remember. I remembered passing out in Kristoff's house. How could I possibly have forgotten waking up and getting into a car? Even the memories of the fight were vague and surreal. I tried piecing together small details of things I had seen. I remembered the blood smears on the walls and the dark shine in the wolf's coat. I remembered the paralyzing fear when Zane came after me. It all seemed like it had happened to someone else. I was trying to force myself to feel the fear and the pain, but none of it was really hitting home. It was all like something—from a dream.

Jess entered the room again and sat in the chair beside the bed. "I'm so sorry this happened to you."

I nodded. "I know. I didn't think this could happen again. The odds—"

"Again? You mean this happened before? I never heard about that."

"I mean the crash. I mean I didn't think I would get into another wreck."

"No, I know," she answered. "Were you in a crash when you were little?"

"What? No. Jess, I was in a crash a year ago. Don't you remember? The crash that ruined my eyes...and then the dreams."

She didn't answer, just shook her head mechanically. "I... Daisy, I don't know what you're talking about."

"Jess, if you're kidding, it's not funny, and you need to stop."

"Do you need me to call the nurse?"

"No, I don't need you to call the nurse," I snapped. "I need you to stop whatever act this is."

"Okay, I really don't like being yelled at when I honestly have no idea what you're talking about."

I tried to calm my voice before responding. "I don't mean to be accusatory, but you were there through all of it, Jess. How can you say you don't remember?"

"Don't remember *what*?"

I sighed, fighting back the sting of tears. "Not again."

"Daisy, please talk to me. Tell me what it is that I don't remember."

"The crash...about a year ago. There was a boy who pulled me from my car. He saved my life."

"What else?"

"Do you really not know this story?"

She just stared at me with a lost look in her eyes. I sighed again, trying to regulate my breathing to get through the story.

I told her everything, from the crash to the fight in Kristoff's house.

She didn't say a single word until I was finished. "You...you have some *crazy* dreams."

"Jess, this was *not* a dream."

"Dais, none of that happened, okay?"

I was about to argue when something hit me. "Wait, none of it? So...my mom...?"

She shook her head. "I'm sorry. Almost none of it. There was a break in. Don't you remember?"

"So...so my mom *is* dead?"

"I'm sorry, but that part happened. Are you okay?"

I covered my face with my hands. "No, I'm not okay. I can't believe you don't remember any of it."

"Daisy, listen, you were in a pretty serious accident. You have been unconscious for a while. It makes sense you would have very vivid dreams."

I shook my head. It couldn't be. I couldn't be waking up from the crash that happened over a year ago. There were too many details, too much time I had lived through. There was no way I had dreamed it all.

"I'll be back," she said calmly. "Try to rest."

I rolled over and closed my eyes, hoping rest could help me make sense of things.

Much later, I stirred when I heard the sound of movement. I turned my gaze to the door and saw him slowly stepping into the room. My mind was immediately assaulted with a collage of memories. The images raced through my head, from the crash, to the death of my mother, and the near-death experience that landed me back in the hospital. His white-blond hair was tousled, and a light stubble speckled his jawline and chin.

I tried to speak, but nothing came out. I pressed my fingers to my temples in an attempt to stop the memories.

"I'm sorry."

His voice was so familiar; it was as if I had just spoken to him moments ago. "Kristoff."

"It's better she doesn't know. It's best she believes you were merely dreaming."

I shook my head. "You can't mean that. She was the only one I could talk to about this. If she doesn't remember, I have no one."

"Maybe it's best for you to forget too."

"No. That's not what I want."

"It's not what I want either."

"Then why are you doing this?"

"Because it is the only way you can stay safe. It's the only way you can truly have a life."

"Nothing made sense to me before I met you and Lucas," I exclaimed. "Everything seemed like some sick luck of the draw that I came out at the bottom of."

He shook his head, his lips curled up at the corners in an almost smile. "I wish I could stay with you. I do...more than anything."

"Can't you for once just do what you want?"

"I wish I could, but there are rules, Dais."

"You can't just leave me like this."

"Daisy, my intention is not to abandon you, but you are safe now. There is nothing left in our world for you. There is nothing but danger."

I didn't know how to respond. He was right. All I wanted was to be safe again.

"Daisy, I'm sorry. I'll miss you."

I nodded, feeling tears filling my eyes. "I'll miss you too…a lot." All I saw was his departing back.

As my eyes closed again, trying to rest, I remembered the brawl that had put me here. I remembered being flung into the wall and passing out. There was something that drew my attention before my eyes went dark, something that made me want more than anything to stay awake. I replayed every moment I could recall slowly, over and over—until my memory flashed with the vague image of the tiger.

I shook my head, trying to make sense of it. Kristoff was alive; that mattered. Somehow, I couldn't shake the feeling there was more. I couldn't stop myself from desperately hoping for the one thing I wanted more than anything else.

Jess came back in, distracting my thoughts. I immediately felt lost, knowing I couldn't tell her about Kristoff. She wouldn't believe me. I didn't want her thinking I was crazy.

"How are you feeling?" she asked softly.

I shook my head. "Lost."

"You've been crying." She sat in the chair beside the bed and took my hand. "Daisy, you're going to be fine. The doctor said you can come home tonight."

Nothing she could say was going to make me feel better. I tried to smile. "That's good."

"Is your head hurting?"

I shook my head. "No. I'm okay."

She nodded. "Then we can get you out of here soon."

"You don't have to stay."

She laughed. "Daisy, of course I'm staying. I am not leaving you."

"Jess, really. You look exhausted. Why don't you go home and get some sleep for a few hours. I'm not going anywhere."

She smiled and nodded. "Well, okay. I'll be back in a few hours, and we can take you home."

I forced a smile once more, actually liking the idea of getting out of here and back to a familiar place.

I closed my eyes again in a vain attempt at sleep. Kristoff crowded my mind, keeping me awake. I replayed our days together with Lucas and the almost-romance we had shared. It did feel somewhat like a dream, surreal, as if maybe it never really happened. An uncomfortable anxiety began bubbling up into my chest. I shook it off. There was *no* way I dreamed all that. *No* way.

I rolled over, trying to think of anything else. It seemed impossible. The room was silent, but I felt as if I wasn't alone. I felt eyes on me, as though I was being watched. I immediately shot up in bed in a sort of panic.

I saw the soft hair hanging in front of deep, familiar eyes, hiding his gaze and the smooth skin of his beautiful face. I tried to speak but didn't know what to say. He smiled at me, staring into my eyes.

"Daisy." His voice was barely a whisper, but it brought tears to my eyes.

"Lucas," I finally choked out.

His smile didn't fade. "I'm so sorry, Daisy."

"I...I thought you were dead. I thought I'd never see you again."

He nodded. "I thought so too."

"I heard you...screaming. It was horrible. Even when Moe told us you were alive...I..."

He stepped closer and leaned over me. "I'm here with you, Daisy."

"Am I dreaming?"

He shook his head. "I'm here, love. I promise you."

I felt joy bubbling up inside me, but with it was so much confusion I didn't know what to do. I reached out my arms, and he leaned over, letting me embrace him the best I could.

"I'm so sorry," he whispered.

When he pulled away, I could see his eyes were filled with unshed tears.

"For what?"

"For things being this way. I can't stay."

The joy I had felt only moments ago began wavering, causing me to tremble almost violently with grief. I knew it only made sense if Kristoff told me the same thing. Somewhere I knew this was the only thing he could have said.

"That's what Kristoff told me."

He nodded. "We set out to make you safe, Daisy."

"And now?"

"Now you are," he said, finally shedding the tears. "But if I stay, you can never live that life we so desperately tried to save. Things will never be normal for you. That is why we chose to let Jess forget."

"*You* did that?"

"Well...The Order. Moe, really."

"Lucas, I don't care about this 'life,' as you put it, unless I can spend it with you."

"Daisy, don't say that."

"It's true."

"You may feel that way now, but someday you will realize that moving on might not be such a bad thing."

I shook my head. There was no way he was going to convince me that losing him again could possibly be a good thing for anyone.

"I have to go, Daisy. I only came to say goodbye."

"Please," I cried, not even trying to stop from sobbing uncontrollably. "Please don't leave me again."

"I can't stay."

I reached for him, and he leaned forward, kissing me softly. I tried to hold on as he pulled away.

"I love you, Daisy. That will never change. I will always look after you even if you don't know I am there."

Chapter Twenty-Four

I WAS UNUSUALLY QUIET. I didn't have anything to say. Jess sat just as still, possibly afraid to say the wrong thing. She finally broke the silence.

"Daisy?" she began cautiously. "Please don't be mad at me."

"Jess, I'm not mad. I'm…upset. Frustrated even. It really has nothing to do with you."

"It does," she argued, "because you think I don't believe you."

"You don't."

"It's not like that. I trust you, Daisy, and I believe you. I just can't believe —*this*."

"That's the same thing as not believing me. If I am telling you this happened and you think I was dreaming, how is that different?"

She sighed and bowed her head. I waited for her to say something, but she didn't. She reverted back to the uncomfortable silence. I guess there was nothing left to say. There was no way of convincing her of what really happened. There was no way that anything I could say or do would be enough.

I got up and peered out the window—no cat, nothing but the light breeze stirring the gray trees. I flopped into the armchair, staring, waiting for the little gray kitten to appear. It never did. The shadows darkened, and I glanced at the clock. I stood up, stretching the kinks out of my back. I must have been sitting a lot longer than I realized.

I felt the unnerving pressure of an oncoming dream as soon as I began to feel sleepy. *Oh no. Please…not the dreams again.* I thought they had stopped—at least for a while. I tried to stay awake, but my mind was so exhausted my body eventually succumbed to the same weakness.

It began the same as the previous dreams of my Lucas—standing in the grass, waiting for him to turn to me, telling me things in half riddles. When he circled around to face me, he was smiling warmly.

"Daisy," he cooed.

I smiled and ran to his arms, jumping into his embrace, wrapping my arms around his neck.

He chuckled. "I missed you."

He set my feet back on the ground, and I snuggled into his chest. I felt so warm and safe. I never wanted to let go.

"Daisy..." He laughed, pushing me away. "I want to look at you."

I smiled and looked up to meet his eyes. He held my face in his hands, and the heat of his skin flooded into me, warming my entire body.

"Is this real?" I asked.

"As real as it has always been. This was the only way I could see you. You are so beautiful."

"If this is how we can be together, then I want to stay asleep."

"Daisy, don't say that. I said goodbye so you could have a life, so you can start over. I am too ashamed to admit I was not strong enough to stay away from you. But I missed you too much. That's why I am here."

I didn't know how to respond. I thought he was dead once, and now I was losing him all over again.

"I won't see you again. Will I?"

His face furrowed into a horrible look of pain. He shook his head slowly. "No. Even through your dreams, it is a violation of The Order's rules. I am to have no contact with you."

"Why?"

"Daisy, I almost gave my life to save you when you were supposed to die. I'm lucky The Order didn't tear me limb from limb."

I sighed. "It isn't fair that they get to choose this for us."

He nodded. "I know. I don't know how much I trust their decisions. Kristoff is so loyal, and he's angry at me because I cannot be."

"You think they aren't what they claim to be?"

He shrugged. "I began thinking that after what they did to me."

"What...what did they do to you, Lucas?"

He waved me off, turning away. "Nothing. I'm fine. You don't need to worry about what happened. It's over now."

I could feel the pain of the memory emanating from him, stripping the previous warmth from my body.

"I have to go now, Dais."

"No, Lucas, please don't."

"I have to. I have no choice."

"We can fight them. If they aren't who they claim to be—"

"Daisy, stop," he demanded. "Even if they are liars, they are too strong to go against. This is just the way my world works. It is not a place for you."

"But...I love you, Lucas."

"I know. I love you as well, more than anything else."

He wrapped me in his arms and planted a soft kiss on my forehead. "Don't forget me," he whispered.

"Never."

I tried to hold on to him as tightly as I could, as if that would keep him from disappearing. I held on until the muscles in my arms started burning, but it was to no avail.

I felt the pull from my sleeping state and found myself wide awake in the late morning, my face wet and sticky from tears.

Jess was up, rummaging through her closet. I sat up, already feeling the dream slipping away like sand.

"What are you looking for?" I asked, trying to sound casual.

She turned to look at me. "Hey. My blue sweater. Have you seen it?"

I shook my head. "Sorry."

"Are you okay?"

I sat up, sighing. "I just had a...weird dream. I'm fine."

"Yeah, you aren't the only one," she said with a soft laugh.

"What do you mean?"

She turned to look at me again, pulling a black sweater over her head. "I had this strange dream about you."

"About me?"

"Yeah," she mused. "Like...a memory almost. We were just standing in an empty road, talking about a boy you met."

I almost choked on my breath. "A boy?"

She shrugged. "Something like that. I don't remember exactly. It was just weird. Probably stress from all that's happened."

I wanted to press for more. But I realized the more I tried to convince Jess of the truth, the further I would push her away from me. I decided to keep quiet until I could think of the right response.

"You know…it wasn't just last night though," she continued.

"What?"

"Yesterday when I was doing my hair, it was almost like I had a vision."

I narrowed my eyes.

She laughed. "I'm sorry. That sounds crazy."

"No. No, really it doesn't. Tell me."

"Well, it was so strange. It was like a dream, only I was awake. I was with you in the café, and we were talking again about some boy you met. There was also a lot of talk about the crash and something about dreams. I am a bit unsure of the details."

"Jess, don't you think…?" I stopped myself.

"Think what?"

"Well, that maybe what I told you…"

She shook her head. "I want to believe it. Maybe that's why my mind is showing me these things."

I shook my head, sighing. "Maybe you are seeing these things because somewhere, you remember them happening."

She bowed her head but didn't respond. It was hopeless. I flopped back down before rolling out of bed. It was getting cold out, so I wrapped myself in my robe.

"Daisy, I'm sorry."

I could hear the concern in her voice. I couldn't blame her, could I? If I hadn't lived through it, I wouldn't believe it either. It didn't make sense. I could only expect her to believe the most logical conclusions, the ones the doctors told her were true.

I sat in the armchair again, gazing out the window. I watched the leaves billow through the air and flutter to the ground. Summer was gone, taking the sunshine and warmth with it, leaving us with a crisp chill and dying leaves. I tried to imagine the oranges and reds of the foliage in the coolness of autumn. I knew it must have been beautiful. I remembered loving it once…back when things were normal. I remembered my mother making hot cocoa and tea in the cooler months. The thoughts made me miss her terribly. I sighed, trying to break away from the oncoming depression.

"Maybe we should do something," Jess announced.

I turned to look at her, not sure what to say. "Like what?"

"Just go somewhere."

I felt a sickness start churning in my stomach. "I don't know. I don't feel like doing anything today."

"I really think it would make you feel better."

I shook my head. "No, thanks."

She sighed. "Anything I can do to help?"

"I can't talk to you about things. That's the only thing that can help."

"Daisy, you can always talk to me."

I shook my head. "It's pointless when you don't believe me."

"I wouldn't say I don't believe you."

"What do you mean?"

"Well, what you said about me remembering?"

"Yeah?"

"It sort of makes sense. I'm not saying that I am ready to believe the whole story you told me was true, but I am seeing things that seem so…"

"Real?"

She nodded. "Yeah."

I sighed, not sure how to respond.

"I want to believe it. I do. I just also want to be realistic."

"I understand that, Jess. I just wish there was some way I could prove it to you. I'm not crazy."

"Daisy, I don't think you're crazy. We have been through this. I would never think that about you."

I prepared myself to reply when I remembered those words from a previous conversation. "Jess, do you remember that day at the café? The day I told you I was having dreams again?"

She bowed her head and nodded. "Yeah," she whispered, "I do."

"Jess, why didn't you tell me?"

She looked up, meeting my gaze. "I did. I just didn't tell you how much of it I remembered."

"And how much do you remember?"

She shrugged. "Basically, the whole thing."

"Why didn't you tell me *that*?"

"I don't know. I wasn't sure it was real."

"I remember it too," I said. "It was real."

She shook her head. "I don't understand. Why can't I remember?"

"It's a long story."

She raised her eyebrows. "About Lucas?"

I nodded.

"Have I ever met him?"

"You have," I said. "But you wouldn't remember."

"So, what you told me...?"

"I swear to you it was real. Kristoff came to see me at the hospital."

"Really?"

"Yes. Lucas did too. He told me we can't be together."

"Well, why not?"

"The...rules? It's complicated."

"Daisy, I have all the time in the world."

I sighed, not sure how to begin. "Do you remember The Order I told you about?"

"A little. They make the rules, right?"

"Right. They're the ones who are forbidding us to be together."

"What would happen if...if you went against them?"

I scoffed. "Nobody wants to find out. Chances are they would kill us both."

She shook her head.

"I know it sounds crazy. Trust me. I know."

"It's not easy to understand."

"I know."

"But I'm going to try," she said. "I'm going to try to believe it. Let's say this is all true. What do we do about it?"

I bowed my head. "Nothing," I whispered. "There's nothing we can do."

"Daisy, you love him."

"Unfortunately, that doesn't matter."

"Why? Why can't you be together?"

I shook my head. "I don't really know exactly. I'm not...like them. Not to mention the dreams I sometimes have."

"The...premonitions, right?"

I nodded. "According to The Order, it's some sort of flaw in the pattern. I guess they think I will cause chaos."

"The dreams will happen whether you are with Lucas or not."

I shrugged. "It doesn't matter. The Order doesn't like outsiders, and that's what I am. They can't have people challenging them."

She nodded. "I'm sorry."

I shrugged. "There really is nothing we can do. Lucas wants me to forget. Even though that will be impossible."

"Could he...*make* you forget?"

I shook my head. "Lucas does have a weird gift that can encourage people to do things or make decisions, like I told you. But it is *only* effective if that person *wants* his suggestion."

She nodded. "I don't want to forget, to be in the dark."

"Unfortunately, that wasn't Lucas. That was the damn Order."

She sighed again, fidgeting with a loose string on her sweater.

"What are you thinking?" I asked.

She looked up and smiled. "That we are both crazy, and I want to believe all of it."

I mirrored her smile. "Get ready to."

.

Chapter Twenty-Five

I FELL ASLEEP EASILY, but something about the night felt off. There was something on its way, but it didn't feel like the familiar pressure of a dream on the horizon. It felt more like dread—like fear, maybe.

I opened my eyes to see myself in the field again. The colors were vibrant, and Lucas's brown coat swayed in the breeze as he walked hastily in my direction.

"Lucas?"

He didn't reply.

"I thought you said you couldn't see me again. I—"

"It's a risk, but I had to. There is something you need to know." His voice was frantic and swelled with panic and nervousness.

"What's wrong?"

"I don't have much time. They could be watching at any moment."

I tried to speak, but he cut me off.

"The Order," he said. "Like I explained, I am not supposed to be here, but I need you to see something. Come back here tomorrow. Under the tree..." He broke off, whirling around, checking behind him. "I have to go. Now."

"Wait!"

But he was already gone, leaving me alone in the field, afraid for him once again.

. . .

I roused slowly. The sun was up, and the shadows in the room were light. Jess was still asleep, so I walked into the bathroom to wash up. The dream was just as vivid as always, and I was afraid of what I may find if I were to return to that field. Lucas had put his life at risk just to talk to me, so I knew it had to be important.

I got dressed and walked back into the room. Jess was sitting in the armchair, peering out the window.

"Jess, I need to go out," I announced.

She turned to look at me with her eyebrows furrowed. "What?"

"I can't explain right now, but I need to leave for a while."

"Daisy, what's going on? Do you want me to come with you?"

I shook my head. "I'm fine."

"Okay," she said, standing up. "Then I'm coming with you anyway."

I sighed. "Jess, I don't want to put you in the middle of this."

"The middle of what?"

"Lucas…he came to me…in a dream."

"In a *dream*?"

"Yes. He told me to go to the field. He didn't get to finish what he was saying, but I know that's where I'm supposed to be."

"Umm…"

"Jess, just trust me. I know it sounds crazy."

"No more crazy than all the other things I am beginning to believe."

"Fine. So you're coming?"

She nodded. "I'll drive."

She drove quickly without saying a word. We parked on the curb and stepped into the meadow. It looked so ordinary and dull without the color. It seemed vast and empty without Lucas.

The tall grass tickled my ankles, and the air had a crisp bite. I wrapped my sweater tighter around my chest. "He said something about a tree."

"Hmm," was all Jess said.

"There are only a few trees in this entire field. It can't be that hard to find the one he was referring to."

"Well, where were you? When he *came* to you."

I walked closer to the middle of the field, feeling that dreamy sensation of the past, making me miss Lucas terribly. "Around here."

"Okay, then it's probably that one," she answered, pointing to the tree behind me.

I turned around, seeing what appeared to be a tall oak tree. The leaves rustled in the breeze, the sound sending chills through my body. That was the one. I walked closer, staring at it, wishing it to change.

"What are we looking for?" Jess asked.

"I'm not sure," I said, not averting my gaze. I ran my fingers along the trunk. "Like I said, he didn't get to finish what he was telling me."

I heard Jess's feet crushing the grass as she circled the tree.

"I don't see anything."

"Neither do I. Keep looking."

"Maybe he meant *by* the tree?"

"Or..." I started, kneeling down and replaying what he had told me, "under."

She joined me on the ground. I ran my hands over a bare patch of dirt. I started digging, throwing the dirt behind me.

"What are you doing?"

"I just...I have a feeling."

I tried to ignore the freezing earth biting at my fingertips. I could hear Jess digging in a spot beside me.

"I don't think there's anything here," she said.

"Well, keep looking."

I started scooping out handfuls of moist soil until my fingertips brushed against something solid. I swept away the remaining dirt and pulled out what appeared to be a leather-bound book.

"Jess."

"Finally," she huffed. "What is it?"

I shrugged and removed the plastic sheeting. "It's a book."

"Open it."

I cracked it open and saw handwritten words on the first page.

Lucas Black

Sect 1

I stared at the words, feeling that it would somehow change if I looked at it long enough, that it would somehow make sense.

"It's his," I whispered softly.

"Lucas?"

I nodded. "He must have left it here for a reason."

"What does 'Sect One' mean?"

I shrugged. "Each sect is responsible for different things."

"I thought you said he wasn't a member of The Order."

"He isn't. But Kristoff was trying to convince him to join. At one point, Lucas tried to."

I slowly stood to my feet, still staring at the page. Something fluttered to the ground, breaking my attention. Jess picked it up and handed it to me. It was an envelope with my name in the same handwriting. I tore it open and unfolded the paper inside.

Daisy,

I know this might seem strange, but it's the only way I feel you will understand things. The words in that journal are for you. Read it and know me. Feel free to let Jess in so she will believe you. I don't want you to be alone in this. Understand what I must do now. I love you, and I will find a way to make things right for us. I promise. I love you.

~ Lucas

I felt a strange sense of hope in the pit of my stomach. *I will find a way to make things right for us.*

"What does it say?" Jess cooed.

I handed her the letter. "Come on. I want to read this at home."

She nodded and followed me to the car. The drive was silent, but thoughts of Lucas swirled through my head. I felt anxious to read what he had written but wanted to make sure we were safe at home where we could talk about things.

"I'm sorry," Jess said, "for not believing you."

I shook my head. "It's okay. Honestly. I wouldn't have believed it either. I can't blame you."

I heard her sigh, but she didn't say anything. We pulled into the driveway and hurried inside, up to Jess's—*our* room.

We flopped onto the bed, and I opened the book again. I turned past the first page.

July 10th

I sat remembering when I first saw her. The vision, I knew, was something that had been coming for a while now. I felt the impending dread that arises when one is waiting. I tossed and turned, wanting only to wake up. I didn't want to see this.

It was a horrific sight. A girl lay bleeding on the road, her clothes torn and shards of broken glass scattered across her body, some drawing blood from her pale skin. I knew her. I had known her for a very long time, even though she would never know me.

I awoke in a panic and immediately jumped from my bed and headed for the door. It was late in the morning already, and I wasn't sure how much time I had. I drove until the blood in my veins ran cold and anxiety shook through me. I knew that meant I was close. I called 911 from a burner phone before breaking the thing in half.

I saw the car. It was in pieces. I didn't see the girl. I got out of my car and raced to the wreck. I saw she was still inside, upside down, suspended by the seat belt. I reached into the broken window, putting an arm beneath her, and pressed the red button with my other hand, releasing the belt. I pulled her gently from the car and moved her as far away as I could. I set her down, and she stirred slightly and breathed as if she were trying to speak.

I knew I shouldn't have been doing this. I knew this was the worst decision I could make. I should have stayed home and ignored the dream. I should have been running from the scene, letting her die. It was a fact that it was my life or hers. Still, as I knew this, I did what I could to keep her awake. If I could keep her awake, I may be able to keep her alive.

I asked her name, with my hand on her shoulder. I already knew her name but needed her to speak in order to stay conscious.

Her voice was frail and no more than a whisper when she forced out, "Daisy."

"Daisy, you are going to be all right. Can you hear me? Stay awake."

Her beautiful blue eyes opened and stared into mine.

Panic was racing through my entire body. I kept telling her she was going to be all right, but I wasn't sure it was true. I couldn't know this wasn't the end for her. The thought of her dying made me almost sick. I pushed it from my mind, forcing myself to stay composed.

I brushed her blond locks from her face, feeling the softness of her skin as her eyes began to close.

I pleaded with her to stay with me, to keep her eyes open. I felt the sting of tears in my eyes as she fell into unconsciousness. I heard the sirens from down *the road and breathed a sigh of relief. I kissed her softly on her cheek and headed back to my car.*

I closed the journal, feeling almost as if Lucas was sitting right beside me. Reading his thoughts and his love for me was like being with him.

"Are you okay?"

I glanced at Jess. "Yeah, I'm fine. It's just strange. He never told me all of this."

She smiled. "I'm glad you're letting me read it."

"I need *someone* to talk to about this. It can only be you."

"Do you want to read more?"

I nodded. "I do, but…I'm feeling anxious, shaky even."

She smiled weakly. "Want to get out?"

"Yes," I breathed. "I think that's a good idea."

I slid the journal underneath the bed and grabbed a sweater and my purse.

"Back to the café?" she questioned.

"Where else?" I laughed.

She chuckled as she started the car. "So, when do you think you'll be able to drive again?"

I shrugged. "I haven't asked, but I'm assuming I can by now. It's been over a year since the accident, and I haven't had any headaches or loss of consciousness."

She glanced at me. "A year?"

I sighed. "Right. You don't remember. It's been a year…Jess."

She nodded. "Okay. But if I don't remember…?"

"The doctors don't either. I know."

"And your eyes?"

I waved my hands in front of my face. "All gray."

"I'm sorry."

"Jess, it's okay. This didn't just happen, remember? I've had time to adjust."

"Well…maybe I need time to adjust too."

"I know. I'm hoping that someday you'll be able to remember everything. If you're having flashes, then maybe they'll continue."

"I hope so."

At the café, we sat at our usual table, and Jess ordered bagels and mochas.

"So, aren't you curious about the journal?"

I nodded. "I am. I was just getting this strange, sick feeling reading it. It feels almost like…"

"An invasion?"

"Yeah. Yeah, I think maybe that's what it is."

"He wants you to read it."

"I know. I just needed a break from it. I'm still trying to process everything."

She scoffed. "*You're* trying."

I smirked. "Yeah, I can't imagine how lost you feel right now. I'm really sorry."

"It's not as bad as you might think. Since I'm able to believe you now, you're helping fill in the blanks. It's just a very bizarre feeling knowing so much happened and I have no memory of it."

"I know the feeling."

"It's a little frightening."

I frowned and touched her hand, unable to think of something to say.

"So, in the letter," she started, "he mentioned making things right?"

I smiled before I could stop myself. "Yeah. I hope that means he found a way for us to be together."

She mirrored my smile. "You think?"

"Well, I'm hoping."

"When will you see him again?"

I shrugged. "No idea. If I do, it'll most likely be in a dream. It's safer. The Order has a harder time finding out that way."

She shook her head. "Crazy. I wish I could talk to people in my dreams."

I laughed. "Be careful what you wish for."

Chapter Twenty-Six

NEITHER OF US was able to resist opening the journal the second we got home. She sat beside me on the bed like we were kids again, staying up reading ghost stories.

July 12th

There hadn't been any dreams for months. That didn't mean things weren't happening. I knew the day at the road with Daisy was against what I was told. I knew it wouldn't be long before I would have to pay for it. I walked into the kitchen and opened the cupboard.

Kristoff came up behind me yelling at me. Calling me crazy. I tried explaining to him that I had to, that she would have died. He told me she was supposed to die and I should have let her.

He said to me, "This is not one of your rebellious little attempts for normalcy. This is a blatant disobedience of authority!"

I flopped into a chair at the kitchen table, telling him I didn't know what else to do. I tried explaining how much I cared about her.

He came to sit beside me. He lectured me again about how she wasn't of our world and how we had rules to follow. It wasn't fair. I should be free to live my life the way I choose.

I asked him if they were after her.

He sighed and nodded.

I felt sick to my stomach. I snapped at him, asked him if he actually expected me to stand aside and let them kill her.

Just as I expected him to, he told me it's not up to me, that if they found out, they would kill us both.

I told him it wasn't right, but it didn't matter. He said it was the way things were and was in no place to question it.

I huffed and shot up from the table. I had to get out. Kris tried to stop me, but I ignored him.

I grabbed my jacket and drove to the café. I just sat with a cup of coffee, watching the people—people I could never know. Not because I was forbidden to speak to them, but because even if I did, they would never know about it the next day. I glanced around, and then I saw her.

Daisy was sitting with the girl she called Jess. I watched her as she spoke, wishing I could hear the conversation. She was so beautiful. Her golden hair was loose, falling down her back and across her shoulders like ribbons. I wanted to run my fingers through it. Her blue eyes were alive as she spoke, almost shimmering from the lights in the room. She was waving her hands around gently as if she was demonstrating something. She was so graceful and soft.

Just the sight of her caused my heart to actually ache. I wanted more than anything to speak to her again. I wanted to experience life with her again. I knew that if I were to do that, it would only cause me more pain. I tried not to sink into my memories, but it was impossible to avoid. I remembered the first time I saw her. It was a warm day in July, and the beach was bustling, busy with life. Daisy was wearing a yellow bikini that accentuated the golden hue of her hair.

I spoke to her, and she helped me overcome my apprehension of the ocean water. She taught me how to ride the waves to the shore. We spoke of art and literature and our shared love of music. I had never been happier. I knew she would be the way I was going to have a normal life, the life I wanted. That lasted only until the next day when I met her at the café and she had no recollection of who I was. She didn't remember even seeing my face.

I couldn't comprehend how something that felt so real could so easily be swept from her mind. Nobody could explain it to me. Nobody knew how it worked. Of course, those of my kind are not affected by this "curse." It is only the ones who live in her world, the ones who we call "human."

I don't know how long I had sat there or when I realized Daisy had left the café, but she came back, sitting at the table about twenty feet away from me. She looked distraught, as if something had happened. I wished I could approach her and comfort her; I wished I could be there for her the way her friend was. Jess had no conception of how fortunate she was to have Daisy in her life the way I never could.

I opened a random book I had grabbed off the shelf, trying to concentrate on something other than my thoughts and memories. I glanced up and saw Daisy staring right at me. The color drained from her face, and she looked away, trying to get Jess's attention. Was it because she knew me?

No. It's not possible. Don't be a fool!

I got up from the table as fast as I could and quickly raced to the parking lot. I hid myself from her sight and darted behind my car. I watched as she searched for me. I noticed the lost look on her face. I hated doing this to her, but I couldn't yet talk to her.

I closed the journal again and sighed.

"Are you okay, Daisy?" Jess asked.

"It's too much—all of his thoughts and secrets. I feel as if I'm overflowing with things I was never meant to know."

"Do you need to take a break?"

I nodded. "Don't you?"

She smiled. "I don't know him like you do, but I can tell how much he loves you."

"That's what's killing me. I can't believe I was ever able to forget him."

"I'm beginning to think anything is possible." She chuckled.

I tried to smile.

"Want to go out again? Get some doughnuts?" she chirped, stripping the tension from the room and catching me off guard.

"Doughnuts?"

"Yeah. Come on."

"Okay. Sure."

"I'm craving sugar."

I smiled. "You always are."

I concentrated on the cool air as we walked to the car. It was good to feel something. After everything that had happened, feeling cold felt normal—felt human. Jess started the car and turned to me, smiling.

"What?" I asked.

"I don't know. Just something seems…different."

"Different how?"

"Not sure. I'm starting to feel like you have told me all these things before. I think…"

"You're getting your memories back?"

She nodded. "Yeah. I think so."

I smiled but couldn't think of what to say. There was a sense of hope in finally having things back to normal—well, as normal as things could be for us now. I focused on that and the possibility of seeing Lucas again. It was the only thing that made it possible for me to stay sane.

"So, the journal," Jess started.

"Yeah?"

"Are you sure it's his?"

"What do you mean?"

"I mean are you sure it's all…true?"

I smiled. "Yes," I said immediately. "I don't have any doubts, Jess."

"It's so crazy," she said, but I heard a smile in her words. "I mean, think of all the stories we heard as kids. They could all be true. Nothing seems impossible anymore."

"I know exactly what you mean."

"It's a little scary. If anything can be out there—"

"Stop. Don't do that to yourself. Trust me. It won't end well."

She chuckled. "Yeah, you're probably right."

She sighed and lowered her head. I saw a strange expression flicker across her face, but it left almost immediately. I stared at her, waiting for her to say something. I heard her mumble inaudibly under her breath.

"Jess?"

"William," I heard her say just loud enough to hear.

"What?"

"William," she said. "Why do I remember…?"

"Oh. You remember that?"

She nodded. "What you told me…I knew it. I knew there was something off about that kid!"

I shook my head. "I know. I can't believe I didn't see it."

"You were scared, Daisy. We both were. It would only make sense to have hope that someone could help."

I nodded. "I guess. I'll listen to you next time."

She smiled. "Maybe you should."

Chapter Twenty-Seven

I WAS BEGINNING to feel like Lucas was going to come to me again. I wasn't sure if it was simply wishful thinking, but I knew I had to finish the journal. I had to finish it before he came back.

July 15th

    I awoke to Kristoff banging on my door. I opened up, annoyed. "What?"

    He was almost shouting at me to get dressed. I was groggy and confused as to why he was waking me up so early. He reminded me we had a meeting with Moe.

    I sighed and nodded. I shut the door, raced into the bathroom, and showered as quickly as I could. Kristoff was not a patient person, and neither was Moe. I dressed myself in a dark blue suit and made sure I was cleanly shaven. I met Kristoff in the kitchen. He was already standing at the back door, with his keys in his hand. His suit was black, and his blond hair was slicked back away from his forehead.

    I asked him what was going on, but all he said was that whatever it was, it didn't seem like good news.

    I followed my brother to his car and climbed into the passenger's seat. Kristoff drove quickly and pulled up to the house where we had spent our childhood. The yard was still the same: dark green grass perfectly clipped and red and purple flowers in the planter. We walked to the door, and before Kristoff even knocked, my father, Moe, opened up, inviting us in.

He was wearing almost the same suit as Kristoff and had his gray hair tied back with a dark ribbon. He gave me the typical, "Good to see you, Lucas."

I nodded nervously.

My brother and I trailed my father to the kitchen, where another older man was seated. He had thick, white hair and deep wrinkles in his cheeks and around his mouth.

Moe gestured to my brother. "Kristoff, you remember Mr. White."

"Good to see you," Kristoff answered, shaking the man's hand.

He introduced me as his younger son but with a sting behind his words. I reached across the table to shake Mr. White's hand, but he just stared at me. I dropped my hand.

Mr. White tried asking me if I was interested in joining them in the coming year. I was already a year late in applying, but I didn't care. I told him I didn't feel like I deserved a place in his establishment, though that was not really how I felt.

He told me Kristoff felt I would be a great fit and they would let him be the one to train me.

I grimaced but did my best to stay composed.

My father interrupted. He said he'd called us for another reason. Something had come to their attention that had to be addressed immediately.

Kristoff and I kept our eyes forward and waited for him to carry on.

He asked if I was still having the dreams. I told him it had been months, but sometimes that happened.

He was anxious when he said a tear had occurred in the world, a flaw in the pattern of the universe. He said there was a human out there having dreams like mine.

I felt my blood run cold, and my entire body started to shake. I yelled out that it wasn't possible. He told me it was true.

Kristoff asked who it was. Mr. White said they were looking for her. He explained she was supposed to die over a year ago, but something they could not explain happened.

Kristoff shot me a look, and I knew what Mr. White was saying. They were looking for Daisy. Daisy is having my dreams.

This is more than bad; this is a complete catastrophe. If they find out I saved her, they will kill me and possibly Kristoff if they find out he had knowledge of it. If they find Daisy, they will kill her. I made a huge mess breaking the rules. I know things can not get worse, so there's no reason to do anything else but try to protect Daisy.

Moe said he will keep us up to date on their progress, but I'm not to be involved.

I nodded and told him I understood.

He told Kristoff he was only allowed to talk to me about specifically permitted things and nothing discussed in council. He went on, telling us Zane Edelstein from Sect Two isn't to be involved. He had broken the first rule and has been officially exiled from council—a surprising bit of news for certain. A member of council breaking the first rule means only one thing—he let a human witness his orders. He let a human see him kill.

Moe looked to me and started with the typical 'Now, Lucas.' That meant he was going to say something I didn't want to hear. He told me my brother's acceptance banquet is in six months, and I'm expected to attend.

I fought back the sarcastic response trying to fly from my lips and just said I wouldn't miss it for the world.

We bowed formally and headed for the door. As soon as we got in the car, Kristoff started scolding me, asking me if I understood the magnitude of what I had done. He said there was no way they wouldn't have found out. They have eyes everywhere and are trained to know these things. I asked him not to hurt her. He said, "I am going to be a member of Sect One. It's not my job to terminate her. That's the job of Sect Two. However, if I know where she is and I don't turn her over, they will kill me."

I knew I had messed up. But Kristoff said he understood, and as my brother, he still wouldn't do anything to hurt me.

I decided I should tell him about the strange feelings I was having—feelings that Daisy might remember me. He tried telling me it isn't possible. I reminded him The Order had also said it was impossible for anyone else to be having premonitions too. He said it doesn't make a difference. I can't be with her. He said we'll take it a day at a time, and the less Moe knows, the better. I know what Moe will do if he finds out we're hiding something from him.

Kristoff promised he wouldn't. He said if he suspected us, he won't pursue it. He would never want to have knowledge of things that could hurt us. He is our father, after all.

I didn't know how to respond, so I stayed quiet.

The evening was cool, and the setting sun's colors were splashed across the sky. I went for a walk and ended up in a field. I've been there many times before. I've even stood in that very grass with Daisy. I almost kissed her that day. I wish I had. It wouldn't have made a difference if she couldn't remember me. I sighed, closed my eyes, and inhaled the crisp air, feeling the breeze ruffling my hair. I love that place. I love feeling human. I want to go to school and be annoyed by arrogant, callous kids. I want to go to the school's football games and join in on gawking at the cheerleaders. I want to have friends, enemies, and everything in between. I just want a normal life away from all the rules and order.

I just want a life with Daisy. If only that could be.

July 16th

I knew the chances—the chances of attempting contact with Daisy. I knew it may only hurt me. The idea came to me years ago, yet I never had the courage to actually try it. Now there's a possibility she remembers me. I decided it was as good a time as any.

I walked this time, wanting to feel normal for once. I enjoyed the cool air, waiting for dawn to break in tiny rays over the mountains. I sat near a tree at the road where I first saved my Daisy. I closed my eyes, envisioning her face. I tuned out everything around me and thought only of her. I felt a kind of numbness come over my body as if I were falling asleep. I slipped out of this world and into the moon lands.

The road was empty except for her. She stood with her back to me, staring into the distance.

We continued on, reading about the time he came to me, the time he told me about the dreams. I skimmed over some passages, then picked back up once I found something new. It was about when we'd met again.

I came to slowly, still leaning against the tree. It took time for my breathing to steady. I wanted to stay there with her, but I didn't have the strength.

I was about to head home. That's when I saw Daisy getting out of a car in a hurry. Jess followed her. I slipped behind the tree and hid the only way I knew how. They raced in my direction, but I knew they wouldn't see me.

In a way, I wish I didn't have to hide like that. I want Daisy to see me and speak to me, but I can't risk it. Not yet. Not until I know how to save her.

When I got home, Kristoff was sitting at the kitchen table in an expensive suit.

"Another meeting?" I asked him.

He looked at me through narrowed eyes and asked me where I'd been. I told him I went for a walk, but I knew he didn't believe me. He said I looked like I hadn't slept in days.

He knew that slipping into the moon lands takes all the energy out of me. He didn't press me.

I asked him where he was headed, but as I expected, he couldn't tell me.

"Right," I said. "Top secret business."

He smirked. He promised if there was a chance to lobby for Daisy's life, he would make it happen.

I gave him a look. He knew what it meant and begged me to trust him. I tried assuring him it wasn't him I didn't trust. He said he would figure it out no matter what it took.

He left through the back door, and I headed to my room, planning to sleep away the afternoon.

July 17th

He walked in, disheveled. His jacket was wrinkled, and his hair was hanging in front of his eyes. I tried not to laugh when I asked him what the hell happened. He looked annoyed but wouldn't answer me. When I pressed him on it, he said he got into it with Moe again.

That means it was about me. Apparently, my father thought Kristoff had the ability to convince me to join The Order. When he explained to Moe there was nothing he could say, they argued. It isn't the first time. I thanked him for defending me, but he said he didn't. He said I need to learn about loyalty. I immediately became defensive. I've always been loyal to Kristoff. He didn't think it was enough since I wasn't loyal to my kind.

I've always thought he understood that. I told him it's the reason we lost Mother. He yelled at me not to talk about her. He always reacts that way when I bring her up. I told him she's the reason I want to leave, but he just said I'm selfish.

"Yeah, that's right. I'm a selfish bastard," I answered. It didn't matter what I said at that point. He's right about the chaos I unleashed by saving Daisy. He can't deal with the stares and the rumors from The Order. I told him he's an idiot for even giving a damn what they think.

He came at me again and struck me hard across my nose. I boiled over and *wrestled him to the floor. I sat on him and hit him as hard as I could until he grabbed my wrist. He glared at me and used his body weight to roll me over. He swung at my face, but I turned my head, so his fist crashed into the floor. He howled and shot to his feet, holding his wrist. I stood up, still with my hands up in defense. Kristoff just glowered at me and turned away, heading to his bedroom.*

July 19th

I know what Kristoff was telling me means I have to do something. If Daisy is in danger, that could mean her loved ones could be too. Things tend to spiral out of control more often than The Order of our world wants us to believe. I have to warn her. There's only so much I can do to keep her safe. If they see me as much as talk to her, it would be disastrous.

I decided to simply encourage a dream for her—a simple warning to keep her loved ones close and safe. I didn't stay to watch the dream play out. I was sure her mind would fill in the gaps.

I stayed in bed for most of the day, not sure what to do. I was almost going mad with boredom. I knew I had to wait for Kristoff to get home before doing anything drastic. I knew he would help me through all of it. He always does.

I picked up a book and opened it to a random page, just trying to think of something else. I couldn't focus on the words, as if I had completely forgotten how to read. I had to get out of the house. I stuffed a few bucks in my pocket and headed to the café.

When I walked in, I saw Daisy sitting at her usual table. I brushed past her at the register and quickly disappeared near the other side of the café, praying she hadn't seen me. I didn't want a confrontation yet, and I was still thinking about how she can remember me. There are too many variables and things to consider before I can be anywhere near her.

I watched her as she talked with Jess. She moves so slowly and fluidly. She is so much more than just a girl. She's different—beautiful and innocent inside and out. I need her in my life. It's just that simple.

I could feel my self-control depleting. If I stayed, I would give up completely and approach her. I thought it was best I leave before completely screwing up—again.

When I got home, Kristoff was just walking in. I asked him what they'd said, but they haven't yet brought up her case. I am going crazy. I have to know. He said he did talk to Moe, and he said there's a possibility we can lobby for the life of the girl. He said Moe is angry but agreed they may be able to come up with a good enough reason.

I reminded Kristoff she might remember me, but he said that's even worse. Her being special is the reason they want her dead.

We have to do something!

July 19th

A knock came at my door.

"It's open," I called.

Kristoff opened the door but didn't come in. He just asked me what I was doing. I knew what he meant. He wanted me to tell Daisy what was going on.

He feels she has a right to know. I'm trying to do the right thing by staying away.

He promised he would keep me safe while I went to her. I asked him how much I should tell her, but he said it was up to me.

I told him I knew where to find her.

I walked to the café to clear my head. I know Daisy well enough to know she would be there at some point. I sat with a cup of coffee and a paperback book. I had no interest in either. I only wanted to see Daisy. Kristoff's permission to speak to her felt like the greatest gift imaginable. I was beginning to feel panic and anxiety, thinking she wouldn't show. I tapped my fingernails on the tabletop.

Finally, she came in with Jess on her heels as always. It took no more than thirty seconds before she looked in my direction. Her eyes locked on mine, and I hurried out to the parking lot. She followed, as I knew she would.

"Mind if I skip ahead?" I asked. "It's about the first time we met."

Jess shook her head. "Not at all."

July 20th

I walked into the living room to see Kristoff dressed up and heading out. He immediately started scolding me, telling me I was supposed to be dressed an hour ago and he shouldn't have to remind me of everything. I had completely forgotten about the pre-acceptance dinner party we had to go to.

I rushed through my morning routine and raced out the door. Kristoff was staring at his phone when I climbed into the passenger's seat.

He looked at me accusingly and said, "Cayucos is a small town. It's easy for them to find her."

I asked him if he thought they had hurt her. He said they want more information about the cause of her dreams before doing anything. I asked him what we should do, but he was as lost for ideas as I was. He said Moe had agreed to stand down for now, but there wasn't much else to do. Moe would talk to the others about waiting.

He changed the subject, eyeing me, looking annoyed, and told me I could have picked a better suit. Guess mine was pretty wrinkled. Oh well.

I shrugged and told him to shut up and drive.

I zoned out during dinner and the bland, drawn-out speeches about Kristoff's amazing promise and potential. I rolled my eyes and slouched in my chair. Moe gave me a glare, and I got it together. I hated having to deal with this like it was part of who I was. They didn't know anything about me.

Kristoff walked with me to his car after the banquet ended.

I complained about how dull it was. Kristoff tried again to convince me to join. I shot him down before we got into a fight. It wasn't happening no matter what he said. He gave me an accusing look but didn't bother to argue.

Back home, Kristoff went straight to his room. I decided to get back to work. I still had a pile of paperwork to file for Moe. If I didn't get it done, it wouldn't be a pleasant situation to deal with. He was very specific about things getting done efficiently.

It's a tedious process entering in subject codes and order numbers. They aren't people when they are on paper. They're only numbers. If I kept my focus on the numbers, I didn't see faces.

I sighed to myself, imagining I was somewhere else. I was on autopilot, entering the information as I pictured myself in the open field with Daisy at my side.

July 22nd

Daisy wanted me to meet her friend. Kristoff said it didn't make sense. Jess wouldn't remember me anyway. I told him I hadn't mentioned that part to Daisy yet. He started laughing. It wasn't funny.

He smiled, shaking his head, and said, "You can't expect me to watch you do this and not laugh, Brother."

I just glared at him.

He pressed me to be careful then snorted and walked away, leaving me alone to think. I know it's going to be confusing for her. After spilling half-truths without telling her what I am, it's already eating away at me. She deserves to know everything. I just have to figure out the best way to tell her—a way that will assure she will believe me.

I sighed, opening up the file system on my computer. I wasn't looking forward to working, but the longer I put it off, the more agitated Moe would get. Again, I just focused on the numbers and letters, ignoring the fact that some of these people would be saved and others destroyed. I have no control over it anyway.

My eyes were beginning to hurt when I finished the last report. I had promised Daisy I would meet her again. I decided to get as much sleep as I could with my mind as heavy as it was. I was able to rest just enough for the energy to make it to the field. This was going to be the conversation I was dreading. I was also terrified of being followed—of being seen talking to her.

I could literally feel her there, waiting for me. I stepped into the grass, feeling the breeze ruffling my hair and inhaling the crisp air. I focused on the sheer freedom of the outdoors, wishing I could stay there forever.

July 24th

I tried telling Kristoff she remembered me. He said he didn't know what that meant. We argued again about The Order. He tried telling me they don't make the rules, that they only keep the balance. I didn't believe it. I still don't. He told me if I keep questioning things, it will end badly for me. I explained I know I am going to have to pay for what I did eventually. He said he wouldn't say a word to anyone, but it doesn't matter. Lobbying for Daisy's life will reveal that I saved her. I will still have to pay. He said he will look out for me, but I shot him down. I told him to just take care of Daisy. He got angry, saying they might kill me.

A chill went up my spine; it wasn't something I hadn't thought about. I said I knew Moe wouldn't let them.

He told me if it's what they decide to do, Moe can't stop them. It doesn't matter to me. If it saves Daisy, it's a fate I have to accept. He knew there was nothing he could say to talk me into stepping aside and letting them take Daisy. He knew his only choice now was to help me.

I sat in bed, not wanting to fall asleep. I was worried about dreaming. I couldn't handle any distractions. I had to focus on Daisy and Daisy alone. As my body began to slip into unconsciousness, I was pulled almost violently out of my bed by a horrible feeling of impending dread. Daisy's face flashed through my head. She was in danger.

I scrambled from the bed and headed for the door.

Kristoff tried asking me where I was going. I just said "Daisy" while grabbing my jacket off the hook. He said they hadn't ordered anything yet, but I knew something was wrong.

I raced down the dark streets, not even stopping at red lights and rolling through every stop sign along the way. When I got to Daisy's house, the front door was open, and a shadow was slowly moving through the living room. I entered the house, following silently behind the intruder. He turned around and came at me with what looked like a knife.

I twisted away from him, shoving him out the door. He had a ski mask concealing his face. I reached to rip it off, but he swung at me, striking me below my jaw. I growled and advanced on him, but he took off running down the street. I wanted to follow after him, but I had to make sure Daisy was okay. I turned back to the house and silently made my way upstairs.

It was quiet—too quiet. The lock on the door must have been broken because it cracked when I turned the handle. I stepped into the room, and Daisy immediately came at me with a huge kitchen knife. I grabbed her arm and flung her onto the bed. Jess came to her defense, so I gripped her by the shoulders, pushing her away.

"Daisy," I said before either of them could come at me again. "Daisy, it's me. Relax."

July 25th

I was entering data on autopilot. I came across a file with "Sect 2" stamped at the top. Normally, I would place it in the pile of files not belonging to Moe's sect, but I felt I had to look it over. Sure enough, it was an order of termination. Subject was said to have been located, and an order of termination was in place.

I knew it had to be Daisy. I couldn't simply not send out the file, could I? They already know about her, and if the file went missing, they would know I had something to do with it.

I started mildly trembling. I couldn't let the sect get hold of that file! But I also knew I couldn't withhold it either. I sat, stiff and completely distracted. We had to do something right then—not later. I got up and went to the kitchen to find Kristoff.

I said, "She's not safe." I had to try to keep my voice even at the thought of something happening to her.

Kristoff said if Moe found out what I was up to, he would have no choice but to turn me in. He said I couldn't bring her here, that it was crazy. But I knew it was the only way to keep her safe. I begged him to do this for me. I told him they sent out the order, that I saw the file. I just needed to keep her with us until after the hearing. He informed me the hearing wasn't even a sure thing yet. I knew he would figure something out. I was afraid The Order had eyes on me, so Kristoff had to be the one to get her. I asked him to use his ability to find her. She doesn't know about it, so she won't be able to block him.

July 26th

I waited at home impatiently. I got up, as I couldn't sit still, and found myself pacing. I was beginning to wonder what was taking Kristoff so long. I grabbed my coat off the hook and stepped outside. I was going crazy sitting inside. I walked through the backyard, hiding in some of the woodland to change form into the gray tabby and hurried down the street to run. It felt amazing to be free. I ran until I lost track of time. I turned back and returned to my usual form.

Before I had even gotten my clothes on, I heard my cell phone vibrating in my pocket. I grabbed my pants off the ground and quickly snatched my phone.

"Kristoff?"

"Lucas, get here. Now."

"Did you find her?"

"Yes."

"What's wrong?"

"Just get here."

I pulled my clothes on and ran back to the house. The door was locked, so I knocked lightly. Kristoff immediately came to the door. He said Moe had found them at the park and threatened them. He said Moe let them go, but we both know this is bad. He'll tell the others before too long.

He opened the door the rest of the way, and Daisy shot up from the couch and ran to me.

I leafed through a few pages, skipping the parts I remembered.

· · ·

July 28th

I thought back to the night before.

I saved you because I knew you, because I loved you.

I told her that—exactly what is in my head—for the first time. It felt amazing, and when she kissed me, she remembered. She remembered the first time we met and everything after. She had fallen in love with me countless times before, but now—now maybe I could have her for real. If she remembers me, everything is different!

I knew I had to tell Kristoff before Daisy woke up. He was still in his room, so I knocked on his door. He opened up immediately and asked me what was wrong.

"I just need to tell you something," I said.

He raised his eyebrows, waiting.

I told him she remembers me. She remembers everything. He ran his fingers through his blond hair like I had seen him do when he's frustrated. He said The Order can't find out. We have to keep it quiet.

I headed back to my room. I walked in and almost lost my breath. Daisy wasn't there. I went back into the living room, but she wasn't there either.

I yelled for Kristoff. He came charging into the room.

"Daisy's gone," was all I could say.

He huffed, lecturing me, asking how I could lose her after one day. We knew it wasn't The Order. If it were, we would have been dead. I asked him to help me get her back. I reminded him he could find her like he did before. He called me an idiot but reluctantly agreed.

Kristoff sat on the couch, eyes closed, still and silent.

"She's in a house," he murmured. "Close. Small room. Dark."

I wasn't sure if he was speaking to me or himself, but I listened intently.

"Her head aches. Ropes. Ropes on her wrists."

Oh God. She must have been tied up. I tried not to ask any questions. I couldn't risk pulling Kristoff out before he found out where she was.

"A voice. Familiar."

"Cut the ropes. The lamp." A whoosh escaped his lips as he exhaled. "The light bulb. Cut the ropes."

I stared, covering my mouth with my hands to stop myself from saying anything.

A groan sounded from Kristoff as if he was in pain. "Run. Run fast. Out the door."

I felt the fear and worry in me depleting. If she was running, she must have escaped. Keep running, Daisy.

Kristoff huffed loudly and shot to his feet. "I know where she is!"

I waited for him to continue. He asked me if I remembered Moe telling us about Zane. I thought for sure he was joking. He wasn't. Apparently, the idiot thinks he can get his place back if he finds Daisy. At least Zane can't turn us in. He would have to set something up just to talk to them, and since his disbarment, they will never agree to that. It didn't matter though. Nothing about this was good.

Kristoff explained they want Daisy, and Zane will never stop trying to get her to turn her over. We had to get to her as soon as possible.

We climbed into Kristoff's car. He drove quickly down the dark streets. I stared out the window, looking for any movement. I didn't see her. He started mumbling things.

"Did you know she's…?"

I glanced at him. "What?"

"Her eyes. She's…"

I nodded. "Yes, I knew. She's colorblind. It's not a big deal."

He scoffed, complaining I should have given him a warning.

The car screeched horribly as he pulled over. Daisy was walking quickly down the street, looking completely disheveled.

I rolled down the window. "Daisy!"

When I got out of the car, she immediately ran to me. I wrapped her in my arms. Guilt was eating away at me. I couldn't believe I let this happen to her.

I briefly told Jess about the conversation that had taken place in the car after they rescued me and started to skip ahead again, but I closed the journal without warning.

"Wait," Jess said, reaching for the book. "Don't you want to finish it?"

I shook my head. "I need a minute. I just need to breathe."

She nodded. "Sure. I don't know how you did it, Daisy."

I smirked. "Yeah, reading this, all of it comes back. I don't know how I did it either."

"It's all so…unbelievable. Yet I find myself somehow knowing it's true."

"I know the feeling. I really don't want to relive the meeting with The Order."

"We don't have to read that part."

I nodded. "There also are a few personal things, something Lucas showed me…"

"His gift?"

I nodded. "If we could skip that part too…"

"Say no more," she said, raising her hand. "It's totally fine, Daisy. It's up to you what you want to share with me."

"I'll share all my experiences with you." I clutched the journal to my chest. "It's just that these are *his*."

She nodded. "I understand."

I flipped through a couple pages, reading a few lines at a time until I found what I was comfortable sharing with Jess and what I was comfortable reliving.

Chapter Twenty-Eight

WE READ a few pages about the nightmare I had about Lucas's death—about Kristoff killing him and him convincing me it didn't mean anything.

I worked Daisy to get her back to sleep and grabbed a pillow and a blanket so I could lie on the floor beside the bed. I was sure I wouldn't be able to sleep, but I was too afraid to leave her alone. I heard Kristoff rummaging around in the kitchen. I got up and found him digging through the cabinets.

"Kris, it's three in the morning."

"Yeah, I'm sorry."

"What are you looking for?"

"Nothing," he said. "Go back to sleep."

"I wasn't sleeping."

"Then go to sleep anyway."

"Why won't you talk to me?"

"Damn it, Lucas. I can't tell you everything."

"Well, you should tell me something. You're in here throwing things around in the middle of the night."

"And you're being a pain in my ass."

"Kristoff, come on. Don't be like this."

His face twisted in that familiar look of anger, and he immediately turned from the cupboard and punched me square in the jaw.

I staggered back, wide-eyed. "Kristoff, what the hell?" I yelled, my hand on my lower jaw.

"Leave," he growled.

"No, not now. You started it."

I lunged at him and struck his cheek with my fist. He stumbled backward and pulled out the family dagger. He came at me. Before I had time to react, he had already dropped the knife to the floor. His hand was covering his mouth. He tried to apologize, but I just glared at him.

He rushed out of the kitchen and locked himself in his room. I sighed and dropped into a chair at the table, covering my face with my hands, still trembling from the fight response flowing through me. I suddenly remembered Daisy's dream—the one where she said Kristoff killed me. I knew I had to tell him. Angry or not, he needed to know.

I went to his room and knocked on his door.

He yelled at me to leave him alone, but I told him I had something important to tell him.

He opened his door, and I prepared myself for his usual antagonism. He didn't appear angry anymore. He apologized again, assuring me he would never have gone through with it.

"I know," I said. "It's okay. I just thought you should know—Daisy dreamed about that."

"What? About what?"

"You...with the knife."

"When?"

"The other night. She thought you were going to kill me."

He sighed. "So it's real?"

I nodded. "I told you it was."

He shook his head. "I was hoping it was a fluke, like maybe she had a few dreams for some reason and that was it."

"I guess there really is more to it than that."

He nodded. "I guess she really does have your gift, Brother. It doesn't make any sense. She's human."

"I know. But she's special. Her brush with death brought this on. She's linked to me because I saved her. I've never heard of that happening before, but that's precisely why she's so special and unique. She's more like us than she is one of them."

"Don't be fooled into thinking that's a good thing."

"I know it isn't."

"Good to know. Before you go, do you know where the tin is?"

212

"Tin?"

"Yeah, I kept some extra cash in it, remember?"

"Oh, that's what you were looking for?"

He nodded.

"You should have just told me. It's in the bottom drawer of my work desk. You moved it before you brought Daisy here."

He thrust his hand to his forehead. "Right. Thanks. Now, will you go to bed?"

I smiled. "Sure."

"Oh, and Lucas?"

I turned around. "Yes?"

"Don't tell Daisy. Please."

I nodded. Although I know that not telling her may not be the best thing for her, I can't refuse Kristoff when he looks at me that way. He appeared so utterly defeated. I know he felt terrible about what happened. I don't need to add to his shame.

"He never told me that," I said.

"He was embarrassed, Daisy."

I nodded. "Yeah, but it would have made me a lot less anxious. I was freaking out the whole time. At one time, I even thought Kristoff may have been the one who turned him over to The Order."

"Men."

I laughed. "Exactly."

I flipped a few more pages and looked to Jess. She smiled at me, as if she knew exactly what scene I was skipping over.

"Just a little—"

"Daisy, it's fine. You don't have to explain anything to me."

I nodded. "Thanks."

I found the right part and continued reading.

August 5th

Daisy was pacing and sighing but otherwise quiet. I knew what she was thinking, and nervousness and anxiety were building up in me as well. I knew Kristoff was smart, and I knew his place in The Order was of use. But all the same, I couldn't shake the feeling it may not be enough.

Daisy stopped pacing and faced me. Her cheeks were red and her eyes tense. She complained she was going crazy waiting.

I told her I understood, but Kristoff would work it out.

She smiled and sat beside me on the couch, leaning against me. I could feel her heartbeat and the faint scent of lavender that clings to her. I could feel her anxiety emanating from her, adding to my own.

A strange tinge of panic washed over me. I shot to my feet, pushing Daisy behind me. I heard her scream as a familiar gray wolf charged into the room.

"That's…crazy," Jess murmured after reading about the fighting wild animals in Lucas's living room. "That really happened?"

I nodded. "It's right here. Just like I told you."

August 6th

It wasn't until Daisy was asleep that I noticed stinging in my arm. I had three deep slash marks from Zane's claws. I went to the bathroom to wrap it up before she noticed. It wasn't worth upsetting her. I crawled into bed beside Daisy, careful not to wake her. My body was just drifting off to sleep when she shot up in bed, panicking.

I grabbed hold of her immediately, telling her it was just a dream.

I put my arms around her, but she pulled away without saying a word. I followed her to the living room. She was staring out the window as if waiting for something. I asked her what she was doing, but she just stuttered out something incoherent. I pressed her, and she apologized.

I told her it was just a dream brought on by the recent stress. The dreams wouldn't stop until she relaxed.

I led Daisy back to bed, hoping I wouldn't have to work her to get her to relax.

I stopped then, deciding to skip Lucas's description of our encounter that night. Jess didn't say a word, just let me skip ahead to where I was comfortable resuming.

· · ·

Daisy was bouncing in her seat. I told her to relax and set a plate in front of her. I asked her if she was okay. She kept saying she had to know what they said.

Kristoff stepped in from the back door, and Daisy was on her feet instantly. "Well?" she pressed.

He laughed, asking if she'd been like that all night.

"Pretty much," I said.

She began pressuring him to tell her everything. He sat at the table and said he'd told The Order about our situation, and they've agreed to a hearing.

Daisy was confused. She said she thought that's what the meeting was for. I explained.

"No," I told her. "He lobbied to get you a hearing. That is where you will go before them and tell them why they should renounce their claim. Tell them why you should live."

We told her not to worry, that we knew exactly what to say. I promised her we would handle anything that came our way.

"Sorry, Jess, but this is too much for me. I'm going to need to skip pretty much the entire council meeting and some details before it.

She nodded. "You already explained that. It's okay."

I sighed, trying to muster the strength to continue reading. The memories were causing a horrible shaky feeling in my limbs—almost like a sense of fear.

August 15th

I took a deep breath and quickly swept down the pages, not allowing myself to form the full memory of the council meeting in the words my eyes plucked from scanning Lucas's recollection of that horrible day. I flipped a page and caught the part I wanted to read yet feared the most. I let myself begin reading, my heart hammering in my chest.

I heard Daisy screaming for me, calling out my name with sick desperation in her tone. Her grief echoed off the stones, causing it to sound even more horrible. I couldn't stand doing this to her. I hated how I had lied to her. I clearly would have known The Order would have to punish me. It was not just a minor offense. Disobeying orders is usually a death sentence. Although I was hoping for a quick execution, I knew I would not be that lucky.

I was still in the mausoleum, where nobody could hear me scream. Mr. White came in.

"Mr. Black," he said apathetically, "do you know why you are here?"

"Of course I do," I spat. I didn't care about being polite. If they were going to kill me, what did it matter?

He and another man pulled my arms above my head, chaining my wrists to the walls. I winced at the strain in my muscles but tried to hide my discomfort. I didn't want to give them the satisfaction.

"Don't even think about attempting a shift, Mr. Black. It will be to no avail."

Even as I believed him, I tried anyway. He was right. Nothing happened— not even the familiar ache of an almost change in form. It must have been another one of The Order's tricks or spells.

Mr. White left without striking me for my disrespect, which I was quite surprised by. I tried controlling my groans and moved my arms, looking for some relief but to no avail. I heard footsteps at my side but couldn't see who was there through the darkness.

"Moe?" I asked, straining my neck to see who I was speaking to.

"No," said the harsh, authoritative voice of Mr. White, seething. "I don't think Moe will be here for a while, Mr. Black."

I swore to him Moe didn't know anything about it. I tried telling him my father was innocent.

"No matter," he answered impassively. "I'm taking the responsibility of enforcing your punishment."

I felt fear slither into my body. I knew whatever Mr. White did would be much worse than what anyone else would do. He already disliked me for declining his offer to join The Order, and he was cold and sociopathic.

I heard shuffling at my side but still couldn't see anything.

-----------------------*happened again. I heard the loud snap of the whip.*

"Wait…" Jess ran her fingertips over the page. "Lines are blackened out. What happened?"

Realization assaulted me like a punch to my stomach. "I…I don't think he wanted me to read those parts."

Jess tilted her head, her soft eyes exuding compassion. "Do you want to keep reading?"

I nodded slowly and took a deep breath. "I have to."

I didn't try to contain my cries, although --
--- --

--- I heard the shuffling of feet, hoping it was over, praying I was alone.

I was still chained to the wall and stood there reeling in pain and discomfort. What a sick bastard. Of course he wasn't going to kill me right away. He was ---

I felt myself weakening. I had been given no food and no water, and my body was exhausted. I slipped into a light sleep and found myself involuntarily in Daisy's head. I was standing in the field. I could see the grass and trees were tall, and the breeze ruffled my fur. I was not in my human form, by no choice of mine. I saw her there, her face sullen and blank, her eyes rimmed with tears.

I pleaded with her to not be sad for me.

She turned around, searching for me. She was so beautiful, and I hated seeing her looking so lost.

"I'm here."

She peered down and met my eyes. She told me she missed me, and I begged her again to not be sad.

It was hard to look at her—hard to see what I had caused. Her face was ashen, and her gaze was confused and far away.

Soft tears slid down her cheeks. She asked me why I'd left her, how I could leave her all alone.

My own pain was almost unbearable. I couldn't stand inflicting it on Daisy. My chest burned, but I tried to stay composed for her sake.

I explained to her I always have a reason for the things I do even if she doesn't understand them. I told her I loved her but that I had to save her. Someone had to pay for my mistakes, and the only person who should be punished is me.

A splash of water on my face pulled me from my dream. I shook my head, trying to shed the fogginess from my eyes. My vision cleared, and Moe was standing in front of me.

"Oh, Lucas," he murmured.

I was barely able to choke out, "Moe...please."

He said he shouldn't have been there, but he'd convinced them to let him see me. He had brought me water. My mouth was dry, and my lips were parched and cracked. I almost felt ravenous at the thought of water. He held a small cup to my lips, and I drank hungrily. He pulled away.

I begged for more.

He lifted the cup again, and as he pulled away, I leaned forward, trying to get more.

"Lucas, you can't have too much. It's going to go right through you."

I hadn't even thought of that. At the time, I didn't care. I felt as if I could drink an entire gallon of water and still be thirsty.

I begged him again. He pursed his lips for a moment but let me drink a bit more from the cup. The coolness coursed through my body, relieving some of the discomfort.

He promised me he would come back later with something for me to eat. He ordered me not to say anything to them about it.

"Why would I say anything to those pigs?"

"You need to keep your mouth in check too, boy. It will be worse for you if you don't."

I didn't respond. He disappeared into the dark, and I found myself, for the first time, wishing he would stay.

I tried to soothe some of the pain in my shoulders, but shifting didn't help. The cuffs were iron and left little room to move. I groaned and whimpered at the persistent, unvarying misery. I just wanted ------------------ I couldn't stay there like that, just waiting for them to come back and hurt me again.

I desperately wanted to know what was behind the black...yet I was scared to know. I had to keep reading and hope my imagination didn't create content worse than he had actually written.

I was feeling myself slipping into unconsciousness when the sound of footsteps alerted me. I braced myself and --- --- -- Mr. White moved from behind me and stood right in front of me, looking into my tired eyes. He didn't say a word, just struck me hard across my face. I groaned, and he hit me again until I could taste my own blood in my mouth. He hit me over and over until I lost half my vision. ------------------------------

He demanded I show him some respect or he would draw out the torment even longer.

He huffed and stormed out. My entire body was already sore and tired, and now this latest beating had me wishing -- -------- ------------

I cannot say how many more days I was there. Moe was right about having too much water. I tried with every ounce of will power I had to avoid letting my body give in, but it was -- I felt sick and disgusted at how pathetic and revolting I was. I had never been so helpless in my life.

Moe came back a few times with some water and bits of food, only enough to keep me alive. --- -- My body was frail, and my mind was cloudy.

I saw Moe approach me.

"Oh, God, Lucas," he said. "Did he do this to you?"

"You know he did," I choked out.

"Oh, son..."

"What is it?"

He made a sound and leaned in closer to see. "Brace yourself."

"Why?"

"Your jaw is dislocated."

"Yeah, it feels that way."

He raised his hand but hesitated a moment. He grasped under my chin and pulled with an agonizing crack. I cried out briefly, but a wave of relief came over me. I thanked him and told him I had one last favor to ask.

He looked at me, waiting for me to continue. I looked away, then softly ----- ----------------------

He barked at me, asking if I actually expected him to do that.

"I'm asking you to." I felt on the verge of tears. "Please."

"Don't be ridiculous, Lucas. I'm taking you home."

All my thoughts halted, and for a brief moment, I forgot about the pain in my body.

Moe said he had begged them for leniency. He said I'd been through enough.

I sighed, already feeling a sense of relief. Maybe I would get to see Daisy one last time. He released me from the cuffs, and the pain in my arms and shoulders was almost immobilizing. He helped me to my feet and took me to the car. I slumped in my seat, barely able to stay conscious. Moe didn't say a word as he drove, but I could feel his anger and empathy for me. It was the first time I really felt he loved me.

After arriving at his place, he basically carried me into the house. He helped me roll onto my stomach and ripped off what was left of my shirt. He blotted at -------------------------------------- an alcohol-soaked cloth. It stung horribly, and I winced, involuntarily groaning.

He told me to stop whining, coaxing me, saying it wasn't that bad. I scoffed. I tried asking him why he was still with The Order if he'd seen worse by them before. He didn't want to get into it and shot me down. He said, "I just want to get you better first."

There wasn't much he could do for my broken ribs except wrap me up. He left me for a short while to sleep and woke me later to help me into the bath. He took off the wraps and helped me stumble into the bathroom. He gave me some privacy but promised he would be right outside the door if I needed anything.

Moe had never been as much a father to me my entire life as he was in those moments he cared for me. It touched me deeply.

I thanked him for everything he had done for me.

He nodded, unable to know how to respond to sentiments. After my mom left, he just sort of shut down.

I soaked in the tub, enjoying the softness of water on my sore skin and appreciating the heat soothing my tense muscles. I forced myself to stand up and rinse off so I wasn't just sitting in filthy water. It wasn't easy staying on my feet, but I was able to just long enough.

Moe put the wraps back on and gave me some new clothes to wear.

He made me a plate. I asked where Daisy was. Before I even got the whole question out, he interrupted me, saying she was fine, but there was something they had to do. I felt sick with worry.

He went on to tell me that because of what I did, things were a real mess, and the only thing they could do to fix things was to make her forget.

I felt an ache come into my chest.

"It's the only way for things to go back to normal."

I tried telling him it wouldn't work. Daisy was special. He argued, but he was wrong.

He said it didn't matter. If nobody else remembered, they could just as easily convince her she was dreaming. He said there was no other way.

I couldn't stand the thought of her forgetting me all over again. She had fallen in love with me so many times before, and now that I finally had her, I *was forced to lose her. The grief was unbearable. I promised her that she would never forget me—that things between us would be fine. I hated myself for breaking the biggest promise I ever made to her.*

I stared back again at the blacked out passages. Of course he wouldn't tell me what happened. He didn't think I could handle it.

"What they did to him…" I paused, swallowing hard. "He wouldn't tell me. Of course he blacked out all this to hide what he didn't want in my head."

She nodded. "Maybe it's better that way."

I shrugged. "Maybe." I turned the page but found it blank.

"That's it?" Jess cooed.

I sighed and closed the journal. "Guess so."

"Did it help?"

I shook my head. "Not really. Most of this was to help *you* believe me. To help *you* understand what had happened. He didn't want me to go through this alone. The thing is, not only do I remember, but I never forgot. And the fact that you're remembering things too…"

"I know," she said. "It doesn't make sense."

"I have to wait until I can talk to him. He might know why what The Order did isn't working on us."

"You said he can work people, right?"

I nodded.

"Well, maybe that's what he did here."

I narrowed my eyes. "It doesn't really work that way. I mean…he could encourage us to *believe* this was all true, but he couldn't make us remember it."

She sighed. "Then I guess you're right. You'll have to talk to him."

I nodded. "I'm going to the field. He'll be there."

"Are you sure?"

"Yes, I'm sure. He knows things…somehow."

She smiled. "Be careful and call me if you need me."

"I will."

Chapter Twenty-Nine

I WALKED SLOWLY, trying to use the time to calm down. I knew seeing him again would bring me running into his arms. I also knew it may not be safe. There were many ways Lucas could be putting us in danger by meeting with me. I sucked in a cold breath of air and pulled my sweater over my chest. A cool breeze rustled the trees, chilling me to the bone.

When I got to the field, he wasn't there. I turned around, thinking I may meet the cat again.

"Daisy?"

I spun. He was standing in front of me like he always was, as if nothing had changed.

"Did I scare you?"

I smiled. "I should have expected it."

The longing within me came to life, coursing through my veins until I thought it would destroy me. Seeing him standing there, so real and honest, made it physically hurt to stay away. I wanted to be with him no matter what it took.

I wasn't sure what he would do if I ran to him. I couldn't be sure if he felt it was safe to be close to me. Either way, I could no longer stand there staring at him, feeling coolness in the space between us. I ran a few steps and fell into his arms, inhaling that amazing scent of the woodlands. He returned my—our embrace, holding me firmly. The longing I had felt was satiated, and my body had warmed completely. I didn't care about being safe anymore; I didn't care about The Order. All I cared about was him.

"Daisy, I need to talk to you."

I forced myself to move away from him and looked up to meet his perfect eyes. They sparkled in a hazel hue through the gray lens in my vision.

"I read the journal," I said. "You never told me all of that."

"I couldn't. You already knew too much for you to be safe. I had to tell you now. You needed to make Jess believe you."

I nodded. "Thank you for understanding how much I need her."

"I couldn't let you go through this alone."

"But, Lucas—what The Order did…"

He raised his hand. "I know. That's why I'm here, Daisy."

"What do you mean?"

"The charm The Order used is cracking."

I narrowed my eyes for a moment. "Why?"

He chuckled quietly, as if meant only for himself. "Well, because of you, Daisy."

"Me?"

"Yes. Why else? As I have told you before, you're special."

"But how?"

He shook his head. "We don't know. Kristoff is trying to keep The Order out of this for now. They don't need to know Jess remembers anything. That needs to stay between us, okay?"

I nodded. "How do you know about that?"

He grinned at me. "You forget who I am."

I smiled. "Right. Are we safe here?"

He nodded. "For now, yes. They don't know the charm isn't effective on you. The only reason Jess remembers is because you're close to her."

"That's so strange."

"After your crash, you and I became linked somehow. I wrote it in the journal, how you are more like one of us now than you are…one of them."

"Is that a good thing?"

He smiled. "I'd like to think it is."

"I feel…torn, like I'm being pulled in two different directions and I don't know which way to go."

He pulled me into his chest and stroked my hair. I could feel his heart beating, and I knew in that moment I was exactly where I wanted to be.

"You don't need to go in either direction," he said. "I know how it feels to be trapped between two worlds. I learned to find peace in between."

I felt a sort of warmth enter me at his words. I felt a sense of understanding. "I want a life with you, Lucas."

His arms around me tightened, pulling me closer against him. "I know. You need to understand that if I find a way to make that possible, it can never be normal."

"I don't want normal. I want good."

"So do I."

He pulled away from me and held my face in his hands. His eyes were full of adoration, his love for me shining through, mixed with the sense of longing I felt myself. He planted a soft kiss on my lips.

"I need words with Kristoff," he said. "I have to go."

"Wait," I pleaded, reaching for him as he turned away.

"I have to go."

"Then take me with you."

"Daisy, I can't."

"Of course you can. I already know everything. Besides, I would really like to see him."

He sighed, staring at me. I frowned, giving him the saddest look I could muster. It always worked on my mom.

"Fine," he groaned. "Come on."

I smiled proudly and followed him to the road. "Where's your car?" I asked, scanning the empty street.

"Not here. I didn't drive here, and since I can't turn you into a feline, I guess we're taking the long way."

"Oh," was all I could say.

He squeezed my hand then dropped it. I reached for it again.

"Be careful," he said. "They may not have eyes on us, but that doesn't mean someone won't see something."

I nodded. "Right."

He flashed me a glimpse of his perfect smile before sighing.

"What's wrong?" I asked.

"It's nothing. Things are just a bit complicated. I want things to be easier than this. I want to hold your hand without looking over my shoulder. I want to kiss you without worrying about being punished."

"I want that too."

"I know it isn't fair to you."

"Lucas, it isn't fair to either of us. None of this is on you. I would have loved you whether you liked it or not."

He chuckled. "Thanks."

I smiled back, playing out in my head all I wished for. I envisioned myself walking down the streets, wrapped in Lucas's arms and going on dates like normal teenagers. I saw us laughing and talking about unimportant things and possibly having friends—friends who could remember him. It all looked beautiful in my head, but I knew none of it was possible. Maybe Lucas was right; maybe I did want normal.

It was about an hour before we got to Kristoff's house. Being back there was like I was somewhere from a past life. As soon as I smelled the air, all the memories came flooding back.

Lucas led me to the kitchen. Kristoff was at the table, reading the newspaper. He was wearing jeans and a polo shirt. It was the first time I had seen him wearing something other than a suit.

"Daisy," he said, smiling and standing up from the table.

"She made me let her come," Lucas said.

"That's okay," Kristoff answered, stepping toward me and pulling me into a hug. "It's always good to see her."

I smiled and sat across from him at the table.

"Does she know?" Kristoff asked, eyeing Lucas.

He nodded and took the seat beside me. "I told her. Do they know yet?"

Kristoff shook his head. "No. I plan to keep it that way. Daisy, does anyone but Jess remember anything?"

"I don't think so."

"*Think* so?"

"No," I said. "No, I'm not close enough with anyone else."

He nodded. "Good. It needs to stay that way for now. I have a feeling the charm is going to wear off eventually."

Lucas narrowed his eyes. "Why?" he asked, exasperated.

"Apparently, there is a crack. The charm not being effective on Daisy proves there is a weak point, like a tear, which only means that anyone she comes into contact with may remember things. It is only a matter of time."

"Doesn't that mean they will just try another method?" Lucas asked.

Kristoff sighed. "It's possible. At this point, anything is."

"So we're back to me being in danger," I said. "Great."

"The Order is just afraid to lose control," Kristoff said. "When someone like you comes into their sights, they feel threatened."

I sighed but couldn't think of anything to say.

"I'm going to take a hot shower to try to relax," Lucas said. "I won't be long. Keep Daisy company?"

Kristoff nodded. I watched Lucas as he sauntered up the stairs. I stared, admiring his long legs and broad chest. He was so beautiful.

Kristoff raised his blond eyebrows at me. "So, how are you feeling?"

I shrugged. "Confused."

He nodded and moved to the chair beside me, putting his arm around me. "It'll be okay. I promise."

I nodded again, starting to feel a sense of discomfort at his touch. He started stroking my hair and leaned in as if to kiss me. I pulled away softly, but he didn't yield.

"Kristoff…"

"I remember the way things were before Lucas came back. I felt very close to you, Daisy. We helped each other through losing him. I know you felt something."

"Kristoff, I was grieving. We both were. I cared about you, and I still do, but…it's different. It's different with Lucas."

He leaned in again, and Lucas's voice broke the silence.

"Hey, have you seen my…" He broke off, and a terrible look flickered across his eyes.

I shot to my feet to approach him, but he put his hands up as if to ward me off. Kristoff bowed his head, seemingly afraid to look Lucas in the eye.

"What…what were you just doing?"

"Nothing," I said. "We were talking."

"Talking?" he echoed. "It didn't look like talking."

"Lucas, just relax," Kristoff said.

"Relax? Why don't you answer my question?"

"Daisy already answered you. We were talking."

"Don't lie to me," he spat, his voice edging on anger.

"It's not like you should care, Lucas," Kristoff shot back.

"What the hell does that mean?"

"You left, remember? You left her."

"What?" He stepped closer to his brother with pain and anger littering his features. "Is this…is this what was going on the entire time I was being tortured by those damn sadists?"

"Lucas, please calm down," Kristoff said, getting up from the table.

"How am I supposed to calm down?"

I stepped between them, trying to diffuse the situation. "Lucas, really, it's not what it looked like. I swear."

He softly guided me aside and closed the space between him and Kristoff.

"I never *wanted* to leave her. You knew that, Kris. How could you? Was this your plan all along?"

"Of course not. I never wished you dead, Brother. But when you were, things were finally going my way."

"A damn competition, Kristoff?" he yelled. "Really? So typical!"

"She was supposed to be mine," Kristoff murmured.

I saw the look on Lucas's face and knew he was seconds from losing it completely. I put my hand on his shoulder. He flinched, startled, and turned around. His eyes were calm when he looked at me, but I could almost feel the anger emanating from him.

"Please," I said, "don't do this. It's not what you think. I never betrayed you, Lucas."

"I know, but that doesn't mean my own brother didn't try."

"You were gone!" Kristoff shouted, throwing his hands up. "What did you expect?"

"Kristoff—" I started.

"He's right," he said, cutting me off as he moved away from me. "You're right, Brother. I was gone. I *was,* but I'm not now. I'm not going to disappear again. I leave the room for two minutes…" He broke off, shaking his head, and started back toward the staircase.

"Wait," I said. "Lucas, don't go."

He put his hand up without turning to look at me. "I need a minute."

I followed him up the stairs, not caring if he wanted to talk or not. He stepped into his room and flopped onto his bed.

"Lucas?"

"I'm sorry. I didn't mean to get so upset."

"No, it's okay. I understand. But I promise you it wasn't what it looked like. Kristoff and I became very close when you were gone, but it wasn't like that. He was just trying to comfort me."

"*He* had a different intention than you did, Daisy."

I sighed, sitting beside him. "Maybe, but I would never let that happen, okay? I love you."

He put his arm around me. "I know," he whispered, kissing the top of my head. "I love you too."

"Just relax. Lie down with me."

He smiled. "Always."

Chapter Thirty

I NEEDED to get back home before Jess started to worry. I sent her a quick text message and let Lucas drive me home.

"Are you two going to start throwing punches when you get back home?" I asked.

Lucas smirked. "No. If anything, we'll stay away from each other for a couple days."

I nodded but didn't know what to say.

"I really am sorry for you being put in the middle of that."

"It's fine," I answered. "I never had siblings, so I've never had that rivalry, but I do know it's normal."

"Well, I guess there's one thing that makes me human," he said with a chuckle.

I smiled. "Maybe you're not as different as you think."

He glanced at me but didn't respond. I replayed my words, beginning to wonder if I really believed them. After all, only in the weirdest of circumstances could any of the recent events actually occur.

Lucas pulled up to the driveway and leaned in for a kiss. It was soft and brief but still full of passion, as everything was with Lucas.

"I'll see you soon," he said. "Sleep well."

I nodded, realizing the dreams had stopped again for a while. Hopefully that would last longer than the last break I had. I needed that pause, that sense of stillness with everything that was going on. I sauntered to the door and raced up the stairs to my room. Jess was in the armchair, reading a romance novel as usual.

"Hey," she said, closing the book. "You were out a while."

"Yeah, sorry. I wanted to see Kristoff, so we went to hang out with him for a while."

She smirked. "Okay, so why do you feel so bad about it?"

"Is it that obvious?"

She shrugged. "I just know you."

I flopped onto the bed. "They had a…a fight."

"Ah. Well, that happens."

"That's what I said. Only it was worse because it was about me."

"What do you mean?"

"Well, Kristoff sort of…"

"Likes you?" She leaned forward.

"Umm, yeah."

"Wow. Is he cute?"

"Jess!"

"I'm just asking." She laughed.

"Yeah, because you always 'just ask.'" I smirked at her, but she didn't avert her gaze. "Yes, okay? He's actually gorgeous. But Lucas is too, and he's the one I'm with."

She raised her hand. "Okay, okay. You know…I'm not with anyone."

I rolled my eyes. "I'm not hooking you up with Kristoff, Jess. Forget it."

She laughed. "You're no fun. Seriously though, what happened?"

"Nothing." I sighed. "That's what's so frustrating. Lucas had this idea in his head that Kristoff and I were…involved when he was imprisoned."

She nodded. "Ah. Well, were you?"

"Not really. I mean, he kissed me once, and there was some affection, but it was more about comfort during the whole grieving process. I mean it was for me anyway. Maybe he had a different idea."

"Seems like he did."

I fell backward onto the soft mattress. "It's all a bit complicated. For once, it's not the guys that make it so difficult."

She chuckled. "Yeah, right. Think about it, Daisy. As complicated as it is, wouldn't it be a hell of a lot less complicated if there weren't men involved?"

I smiled. "Sure, but even still, the rules and laws of their world, the fact their world exists at all…"

She sighed. "Yeah, I know what you mean."

· · ·

The room darkened, and my eyes began to feel heavy as the night's events caught up with me. I curled up in bed, and my body collapsed into unconsciousness. The exhaustion had me deep in sleep until the morning came, waking me slowly and softly. I got up from the bed, and Jess shot up, gasping for air.

"Hey, what's wrong?" I asked, rushing to her side.

She rubbed her eyes. "Nothing. Just a weird dream."

"Are you okay?"

"Yeah, yeah." She yawned. "All this talk has got my mind in strange places."

"Tell me about it. At least you aren't dreaming of talking cats."

She laughed. "Well, I think I should tell you something."

I narrowed my eyes at the sudden change in her tone. "Okay?"

"Is it possible for me to…remember Lucas? I mean, the way you do?"

I shook my head. "I don't think so. Nobody else but me has even been able to."

"Uh huh."

"Jess? Why are you asking me that?"

She shrugged. "I don't know. I just…I sort of feel like I do…remember him, I mean."

"Well, that's probably because of how much I've told you. And the journal…"

She shook her head. "But it's more than that. In my dream, I don't remember anything that was said, but I knew his voice, and when he was next to me, he had this certain…smell."

I leaned in closer. My insides were twisted, and a nervous feeling grew in the pit of my stomach. The feelings were boiling up inside of me.

"Explain it to me."

"His voice was soft and almost youthful."

I nodded. "That's true so far."

"He smelled like…like the days when you and I would go exploring in the woods and build things out of scrap wood and tree branches."

I smiled. "That smell of wood and foliage."

"Yeah."

"That…that's crazy."

"So, maybe I really am remembering him."

"Well, Lucas said something about the other charm not working because I'm immune to it and I'm close to you. Maybe that's the same thing that's happening here."

She shook her head. "We have such weird conversations."

I laughed. "Yeah, that's an understatement."

I got back up and headed for the bathroom when a knock came at the front door. Jess shot me a look. I drew my hair up in a bun and headed downstairs, with Jess on my heels.

I opened up to see Lucas. A smile involuntarily stretched across my face.

"It's…you," I heard Jess murmur.

I moved away and stared into Jess's eyes. Her gaze was fixed on Lucas.

"Hello, Jess," Lucas sang.

Jess didn't smile. Her face was blank and ashen, but her eyes appeared chaotic. "I… Daisy, I told you I…" Her voice trailed off, and she finally looked at me.

"Are you sure?" I hummed.

She nodded mechanically.

"Lucas, you should come in," I said. "Come sit."

"What's going on?" he asked. "Are you two all right?"

I grabbed his wrist and almost dragged him to the living room. "We're fine. Just come sit."

His eyes were filled with layers of confusion and annoyance, but he didn't say a word. He sat beside me on the couch.

"Something…happened," I started.

"Like what?" he asked.

"Like…something weird."

He sighed. "Daisy, please. None of the way you tend to beat around the bush. Out with it."

"Fine. Jess sort of remembers you."

"Wait. Sort of?"

"Mostly."

He got up from the couch and stared at Jess. "Is that why you were staring at me as if I were from outer space?"

She looked up, meeting his eyes. "Yeah."

"Oh, that's just great."

I was instantly aware of his tone. "Lucas, why are you so upset?"

"Daisy, you still don't understand. When things go haywire, it causes a lot of chaos and danger for us."

I shook my head. "Well, there's not much we can do about it."

"If she remembers me and her other memories returned… The Order must *never* find out about this. Understand?"

I nodded. "I get it."

"I came here to tell you something though—something that Kristoff told me."

"Okay…"

"There was a death," he started. "A car crash similar to yours. The man who was hit…died."

I frowned. "That's really sad…but what does that have to do with me?"

"Nobody saw it coming, Daisy."

"Nobody?"

He shook his head.

"Nobody but…The Order, right?"

"No," he said, placing his hands on my shoulders. "Nobody."

"But that's not possible."

He bowed his head. "It's not supposed to be." His voice turned almost acidic when he spoke again. "But at this point, anything is possible, and this could cause everything The Order says to be called into question—which is bad, very bad."

"You *already* questioned them," I said.

"Yes, well, I was just someone they assumed to be a disobedient child. If others start to doubt…"

"What?" I mused.

"I don't know. I don't know what might happen."

"If nobody trusted them, couldn't that be a good thing?"

"Obviously they are not who they say they are, Daisy, but they will always have followers—people who believe in them. If others try to go against them…" He stopped again, looking away from me, clearly afraid to continue.

"What? What is it?"

"You know what they are capable of. What they did to me? That was nothing—*nothing* compared to what they may do to others. People who betray them and go against them are given the highest of punishments. The only reason I am still alive is because Moe has standing in The Order and happens to be my dad."

"Well, what can we do? Or what can *you* do?"

He shook his head. "Probably nothing."

"Nothing."

"Nothing. Things are about to get more than just bad. Things are about to get bloody."

SARA J. BERNHARDT

Lucas drove me to his house; Jess stayed back, feeling a bit overwhelmed and wanting to lie down.

"Oh, good," Lucas said, pulling up next to Kristoff's car, shifting into park. "He's back. Let's hope he was able to find out more from Moe."

He led me through the front door, and we found Kristoff sitting on the living room couch, leaning forward, his elbows resting on his knees, his hands twisting in front of him.

"Glad you're back, Kris," Lucas said. "Did Moe have anything to...?" His voice trailed away as his brother slowly turned to face us.

Kristoff's eyes were sad and his face sullen.

I took a small step forward. "Kristoff, are you okay?"

"What's going on?" Lucas asked, his tone urgent and concerned.

Kristoff stood. "Something has happened."

Lucas grasped my hand but didn't break eye contact with Kristoff.

"Moe didn't have anything new about the unseen death, but..." He inhaled and exhaled deeply. "He...wanted me to tell you myself."

"Kristoff, just tell me what it is."

"Well...Mr. White..."

"Yes? The bastard who tortured me. What about him?"

"He's...dead?"

"Dead?" Lucas almost shouted. "What the hell happened?"

Kristoff shook his head. "I don't know. But some of them have claimed to have seen something...strange."

"Strange how? Spit it out!"

"They say he was killed by a...a bear—a huge, brown grizzly bear."

Lucas's mouth fell open, and his hand in mine went limp. "Could it...? Do you think it could be...?"

"Mother," Kristoff whispered. "Yes. I think it is."

234

About the Author

Sara J Bernhardt is an author and poet who has been writing since a very young age and is a winner of several poetry and short story contests. It is clear that Bernhardt writes in a realistic tone while still creating the enthralling feeling of fantasy. Her writing puts readers in a world that they will truly love to be a part of. Though the writing is edgy and catching it is also not too complex which makes it a comfortable and enjoyable read for everyone.

You can follow Sara at these locations:

Facebook: www.facebook.com/Sara-J-Bernhardt
Amazon: www.amazon.com/Sara-J.-Bernhardt

Also by SARA J. BERNHARDT

https://www.amazon.com/Sara-J.-Bernhardt/e/B07DNFCH5J/

Summer's Deceit (Hunters Trilogy – Book 1): Jane Callahan is a reclusive, seventeen-year-old high school student dealing with the death of her beloved brother. Her home in Southern California with her mother is a constant reminder of her loss and pain. In hopes of escaping her past she moves to North Bend Oregon to live with her father, where she meets a beautiful boy named Aidan Summers. Jane is intrigued by his looks as well as his unusual ways of attempting to get her attention. After months of uncommon conversation and frustration, an uncertain romance brews between Jane and Aidan, but Aidan has a ghastly secret that could destroy everything.

Summer's Shadow (Hunters Trilogy – Book 2): Aidan Summers, a seventeen-year-old, stunningly beautiful genius, somehow finds his way into the life of Jane Callahan; a lovely girl trapped in soggy North Bend, Oregon. In this new Tale by Sara J. Bernhardt, Aidan relates his side of the story. All of his dark secrets are revealed and all of his motivations behind his strange ways become known as the story unravels in a captivating narrative of suspense, romance, courage...and murder.

Summer's Redemption (Hunters Trilogy – Book 3): The secret alliance of The Silver Wing and the waging war with their evil rival, The Sevren, come into full view in a new light. The evil that still lurks and stirs behind the supposed destruction of The Sevren steps out of the shadows and spins a new tale of adventure, suspense, romance, mystery and terror.

Behind Blue Eyes Series

A father's desire to save his child presents him with an unthinkable choice that leaves him darker than human, forced to roam through time alone as he searches for the place he belongs.

Adam Gold – Book 1: Fleeing the French invasion of Geneva Switzerland in the 1700s, Adam Gold books passage to America with his family. On the ship, Adam's daughter falls fatally ill. A mysterious man comes to Adam with a way to save his child by turning Adam into something darker than human.

The Medallion – Book 2: Adam Gold, an immortal with sweet eyes of blue, rushes through the centuries on a quest for reason and a thirst for revenge. To cope with his pain and regret, he sleeps away the years and awakes in a new era with a powerful, ancient vampire who sets her sights on him.

Golden Shackles – Book 3: When the ancient queen, Sekhmet snatches up Adam, he is faced with a terrifying decision. To help aid her in her vile plans or dare to stand against her.

Plus 3 more segments!

Also from our Lavish family

Irrevocable Series
Samantha Jacobey
http://myBook.to/TheIrrevocableSeries

The end of the world is coming, or so they say, and that puts Bailey Dewitt on a crash course with Armageddon. Orphaned, she and her young brothers find themselves living with their renegade uncle as part of a group of survivalists. She struggles against them, searching for a way to escape, but every discovery only terrifies her more.

For Caleb Cross, the Ranch is a way of life. The members of their group are family, and none should come between them. Smitten from the moment he met Bailey, his choices are no longer easy, his path no longer clear. He wants to welcome her and the twins into their fold and hopes his kin will agree.

But the elders who lead them aren't interested in the troublesome girl. They are plotting for the time they will be rid of her and expect Caleb to go along with their plans - he is after all one of them.

At first, Bailey resists Caleb's charms, but soon must admit that she desperately needs a friend. She has no intention of anything more, but when the elders make their move, she is forced to trust him with her very life.

They both have hard lessons to learn. Relationships built on secrets and lies don't come with guarantees. When the world falls apart around them, some things are Irrevocable.

The Norn Novellas
A. Nicky Hjort
http://myBook.to/NornNovellas

The Norn Novellas are all chapters in the epic saga of the youngest and most fickle of the four Norn Sisters. The same feisty immortal creature who must escape her inherent inner darkness to learn the meaning of life.

Each story takes a classic fairytale and spins it on its head, as we learn that maybe Norse Mythology was so much more than legend. And to think, you thought you knew those old tales so well.

Meet Za and find out what really happened...

When Tyndra Turns to Ardnyt - Book 1: In the center of a magical world there grows a beautiful and terrible chasm of climbing plants. On one side of the Ivy Wall we find the hell-of-Tyndra, on the other, the heaven-of-Ardnyt. But legend has it that in the middle...lives a preternatural beast that imprisons and tortures the children from both sides.

When the war against time begins, Azza will have to cross over the Ivy Wall, something that has never been done before by a living being. But if she does make it through, she just might discover who she really is and how she became trapped in this alternate reality.

A fairytale at heart, this is the first chapter in the epic saga of the youngest and most fickle of the four Norn Sisters. The same feisty immortal creature who must escape her inherent inner darkness to learn the meaning of love.

A veritable palindrome from start to finish, the narrative of Where Tyndra Turns to Ardnyt journeys through duality to discover what shocking truths emerge when up becomes down, life becomes death, suffering becomes release, and the most unexpected endings become the most surprising beginnings.

Welcome to a place where forwards and backwards are exactly the same direction. Here Where Tyndra Turns to Ardnyt.

Where Ebon Sounds Like Ivory – book 2: Norse legend has it that the arms of the Yggdrasil tree—a sacred instrument of Odin—are ever-reaching, and its survival is necessary for life itself to continue.

During Winter's Solstice, when the search for her mortal mother begins, Za will have to cross over the Ebon Branch of the Dead—a feat that has supposedly never been survived intact. But if she does make it across and back home, she just might discover why she and the other three Norn Sisters of Fate came to be.

A fairytale at heart, this is the second chapter in the epic saga of the youngest and most fickle of the four Norn Sisters. The same feisty immortal creature who must discover her true origins to understand her inherent inner darkness. Only this way can she learn the meaning of unconditional sacrifice in the name of impenetrable love...when, as her destiny would have it, all the branches of such a powerful tree tremble treacherously in her tiny little hands.

A veritable unraveling of Snow White, the narrative of Where Ebon Sounds Like Ivory journeys through the most horrible of realms where shocking truths emerge. Here where death mimics life, obsession masquerades as devotion, and the most unexpected endings become the most surprising beginnings of a classic tale. One...you thought you knew so well.

Welcome to a place where the darkest of melodies births a miraculous tune of surrenderance. Here Where Ebon Sounds Like Ivory and Christmas, as we know it, begins.

Fairfield Corners Series
L.A. Remenicky
http://myBook.to/FairfieldCorners

Small town romance with a paranormal twist! Each in standalone style, read and enjoy any order, any number!

Saving Cassie – Book 1: Some secrets are too dangerous to keep.

After ten years in the big city, Cassie Holt is back in Fairfield Corners. She may look like the same girl who left home a decade before but she's hiding a dark truth from everyone. When her life is threatened by the demons of her past, her best friend—who happens to be the local sheriff—offers his help.

Deputy Logan Miller has been burned by love. He's not looking to get involved but duty calls when the sheriff tasks him with Cassie's protection. Thrown into close quarters with the gorgeous bookseller, sparks fly. Logan is drawn to Cassie, but it's hard to get close to someone who keeps themselves guarded all the time.

To keep Cassie safe, Logan must open his heart but that's something he swore he'd never do.

Ragan's Song – Book 2: One look into his eyes told her she was in trouble – again!

Ragan returned home to celebrate her parent's anniversary hoping they would forgive her the secrets she's kept from them over the last few years. When she discovered that Adam was still living in Fairfield Corners she hoped her secrets were safe, secrets that drove her away three years, secrets that could change both their lives forever.

Adam Bricklin was devastated when Ragan Newlin left town. No note, no email, no text. She was just gone. It has taken three years for Adam to finally move past the heartbreak he suffered when Ragan left town. Now he's moved on and everything was going well until the day Ragan returned to Fairfield Corners. Now the melody that he lost all those years ago is back. It's the same tune he heard that tells him right from wrong—the one that sang Ragan was the one.

Even separation can't silence Adam and Ragan's song, and now that she's back it's time for Adam to decide if he should let the song die or breathe life into it once again.

Where There's Faith – Book 3: A past she can't remember. A love he can't forget.

After losing everything in an accident that he can only blame himself for, Robbie Newlin embraced sobriety and tried to live his life quietly alone at this family's cottage on the lake. Grief being his only ally, Robbie was perfectly content with how he lived until Faith moved into the cottage next door. Now Faith had him questioning whether to keep grieving or to open his broken heart to let love in again.

Faith McMillan had no memory of her life before that day three years ago. The physical scars had faded but the emotional ones were still fresh and raw. Living rent-free seemed like a great way to finish her second book and give her the time to figure out her next move, but then she met the reclusive guy next door and everything changed.

To get past the broken parts, Robbie and Faith must figure out if they want to continue living their lives in solitude or take a chance on finding an ending together.

Made in the USA
Columbia, SC
23 July 2021